ONCE UPON A TIME IN CAMELOT

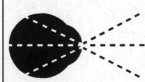

This Large Print Book carries the
Seal of Approval of N.A.V.H.

Once Upon a Time in Camelot

James Patrick Hunt

THORNDIKE PRESS
A part of Gale, Cengage Learning

GALE
CENGAGE Learning

Farmington Hills, Mich • San Francisco • New York • Waterville, Maine
Meriden, Conn • Mason, Ohio • Chicago

GALE
CENGAGE Learning®

LIBRARY OF CONGRESS CATALOGING-IN-PUBLICATION DATA

Names: Hunt, James Patrick, 1964– author.
Title: Once upon a time in Camelot / James Patrick Hunt.
Description: Large print edition. | Waterville, Maine : Thorndike Press, 2016. |
  Series: Thorndike Press large print thriller
Identifiers: LCCN 2016041745| ISBN 9781410493767 (hardback) | ISBN 1410493768
  (hardcover)
Subjects: LCSH: Large type books. | BISAC: FICTION / Thrillers. | GSAFD: Suspense
  fiction.
Classification: LCC PS3608.U577 O53 2016b | DDC 813/.6—dc23
LC record available at https://lccn.loc.gov/2016041745

Published in 2017 by arrangement with James Patrick Hunt

Printed in Mexico
1 2 3 4 5 6 7 21 20 19 18 17

"In the foreign policy establishment, it is far more forgivable to do something incompetent or dangerous inside than to talk about it on the outside."

— Richard J. Barnet

"If people want a sense of purpose they should get it from their archbishop. They should certainly not get it from their politicians."

— Harold MacMillan

PART 1

CHAPTER ONE

1972 . . . in a country that could have been ours.

A Secret Service agent led Mike Mayville to the basement of Terry McCormick's townhouse. It was strangely quiet. Terry had seven children, but they stayed with their mother Erin in the mansion in Virginia. Terry had always said he didn't want his children growing up in hotel rooms, fancy or not. Terry was behind the bar, pouring orange juice into a glass while he spoke on the telephone. He nodded to Mayville and then motioned the Secret Service agent upstairs.

Terry barked out a laugh and said, "Well, you tell that bastard we're not buying anymore votes than we need to." Another laugh.

Mike Mayville felt himself brighten. He knew what it was to be on the receiving end of that laugh. To be accepted, to be charmed, to feel for a moment welcomed into that inner ring of McCormick power and grace. It made you forget the other times when Terry could be wrathful. Terry had a temper, as Danny often said.

Mayville was in his mid-thirties. A trim man with a trim haircut and a quality, no-nonsense suit. Mayville had worked for the McCormick family for almost nine years. When he had met Terry's brother Daniel, he had just graduated first in his class from Harvard Law School. He had been offered a clerkship at the U.S. Supreme Court. He turned it down to work on Dan McCormick's presidential campaign. He had known access to power and soon had acquired power himself. Like many men on McCormick's staff, Mayville had come to believe he was shaping history. A force for good. A part of the team.

The McCormicks were Catholic. Mayville was Yankee Episcopalian. He had the pedigree that the McCormicks sought. Choate, Yale, Harvard Law. But he was tough and disciplined as well. Mayville knew the McCormicks had little patience for liberal eggheads who thought too much and didn't get things done. Mayville's parents had always looked down on Catholics, particularly his father. Mackerel snappers, he called them. But Mayville's father had not known the McCormicks. In the country of an earlier generation, a country that was run by Mayville's father's people, it was incomprehensible that an Irish Catholic family would become an American dynasty.

But how could they not? Mayville thought. The McCormicks were handsome and charismatic and smart and witty. A family of men born to lead. Danny a war hero who stormed the beach at Normandy and, months later, led a regiment to take a key bridge on the Rhine. Danny told people that, after the war, he only had ambitions to become a writer. But no one believed that. And even if it were true, Ben McCormick — Dan and Terry's father — would have never permitted it. No son of his would be allowed to stand on the sidelines and merely *observe.*

Terry himself would sometimes play the humble card. "I only wanted to be a lawyer," he would say. Or he would say that he would have been content to be an appellate judge in his home state of Connecticut. No one really believed that either.

But it didn't matter. Certainly not to Mike Mayville. Like many men who worked with the administration, he had unconsciously and perhaps consciously started aping the

11

mannerisms of the McCormick family. The hands in the pockets, the aristocratic slouch, the somewhat halted speech, the disdain of hats. Reading Shakespeare for pleasure, drinking daiquiris without sugar, touch football on Sundays.

Now, at forty-three, Terry McCormick still retained his youthful looks. He still had his thick shock of hair and his boyish smile. The Vietnam War had taken its toll on many men and aged them prematurely. But not Terry. In what was now the eighth year of the new frontier, Terry still had complete faith in the future.

Terry had formally resigned as Secretary of Defense six months ago to run for president. The election was now a few weeks away.

When he got off the phone, Mike Mayville showed him the cover of the *Washington Post*.

Mayville said, "Polls say you're ahead by five points."

Terry said, "Last week it was eight."

Mayville shrugged. "A shift."

"A downward shift. The paper say anything about California?"

Mayville hesitated. "I don't know."

"You know, Mikey. The *Times* say that Jorgenson's polling ahead of me in California.

12

If I can't win California, I can't win."

"It's temporary. Jorgenson's this month's flavor. You know that."

"I don't know that. Jorgenson served in the Senate with Andy. Andy likes him. You know what Andy says?"

"What?"

"Andy says we underestimate him."

"Underestimate Andy?"

"No. Jorgenson."

Pete Jorgenson. Junior Senator from Oklahoma. A liberal Republican in a conservative Democrat state. It was joked in Washington that Jorgenson was running for president because he could no longer get elected in Oklahoma. Joke or not, it was more or less true. Jorgenson had been one of ninety-nine senators who voted yes on the Gulf of Tonkin Resolution. But as early as 1970, Jorgenson started publicly regretting his support. Jorgenson wasn't running against the McCormicks. He was running against the Vietnam War.

Terry had beaten candidates opposed to the war in the primaries. And he had presumed that whoever the Republicans nominated would support the war also. But then Jorgenson had come along with his Will Rogers folksiness and populism and, by a slim margin, won his party's nomination.

The McCormicks had been ready for the egghead war opponents, they had been ready for the intellectuals. But they hadn't foreseen a candidate from the American Southwest who wore cowboy boots, channeling the ghost of Will Rogers and using common-sense arguments.

When Jorgenson first declared his candidacy, no political observer believed he would last much after New Hampshire. But then Jorgenson did a very clever thing. He offered to engage in four debates with the leading Republican contender strictly on the Vietnam War. As Lincoln had done with Senator Douglas and slavery a century before, Jorgenson made those debates the centerpiece of his campaign. But unlike Lincoln, Jorgenson had the benefit of national broadcasts. Jorgenson trounced his opponent. The televised debates made Jorgenson a household name. And when it was all done, opposition to Vietnam no longer seemed disloyal.

The McCormicks could still point to Danny's record as a war hero. Danny's book about the experience (written by his speechwriter) was *still* a bestseller and was required reading in some schools in the Northeast. But Jorgenson was a U.S. Marine who had seen combat in World War II *and* Korea.

Accusations of communist sympathy bounced off him. Terry, the former Secretary of Defense, had never actually been a member of the armed services.

Danny McCormick was elected president in 1964. For most of the sixties, the conventional wisdom was that the country would be led by Dan for eight years and then Terry for the next eight. And maybe even led by Andy after that. A genuine American dynasty.

But now Mayville could see that even Terry was unsure.

Mayville asked, "Is something wrong, sir?"

Terry gave him a steady look and said, "You tell me."

Mayville was a cool customer. But at that moment he felt his heart quicken. McCormick enemies — and there were plenty — teased them about their vanity. And they *were* vain. But just because a man is self-absorbed, it doesn't mean he's not aware of what's going on around him. Terry McCormick was almost as good at sizing up men as his brother. And right now Terry could see that Mayville was worried. No, not worried. Scared.

Terry McCormick said, "There's something bothering you. Something other than slipping polls."

15

Mayville said, "There is a concern, yes."

"What is it?"

"You know about Albert Hirsch?"

"Yes. One of your military analysts."

Your military analyst. Actually, Terry had been the one who hired Hirsch. Mayville knew better than to correct him.

It started in 1965, after Danny had been sworn in for his first term. The Old Man had wanted Danny to name Terry as Attorney General. Terry protested, saying he wanted to take Danny's Senate seat. But the Old Man said that was reserved for Andy.

The problem was, Terry had led congressional committees targeting organized crime. And his participation at hearings had been vigilant. Several corrupt labor leaders and some of New York and Chicago's leading underworld figures had been vehemently cross-examined by Terry. Under normal circumstances, such experience could be used to support naming someone to the position of Attorney General. But the McCormicks had not exactly conducted a normal presidential campaign. Or perhaps they had conducted a normal campaign, and that was the problem. The Old Man had sought and obtained support from members of the Chicago Outfit as well as

16

some mobsters on both coasts. Both Danny and Terry claimed they had no idea of what the Old Man was doing in their name. Perhaps Danny didn't know. Certainly, Terry didn't. In any event, promises had been made, assurances given. And one of those promises was that Terry would "lay off the boys."

Danny was born lucky and he knew it. But he was no empty-headed pretty boy. He was a shrewd politician, conscious of the Old Man's demands and the pulse of the nation. If Terry were named Attorney General, one of two things would happen: Terry would continue his public crusade against organized crime or Terry would mysteriously drop his crusade against a problem he had more than once said was, after communism, the greatest threat to the country. Either outcome was unacceptable.

That was how Terry McCormick came to be the Secretary of Defense. He was thirty-five at the time.

Terry was Danny's closest confidant and most trusted advisor. As such, his access and influence to the president was greater than the Joint Chiefs of Staff, the Secretary of State, and the Director of the Central Intelligence Agency combined. Terry had, in effect, become an assistant president. Ter-

17

ry's clashes with the CIA became frequent. Terry resolved this by creating his own intelligence agency at the Pentagon.

In 1966, Terry hired an intelligent young man named Albert Hirsch. Hirsch had degrees in engineering and in law. He had been a captain in the Marines and had come to Washington filled with optimism and a sense of public duty. Hirsch had been an early supporter of American intervention in Vietnam. But around 1969, Hirsch had become disillusioned with the war and perhaps with the McCormicks too. Terry became aware of this and invited Hirsch to his house for dinner. After dinner, Terry persuaded himself that he had turned Hirsch around.

He was wrong. Under pressure from Congress and even some from his brother in the White House, Terry commissioned personnel at the Pentagon to prepare a report. Having convinced himself of Hirsch's loyalty, Terry included him on the report committee. The report was to be top secret, revealed only to Terry and the president. It would come to be known as the Pentagon Report. Terry had told the analysts to be forthright and honest in their conclusions. They mistakenly took him at his word.

The report made clear findings that top

officials of the U.S. government knew as early as 1965 that the Vietnam War could not be won. The report found that members of the White House and the Pentagon had lied to Congress. The report found that continuing the war would lead to far more casualties than had been previously acknowledged. The report found that events justifying the Gulf of Tonkin Resolution had been fabricated. Finally, the report "strongly urged" a complete withdrawal of American troops in Vietnam.

After reading the report, both Dan and Terry McCormick agreed that it had to be destroyed.

Now Mike Mayville said, "Albert Hirsch is missing."

Terry McCormick closed his eyes and opened them. He said, "Do we know where he is?"

"No. We're working on that. But, sir . . . there's a concern that he may have made a copy of the report. That he . . . that he *has* a copy of the report."

"Oh, Jesus."

An hour later, Mayville sat in a restaurant in Georgetown and contemplated the politics of assassination. Not the matter of setting it in motion, for he knew who to contact to get that started. But rather the politics of discussing such things with men like Terry McCormick.

Terry McCormick attended mass regularly. He had received his first communion in Rome from Pope Pius XII and his marriage ceremony had been officiated by Cardinal Spellman. He was comfortable discussing theology with Jesuit priests and bishops. Yet in the past eight years, Mayville had seen Terry McCormick call CIA men "chicken-shit bastards" because they couldn't or wouldn't kill Fidel Castro. Mayville also suspected that the McCormick brothers had had a hand in the assassination of Diem in South Vietnam. That is, that they had ordered the murder not just of a foreign leader, but of an ally. There was, of course, no *direct* proof that the McCormicks had been complicit in that. But the U.S. ambassador to Vietnam had quietly resigned after Diem's death. And the mood at the White House had certainly improved after Diem was out of the picture.

Mayville himself had no politics. The terms "liberal" and "conservative" had about as much meaning to him as different-colored pieces on a chessboard. Red or black, it was all the same. He was drawn to power and didn't have much of an interior

20

life. He believed that self-examination was a weakness. But Mayville knew that men like Terry McCormick had a need to maintain a certain view of themselves. A need to maintain the illusion.

Terry had said, "He might defect."

Meaning, Hirsch could defect to the Russians. But Mayville knew Hirsch wasn't going to defect to the Soviets any more than Johnny Carson would. Hirsch was no commie. Mayville knew it and he knew Terry knew it too. But Terry wanted Albert Hirsch killed. It was easier for Terry to accept his decision to murder an American citizen if Terry could persuade himself — even for a moment — that that American citizen was going to betray his country. Terry would never admit to even himself that Hirsch had to be killed so that Terry McCormick could win a presidential election. It would have to be a matter of *national* interest.

Mayville remembered a spook telling Terry that military tactics were those of the sniper, the ambush, and the raid, and that political tactics were those of terror, extortion, and assassination. Terry did not ask the spook if the tactics remained the same when you were operating in your own country.

"He has to be taken care of," Terry had

said. "Do you understand me?"

Mayville understood.

CHAPTER TWO

The sun was sinking down through the Los Angeles smog, making a haze of the evening traffic, taking it slightly out of focus. Among the blur of vehicles was a beige 1967 Ford Galaxie station wagon with wood-colored sides and a luggage rack on top. A dark-haired man in his late thirties was behind the wheel of the car, driving alone. He didn't have a wife or children but he had selected the station wagon at the Phoenix airport. The man's name was Vince Kegan. He was a big man with thick hair and oak lines in his face that made him look older than his years. He wore a brown suit with a blue shirt and blue tie. He looked like a businessman.

Kegan drove past A&Ws and Tastee-Freeze drive-ins, record stores, gas stations, and apartment complexes. He kept the car under the speed limit and then he braked softly when he saw the flashing taillights

23

up ahead.

There, on the right. An older model Chevy Nova blocking the right lane, the hazard lights still flashing.

There were no police cars behind or ahead of it.

Kegan slowed the station wagon, put on his direction signal, and slipped into the left lane. He saw the old woman then. She wasn't by the Nova, but up on a small porch. There was a bag of groceries on the ground next to her. The passenger door of the Nova was still open.

Kegan passed the Nova. He looked in the rearview mirror and saw the old woman trying to put keys into an iron-framed door. Kegan sighed, shook his head. He made a right turn at the next block and circled back.

He parked the station wagon behind the Nova and turned on his own hazard lights. He was careful to check traffic before he got out of the car. Cars motored by, none of them slowing. The old woman had just unlocked the gate when he came up behind her.

"Ma'am? Do you need some help?"

She turned around and gave him a quick look. She didn't seem afraid. Old people rarely feared him.

"Oh, yes," she said. "Do you mind?"

24

"No," Kegan said. He turned and looked into the Nova. There were four more shopping bags. He got them out and carried them up the steps. By the time he got there, the lady had already gone into the apartment complex. She left two bags on the ground.

Kegan followed her. It was a two-story complex with an empty swimming pool in the center. There were screen doors on the apartments and Kegan could hear television broadcasts through a couple of them.

The old woman's apartment was small, dark, and depressing. She lived alone. On the table between two chairs was a black-and-white picture of a man in a World War I uniform.

Kegan nodded his head to a small table in the kitchen area and said, "Here?"

"Yes. Thank you."

She did not make eye contact with him.

Kegan went back to the front steps and got the other two bags. The cars were still parked on the street, traffic still whizzing by. He came back and put the remaining bags on the kitchen table. The old woman was putting a gallon of milk in the fridge.

"Okay," Kegan said. "Will you be able to take care of your car?"

"Oh, yes."

Kegan said, "Isn't there a parking lot in the back?"

"Yes. But then you have to walk up a flight of stairs," she said. "Out front, it's just that porch."

Kegan wondered just how many other drivers had come close to piling into the back of her car.

"Okay, then," Kegan said, signaling her that he was leaving.

"Oh," she said. She took some change out of her purse and extended it to him. Like he was a boy at a grocery store, rather than a grown man in a suit.

Kegan suppressed a smile. He held up a hand and thanked her all the same.

He stopped at a drive-in a half hour later and ordered a cheeseburger, fries, and coffee. After he ate, he took his time sipping his coffee, listening to a baseball game on the radio. Contemporary music came out of the drive-in's loudspeakers — Stevie Wonder singing "My Cherie Amour." Kids in convertibles and on motorbikes took no notice of him.

At eight forty-eight, he left the drive-in and drove to the Beverly Hills Hotel. Now it was dark. At the hotel, he removed a case from beneath the car seat. From the case he removed a .38 revolver and a silencer. He put the revolver in his inner jacket pocket and the silencer in his side pocket. Then he went into the hotel bar.

In the bar he took a table by himself in the corner. He became aware of all the customers focusing their attention on another table where a young man with long hair, spectacles, and a Northern English accent held court. The young man was telling his friends that getting the Beatles back together for a concert to raise money for world hunger wouldn't do any good. Not in the long run anyway. "It won't *solve* anything," the young man said. The young man seemed to enjoy pricking expectations. People called the young man John. Kegan began to like the young man. The young man seemed like someone you wouldn't want to talk to or know, but he drew everyone's attention.

At nine twenty-seven, a woman in her late thirties came into the bar. The woman had reddish brown hair and a green dress with a chain cinched around her waist. She had a figure; buxom but not fat. Solid build, which the men would like, and one of those surly mouths that looked great on film. She lighted a cigarette and ordered a vodka

27

martini. The bartender called the woman Cassie.

After her second martini, she left the bar. Kegan paid his tab and followed her out.

Kegan kept his distance but kept her in sight as she walked along one of the many winding pathways of the hotel grounds. The path cut through lush greenery and beautiful gardens. The music and laughter of the hotel bar faded out as they progressed.

Kegan stepped into the shadows when the woman started to approach a bungalow at the end of the path. The woman knocked on the door twice. A man in a silk bathrobe answered it and let her in. The man was in his late forties and very handsome. His name was Mickey Gold and he had screen-tested for a couple of parts in the movies.

Mickey Gold closed the door and Kegan thought, yeah, he'd *tested* for a couple of parts but he couldn't get any of them. Maybe because they knew he was a hood — well, everyone knew that — but maybe because it wasn't enough to be good-looking to be in the movies. You had to have screen presence too and maybe Mickey Gold didn't have that. But Mickey was vain. He was that.

Kegan worked his way around to the back of the bungalow. There were French doors in the back, soft light coming out of them onto the garden patio. Now Kegan could hear music. He crept closer. The music was discernible now — Frank Sinatra singing "Let Me Try Again." Geez, Kegan thought, all the L.A. hoods were so predictable. Playing Frank Sinatra music to women, letting them know they knew Frank personally.

Through the French doors, Kegan saw Mickey embrace the woman. His mouth on her neck, his hands reaching behind to unzip her dress. The straps off her shoulders, the dress now on the floor. The woman naked now.

Kegan took the revolver out of his pocket and screwed the silencer on the muzzle.

The woman put a finger on Mickey Gold's nose, a Hollywood move, then she stepped away from him and went into the bathroom.

That's when Kegan went to the French doors. Mickey Gold's back was to him. Kegan put his left hand on the latch and slowly depressed it. It was locked.

Shit.

Kegan stepped back and then rushed forward, putting his shoulder into the door. It gave as he thought it would and the French doors burst open, the wood and door jamb splintering. Mickey Gold turned in surprise but then quickly moved to the nightstand on the other side of the bed and reached down. His hand was on a gun and he was turning back when Kegan shot him twice in the chest. Gold flung his arms up, the gun spinning out of his hand, and he fell back. Kegan came around the bed and saw Gold on the floor gasping. Kegan shot him once more in the chest and then twice in the face.

A face for a face.

That was the directive. It didn't matter whether or not the man was already dead, which he was. A face for a face, they said. The message had to be delivered.

Kegan had one bullet left in the gun. He looked at the bathroom door. It was still closed. He had not heard the woman scream. He had not heard anything from her.

Slowly he approached the bathroom door. He stood by it for a couple of seconds. Then he picked up a chair and braced it under the doorknob.

That would keep her there for a while.

Kegan drove the Ford station wagon toward the exit of the Beverly Hills Hotel parking lot. At the exit he stepped on the brakes and screeched to a halt. The station wagon was still rocking back and forth when a

30

couple of kids drove by in a red Shelby convertible. They had come in the wrong way and almost smashed head-on into him. Kegan heard them laugh. They were drunk or high.

Kegan continued on. It was a couple of miles before he could relax.

CHAPTER THREE

Davidson said, "And what do you expect to get out of this?"

Mayville smiled but did not answer.

"I know," Davidson said. "I'm not supposed to ask questions. I'm not even supposed to know who sent you to me."

"No one sent me," Mayville said.

They were walking on a trail in the woods outside of Bob Davidson's West Virginia home. Davidson wore hiking boots and a houndstooth hat. He was a tall, lanky man and he liked it when people said he looked like Henry Fonda.

"No one sent me," Mayville said again.

It was technically true. Terry had not told him how to go about it. Even Terry knew better than that. Terry could be bad about micromanaging intelligence operations.

But Bob Davidson knew who Mayville worked for. Bob Davidson knew just about everyone and everything. He had been an

FBI agent after the Second World War and had been J. Edgar Hoover's second favorite man. He resigned during the Eisenhower administration and opened up a private detective agency in New York. But it was widely and correctly suspected that the agency was a CIA front. Davidson took on the "impossible" jobs the CIA wanted done but wanted to plausibly deny involvement in. He had other clients too: corporations who wanted union officials tailed and tape-recorded, affairs discovered, Ralph Nader followed, and so forth.

In the late sixties, Davidson closed up shop and started working solely for Jonathon Jeffords, the millionaire industrialist and movie mogul who had lost his mind. Jeffords paid him fifteen thousand dollars a month. It was money hard-earned. Davidson worked sixteen-hour days and on several occasions took three a.m. phone calls just to listen to the crazy old bastard rant about the American way, communists, and rock music. Jeffords fired him after they had an argument over Arthur Ashe.

It happened this way: Jeffords wanted to bring the Davis Cup tennis tournament to Las Vegas, the town where he had gone to live dead. The night before the tournament was to begin, Jeffords called Davidson at

33

four in the morning and demanded they cancel the whole thing. Why? Because he didn't want "that nigger" Arthur Ashe playing in his town. On his courts! Davidson wouldn't cancel the tournament and Jeffords fired him.

Now Davidson was back on the East Coast, working in the security and surveillance business again. But Mayville could see he wanted something more this time.

Davidson said, "All right, no one sent you. Suppose I take this on. What then?"

"A quarter of a million dollars in your Geneva account. A service to your country. What else do you want?"

Davidson said, "Well now that J. Edgar's dead, this country's going to need another FBI director."

FBI Director J. Edgar Hoover had died last May. Terry McCormick wasn't the only one who celebrated his passing.

"We already replaced Hoover," Mayville said.

"Dan McCormick replaced him. I have it on good authority that Terry isn't happy with Danny's pick."

Mayville shrugged.

Davidson said, "Yes or no."

"I'm not authorized to make that offer. But I can tell you that if you do this, it

34

would be greatly appreciated."

"That's pretty vague, Mike."

Mayville said, "What do you want to be FBI director for? You've got money. You don't have to answer to Congress. You don't have kids in the streets calling you a fascist pig. You've already served your country."

Davidson smiled at Mayville's flattery. He almost bought it.

Davidson said, "You're still young. You don't understand. I want to be remembered. And not just by the McCormicks."

"I don't think being remembered is what interests you."

Davidson laughed. "You're right about that." And then they both knew they were talking about power, the real coin of Washington. Davidson was tired of working for the Jeffordses and the titans of Wall Street and Detroit. Tired of being a well-paid cop, a middleman fixer. He felt he was something more than that.

"Oh what the hell," Davidson said. "I'll take the job on. Maybe Terry will give me the post, maybe he won't. I always liked Terry, you know."

"He knows that," Mayville said.

CHAPTER FOUR

Lewis Knowles switched off the vacuum cleaner and said, "You know my policy, right?"

Kegan nodded.

They were in Lewis's suite at the Montclair Hotel in Chicago. Lewis was in his sixties now, but still fit and trim. He wore a white silk shirt with French cufflinks and a blue tie and gray slacks. His jacket hung on a wood hanger in a closet. Now he picked up a can of furniture polish and sprayed some on his desk. He began to wipe the desk with a cloth.

Lewis said, "If you know the why before you do the job, it just complicates things. It's better for you not think about the why. Thinking gets in the way."

Kegan said, "You don't have to explain."

"I know I don't have to explain. Not to you because you're an intelligent young man. How long have we known each other?"

"A long time."

Since childhood. Kegan's mother was Italian. His father was a not-so-bright Irishman who ran bootleg for Capone, then started working for Lewis after Capone went to Alcatraz. Kegan's mother was relieved when her husband died in a car crash. Lewis Knowles lined her up with a job in one of his laundromats. As far as Kegan knew, there had never been more than that between Lewis and his mother.

Lewis said, "You say you don't know, but you heard the rumors. Right?"

"I did."

"You heard that Mickey was stealing skim from the casinos. Right?"

Kegan said, "Something like that."

"Well, he wasn't," Lewis said. "Mickey was dumb but he wasn't stupid. I'll tell you what happened."

"If you want."

"You know Chrissy Jennings, right?"

Kegan nodded. Everyone in the Outfit knew Chrissy Jennings. She had worked for the boys since the fifties, shuttling cash from Vegas to Swiss banks and spying on the New York crime families. She was a beautiful woman and a good soldier. She started out as a showgirl in one of the Outfit's nightclubs but her charm and savvy moved

37

her up the chain of command. She liked men and she liked sex and she didn't care who knew it. When she was called to testify before Terry McCormick's subcommittee, she was appropriately vague about the Outfit's business. And her own. When Terry McCormick asked why Sam Iacovetta would give her eighteen thousand dollars to take to Geneva, she answered, "Do you really want to know why? Then I'll tell you. Because I give the best blowjobs in the city."

Lewis and the other bosses were grateful for her loyalty. In exchange for that, they paid her well and they let her live her life the way she wanted to.

When she started dating Mickey Gold, no one was surprised. Mickey and Chrissy had much in common. They both had hot tempers and overactive libidos. And they both liked to fight. But as usual, Mickey had gone too far. Chrissy returned from Los Angeles one weekend with a black eye and a fat lip. Sam Iacovetta and Lewis Knowles were incensed. In no uncertain terms, it was explained to Mickey that he was to never hit Chrissy again.

Mickey didn't listen. Two weeks later, he beat Chrissy up again, this time breaking her jaw. Christy was put on a plane to Europe to get the best medical treatment available. Vince Kegan was sent to Los Angeles to deliver the Outfit's own message: a face for a face.

This was what Lewis explained to Kegan.

Kegan took it in, nodded at times, but didn't ask any questions. In a way, he was flattered that Lewis explained it to him. Not because Lewis had let him in on something secret. Kegan already knew that Lewis trusted him. But something more. Lewis wanted Kegan to know there had been good reason.

Lewis said, "So you understand, we gave him fair warning."

"I understand." Kegan would not say aloud that Mickey Gold had it coming. Nor would he say aloud that he felt better knowing he had had a part in avenging Chrissy Jennings. Things got tangled when you started thinking too much or saying what you thought out loud. Kegan had met Chrissy once. At a nightclub in Vegas, she had sat next to him and bought him a drink. They knew some of the same people, of course, and they spent about fifteen minutes talking. Kegan thought she was funny and quick and sexy but had told himself she was way out of his league. Movie stars, mob bosses, and bullfighters were her thing. But she had been nice to him and did not talk down to him. . . . Yeah, he felt better knowing he had done something for her.

And there was the fact that Kegan had never much liked Mickey Gold anyway. With his slicked-back hair and capped teeth and Rudolph Valentino delusions. Typical Hollywood hood. Mickey had thought he'd gotten too good for Chicago. Maybe Lewis and Sam Iacovetta had figured that out too.

Lewis finished dusting his desk. He began to straighten out his desktop items.

Lewis said, "You can pick up your money at Sully's."

Kegan realized he had been excused. When he reached the door, Lewis said, "Vince."

"Yeah."

"Lay off the tables, huh? At least for tonight."

"I will," Kegan said.

Kegan parked his light blue '64 Chevy in front of Sully's bar and walked inside. Sully had two customers to serve. On the television behind the bar the governor of California was giving a speech about the silent majority of Californians supporting the Vietnam War. One of the customers said, "Christ." And Sully turned and gave the guy a look.

"Show some respect," Sully said.

"The guy's a crook," the customer said.

"I suppose you voted for McCormick," Sully said.

"This is Chicago," the customer said. "We all voted for McCormick."

McCormick had beaten Senator Jim Lundy from California in 1964. Lundy had returned to California and two years later ran for governor. He lost that election too and then announced at a press conference he was retiring from politics altogether. He said to the reporters, "What will you do? You won't have Lundy to kick around anymore." He ran for governor again in '70 and won. He still seemed bitter.

Sully said, "Well, I still say he's a good man."

The customer said, "You know why he supports the war?"

"Tell me, professor."

"The defense contracts. A lot of those corporations are in California. Lockheed, Douglas Aircraft, General Dynamics. They're all making a fortune keeping the war going. You think Tricky Jim Lundy's going to go against them?"

Kegan spoke before Sully could respond. "Sully."

Sully looked at Kegan. Kegan motioned

41

with his head to the back room. Sully came from around the bar and followed Kegan.

"He's a good man," Sully said.

In the back room, Sully said, "That really bugs me, guy talking like that. What's wrong with people?"

Kegan didn't respond.

Sully said, "You heard about that actress? Henry Fonda's daughter, she goes over to North Vietnam and has her picture taken with the Viet Cong. Can you fucking believe that?"

Kegan said, "I think it was the North Vietnamese Army."

"Same difference. I fought the war for people like her. I don't know what in the hell for anymore. This country has gone to hell."

Kegan said, "Sully."

"Okay, Vince. Okay."

Sully opened a safe and put stacks of money on a table. Kegan put it in his jacket pockets.

Sully said, "Hey, I'll give you another ten bucks to throw that big mouth pinko outta here."

"It's your place, Sully. Throw him out yourself."

Kegan drove to a Goodyear franchise and

bought new tires for his car. They suggested he replace the air filter and wiper blades too and he went along with it. He was flush after all. And part of him knew he was putting money into the old car so he would be less tempted to buy a new one. There were men in his profession who would have gone straight out and bought a new Cadillac if they had gotten twenty grand. Lewis hated that sort of behavior. Lewis said that was how Capone got nailed. Showing off. Flashing his cash and making sure he got his name in the papers.

Kegan started the Chevy and left the parking lot. He went about a mile and realized he needed gas. He pulled into a station and asked the attendant to fill it up. The attendant asked if he wanted the oil checked and Kegan said he didn't. Kegan walked over to a telephone booth.

He dialed a number and waited for an answer.

Kegan said, "Yeah, Tim. It's Vince. . . . Good. . . . Hey, Detroit–Green Bay. What are the Lions getting? . . . Three and a half? . . . Okay, I'll take the Packers. . . . Yeah, fifteen hundred. . . . That's right, fifteen. . . . Well, I'm feeling lucky. . . . Thanks, Tim."

The Doobie Brothers were playing "Listen to the Music" on the jukebox when Kegan walked into the steakhouse. Kegan took a seat at the bar and ordered a double vodka. The bartender brought him his drink and Kegan ordered his dinner. A twelve-ounce filet mignon and a baked potato with sour cream and butter.

The bartender said, "You want a booth, Vince?"

"Sure."

The bartender gestured to a booth in the corner where Kegan usually ate his meals. The busboy was getting it cleared.

Kegan said, "What's with the modern music?"

"Hell, I don't know," the bartender said. "We used to play Dean Martin and Frankie, but the clientele is changing and the boss says we gotta change with them. Some guy came in here the other day wearing a goddamn ball cap. We told him he had to take it off and he started showing us attitude and we had to throw him out. I don't know what the world's coming to."

Kegan said, "That's what people keep saying."

"At least we're keeping some of our decorum."

The decorum was male waiters only, dinner jackets, all bills paid in cash. Jacket and ties required for all male customers. No hats worn at the tables.

Kegan took his seat at the booth. They brought him his dinner and he began eating. A few minutes passed and a man and a woman came into the restaurant. The man wore a three-piece suit and thick glasses. The woman was in her early thirties and she wore a low-cut satin dress, pearls, and a fur coat. Kegan made eye contact with the woman and raised his fork to her. She smiled back at him.

The woman and her date were led to a table. The woman said something to the man and then walked over to Kegan's table.

Kegan did not stand up.

"Hey, Vince."

"Gerri."

"Can I sit down for a minute?"

"Sure."

Geraldine Kegan had kept her husband's name after the divorce. It had been her decision to keep the name, not Kegan's. She had once told Kegan it brought her some respect to be known as the ex-wife of a "made man." Kegan had told her that was

45

nonsense.

Kegan had never told Gerri what he did to supplement his income. She knew though that he worked for the Outfit and that he was on a first-name basis with Lewis Knowles. It was enough for her. Kegan had married her when she was twenty-five. She divorced him when she was twenty-nine. She said he traveled too much and he gambled too much. She said he'd kept too many things to himself. She said they didn't have a real marriage. Kegan hadn't argued with her.

Now she sat across the table looking better than she had when she was in her twenties. Kegan still felt something for her. Not love, because he doubted he had ever loved anyone. Something else, though. Maybe responsibility.

Kegan said, "What's the matter?"

"Why should something be the matter?"

"I don't know. I sent your alimony check, didn't I?"

"Yeah. You've never missed."

"Okay, then."

"Okay, then," she said. She lighted a cigarette.

Kegan looked over at Gerri's date. A Jewish guy in his early fifties, looking back at Kegan for a second, but only a second and then turning away. Few men maintained eye contact with Kegan for very long.

Kegan said, "What is it, Gerri?"

Gerri pulled on her cigarette and said, "I'm pregnant."

After a moment, Kegan said, "Oh."

Gerri sighed and said, "Oh, not him. Jesus, Vince, give me some credit. But . . . ah, the father, he's married."

"Who is it?"

"You don't know him. He's not in your world."

"Does he know?"

"Yeah, I told him. He told me to get an abortion."

Kegan said, "You can't do that."

Gerri looked at him for a moment, shook her head, and smiled. He had never told her what he did for a living, had never told her he had killed anyone outside of his military service in Korea. But she had known and he had known she had known. A professional killer counseling his ex-wife against abortion.

Gerri said, "You think it's murder?"

"I didn't say that, Gerri. I didn't say anything like that. Your beliefs are the same as mine."

"You're right. I don't want to have one. But, Vince, what am I going to do?" Her

47

voice broke.

"I can give you money. You can go away for a while. Have the baby and I'll help you set up the adoption. Lewis can help."

"I don't want Lewis Knowles's help, all right? I don't want to give up the baby. I want to have it."

"The father. What about him?"

"He's a schmuck. I don't want anything to do with him. Listen, don't make me go into that. It's very embarrassing."

"I won't." Kegan was quiet for a few moments. Then he said, "What do you want to do?"

"I want to have the baby," she said. "I want a child. You and I . . ."

"I know," Kegan said. Remembering the months of trying that stretched into a year. The visits to the doctors and the specialists. Kegan being asked if he was ever exposed to any radiation while he was in the Army, Kegan saying he doubted it. For whatever reason, he was unable to help conceive a child.

Kegan said, "You still working for the airline?"

"Yeah," she said. "And you know how they are about weight."

"I remember." Kegan took out ten one-hundred-dollar bills.

"Vince . . ."

"You haven't asked, okay? Just take it."

"But it isn't going to solve anything."

"It's just for now," Kegan said. "I'm going to help you with this."

"Vince, it's not your child. . . . I don't understand."

Kegan shrugged.

"Because you couldn't give me a child?" she said. "Is that it?"

"No, that's not it. You're in a bind."

"I'm not in a bind. I'm going to have a baby. It's not a bad thing."

"I know that too," Kegan said. "Now. You want to tell me the name of this fellah who's the father?"

After a moment, Gerri said, "I don't think so."

"I won't hurt him. I just want to talk to him."

"I don't want you talking to him. I don't want you asking him — persuading him — that he needs to help me. I don't want you going near him."

"I'm not going to hurt him."

"Vince, he's a cop. Okay? He's a cop. A captain. A patrol captain, not a detective or anything, but he's got a lot of friends and he can make more trouble for you than you can make for him. So, please, I'm asking

49

you nice. Stay away from him."

Kegan said, "I don't even know the man's name."

"No, and you're never going to. I'll take your help, Vince. I'm not too proud to do that. I wish I were, but I'm not. But I'm not going to tell you the father's name. When we were together, I always worried that you would end up in jail. You didn't and I guess we both got lucky. But I'm not going to help you go there now."

Kegan went to a whorehouse after he left the restaurant. It was part of his usual routine after a job. A meal and a woman. But that wasn't all. He had placed a bet too. He had money in his pocket and he had to wager it. Lewis had told him to stay away from the tables and he had. A blackjack game or a poker game. But he would find one tomorrow or maybe the day after that. He had once been dumb enough to play a game of gin rummy with Tony Spilotro, one of the best rummy players in the Outfit. That had cost Kegan nine grand. People told him later he was lucky to lose because winning could have gotten him killed. Spilotro was known for his temper, fearsome even by Outfit standards. Kegan gambled after jobs and when he wasn't he was in the

50

process of setting one up. Kegan gambled. And people like Lewis Knowles knew it, knew that after years in this business, he should have had a nest egg of two hundred thousand saved up by now. But he'd saved little if anything. He couldn't afford to retire and they knew it.

A wise guy had once told Kegan the problem with compulsive gamblers was that they had a need to lose. Kegan would have punched the guy if it hadn't made him so depressed. The guy didn't understand the rush.

Kegan watched the last quarter of the Detroit–Green Bay game in his apartment. The final score was a tie, 14–14. Green Bay hadn't covered and Kegan was out fifteen hundred dollars.

CHAPTER FIVE

Dan and Terry McCormick sat at a table near the swimming pool, their chairs close together as they spoke in quiet tones. President Dan McCormick took a small container of pills out of his jacket pocket. He set two of the pills on the table. Then he chased them down with a drink of water. Terry looked away as Danny swallowed the pills. Terry didn't want to know what the pills were.

Dan McCormick said, "You should talk to Pop."

"I did talk to Pop," Terry said. "He said Andy's his own man."

Danny frowned. "Pop said that?"

"I didn't say I believed him," Terry said. "I'm just telling you what he said."

"Andy wants to push through another civil rights bill and Pop said leave him alone. I can't believe that. Did you tell Pop what a civil rights bill would do to you in the

South?"

"Of course I told him. I told Andy too. Andy told me not to worry about it. He thinks we've got the election wrapped up. But he doesn't understand the realities of a presidential election. Andy doesn't see beyond Connecticut."

Danny said, "I can understand Andy telling us to go fuck ourselves. I gave up trying to control him years ago. But I never thought I'd see Andy stand up to Pop."

Terry said, "Who's to say he did?"

"What does that mean?"

Terry McCormick leaned back in his chair. "I don't know," he said.

Danny laughed. "You're not going to sit there and tell me Pop's got a soft spot for the blacks. Jesus, when I first ran for president, I had to tell Pop to quit telling nigger jokes about a hundred times. And you know how he is about the Jews."

"I know."

They both remembered. Ben McCormick's political career had been short-lived. The man was a wizard at making money, but a disaster at politics. During the Second World War, an ill-informed administration had made the mistake of appointing him the ambassador to Germany. Ben McCormick had been charmed by Hitler and had

53

written letters to his sons telling them the persecution of the Jews was fully justified. The Old Man would later say he never knew the persecution would go so far. Even his sons doubted him on that matter. The letters and other records of anti-Semitism had since been destroyed. It also helped that Ben McCormick's eldest son Michael had been killed at Anzio and that Danny had received wounds at Normandy that still hadn't healed. Accusations of being a Nazi sympathizer were met with indignant declarations that the McCormicks had died fighting the Germans.

But Andrew McCormick had not been one of them. Andy had been twelve years old when that war ended. Andy was the youngest of Ben's children and perhaps for that reason, he had not been subjected to as much as his father's influence as the older sons. Danny and Terry appealed to the liberals because the liberals saw in them what they wanted to see. They said the right things about the right causes and told people they read the right books and saw the right films, but their devotion to civil rights and the poor were lukewarm at best. Andy, in contrast, believed. Andy had become a liberal's liberal.

Terry said, "Did it ever occur to you that

the Old Man's going soft?"

Danny laughed again. *"No."*

Terry said, "Danny, the man is seventy-seven years old. And he did have a stroke two years ago."

"His capacities are fine, I assure you. I think you're missing something here."

"What's that?"

"Did it ever occur to *you* that Pop likes to keep us in check? If you, me, and Andy are all on the same page, we're that much stronger against him. He doesn't want the three of us united."

It wasn't as easy for Terry to laugh as it was for Danny. Terry knew this and he envied Danny for it. Many people had underestimated Dan because of his good looks and his charm. But Dan McCormick *was* a cool customer. Dan had managed to crack a few jokes even during the missile crisis while people around him were terrified at the real prospect of nuclear war with the Russians. Even the generals were impressed by his toughness.

Terry said, "So to do that, Pop's willing to support civil rights? He's willing to risk my candidacy?"

"Ah, he won't go that far."

"Dan, he's allowing it to happen."

"You talk with Andy yourself?"

"Hell, yes, I talked to him about it. You know what the little bastard told me? He said, 'I don't work for you.' Can you believe that? I mean, we made him Senator."

"Yeah, but that was eight years ago. He's been re-elected since then. And he had to fight to be re-elected."

"That's what he told me. Like he's earned it or something. Still, you think he'd be more grateful."

Dan said, "Andy's always gone his own way. You look at him and you see that fat little boy who ran around in shorts and cried when we wouldn't let him play football with us. But he's a tough little bastard. You know, he quit drinking?"

"Ahhh . . ."

"No, I really believe he has. Look at his eyes. Clear as a mountain lake. And the son of a bitch is *jogging* now. Every morning, three miles."

"It won't last."

"Maybe, maybe not. But here's something you don't really understand about Andy. See, he really doesn't want to be president."

"Ah, come on."

"No, he not only says he doesn't want it, he really *means* he doesn't want it. Because of that boating thing, he figures he can't ever be elected anyway. When the girl died,

56

he said that was the end of him going to the White House."

"It was an accident," Terry said.

"Yeah, everybody said so. But people will always say the McCormicks paid off the Coast Guard and the local cops and the girl's family. And Andy . . . well, Andy's still got the little Catholic boy in him. He thinks he shouldn't be president because of it. An atonement."

"Some atonement," Terry said. "I don't remember him offering to give up his Senate seat."

"Ah, Pop wouldn't have allowed that. Neither would I, for that matter. And since then, he's tried to be the best senator he can. That's where he wants to make his mark."

Terry McCormick shook his head. It was not something he could comprehend. How much power could there be in the Senate? Listening to lobbyists pimping for the dairy industry, oil, insurance, and steel. Hearings on what legal mediocrity got to be the next judge of the eastern district of Tennessee. All of it so depressingly domestic. No executive office, but just being another *legislator.* How could a McCormick be content with so little?

Terry said, "What kind of mark can you

57

make there? Remember what you said? No one's going to remember anything about a president's legislation. It's foreign policy."

"Andy's not so much for foreign policy. He thinks Vietnam was a mistake."

"Yeah, I know. At least he's keeping that to himself."

"For now. But after you're elected, don't count on him to keep quiet for long."

Terry said, "I don't understand him. When you first ran in '64, he was the biggest red-hater on the seaboard. Now he wants to pull out of Vietnam. He told me the other day that Vietnam going commie won't mean anything in the Cold War. He said to me, he said, 'It's their country.' Can you believe that? I said to him, 'What about the sixty thousand American boys who died there? You want to tell their parents they died for nothing?' He didn't have an answer for that. You know what he wants me to do after I get elected?"

"What?"

"Open relations with China, for chris-sakes. China."

Dan said nothing.

Terry McCormick studied his brother for a moment. No one on earth was closer to Dan McCormick than Terry. Certainly not the First Lady. But even Terry didn't fully know Dan. No one did, really.

Terry said, "Jesus, you agree?"

Danny said, "I don't necessarily disagree. It would help us put some leverage on the Soviets."

"Well, that's the first I heard you say that. China is a communist country, you know."

"I haven't forgotten. Terry. Stop worrying so much about Andy. Worry about your own campaign."

"I am. I just don't want him fucking it up for me."

"He won't. He's with us at the end of the day."

"I wish I could be as sure as you." *About everything,* Terry almost said.

A girl came into the pool house. She was very pretty. About twenty years old with that fair-skinned, finishing school look of a well-heeled Protestant. Danny liked them like that. She went to the other side of the pool and shrugged off the bathrobe she was wearing. Naked, she slipped into the pool and swam out into the center. Terry realized he didn't have much time left with his brother. Dan McCormick was known for getting bored quickly.

Terry said, "You heard about Albert Hirsch?"

Danny said, "I heard something about it."

"He's disappeared. My people think he has a copy of the Pentagon Report."

Danny McCormick looked at the girl in the pool, her dark pubic patch visible in the water. "Is that so?"

"That could hurt us."

"Yeah, it might." Dan loosened his tie. "You want to do something about it, I'm okay with it. You've got more at stake than I do."

"I think we all have something at stake," Terry said. He wanted to believe it. He and his brother had ordered assassinations before. In South Vietnam and in Cuba. They had finally gotten Castro in '69. Dan's belief was that he had to get Castro before Castro got him. The Russians had filed some sort of protest at the United Nations, but nobody could be persuaded that the McCormicks could have sanctioned such a thing. But never had they directly targeted an American citizen. Terry McCormick had never been a man much troubled by conscience. Like his father, Terry saw the world as one in which if you were not a fighter, you were a loser. McCormicks didn't lose. Even so, Terry now wanted something from his brother on this. A word, a gesture of approval.

Terry had been with Dan in the Oval Office when Dan told a general from the Joint Chiefs, a former CIA operative to boot, that they wanted the South Vietnamese president killed. The general looked Dan in the eye and said, "Mr. President, I can't do that." Naturally, Terry jumped on him, calling the general a chicken-shit bastard and lousy patriot. But the general wouldn't budge. They'd had to resort to different channels. They'd had to go around the CIA. Dan had given the word and Terry had managed it. They never told Andy about it. Andy could be soft about such things. In fact, they didn't even tell the Old Man. Not because they thought he would disapprove. Rather, because they couldn't trust the old bastard not to brag about it.

Now Terry said, "Well, what do you think?"

"I told you I was okay with it. Just don't give me any details."

Dan stood up and began taking off his clothes. Soon he was in the pool naked, wading toward the girl. As Terry left, he heard Dan say, "Hey, kid."

He always called the girls kid. Usually, he couldn't be bothered to remember their names.

61

CHAPTER SIX

The FBI Organized Crime Section had a file on Lewis Knowles that claimed that he was one of the three leaders of the Chicago Outfit. The other two were Sam Iacovetta and Jimmy Alfieri. Unlike the others, Knowles was not Italian. He was born in a village in Wales and had come to Chicago when he was eight years old. He dropped out of school when he was twelve and got a job hauling ice. He soon started stealing from some of the homes on his delivery route. After his first arrest, a judge took an interest in him. The judge saw that Lewis was a very smart young man and tried to persuade him to become a lawyer. The judge's assessment of Lewis's intellect was correct, but Lewis couldn't be turned away from crime. He continued stealing until he got into the bootlegging business, working for Capone. After Capone went to Alcatraz, Lewis Knowles took over Chicago's liquor disbursement and then, later, the unions.

He was a born businessman. He knew that prohibition wouldn't last forever and he moved into other ventures. One of them was linen supply. With the right combination of threats and friendly persuasion, he took over all the competition. Soon he was supplying all the hotels and hospitals in the greater Chicago area. He thought in a way most gangsters didn't. More than a few FBI agents had expressed admiration for Knowles over the years. Knowles was not a vulgar man, and he preferred bribes to violence. But he was still a gangster.

The Italians respected Knowles. They called him Chicago's Meyer Lansky, a comparison that rankled Knowles more than flattered him. Like Lansky, Knowles was not above using murder and violence to get what he wanted. But he preferred to use killing as a last resort.

Another thing: Knowles did not crave attention. He remembered what Capone's love of the limelight had done to him. Iacovetta and Alfieri needed Knowles and he needed them. They had been running the Outfit since the fifties and things had been relatively peaceful.

In 1963, they received word that Ben McCormick wanted to meet with them.

Knowles saw what was coming and told Alfieri and Iacovetta he didn't even want to be in the same room with Ben McCormick. Knowles had done some bootlegging business with McCormick some years before and considered him one of the biggest cheats he'd ever known. Knowles told the Italians he'd never do business with McCormick again.

It was agreed that Sam Iacovetta would meet with Ben McCormick.

The meeting was set up by a respected Chicago judge who had never done anything corrupt in his life. When he realized who Iacovetta was meeting with, he told Iacovetta's lawyer, "I wish I hadn't gotten involved in this. Something bad is happening here."

Iacovetta talked alone with Ben McCormick in the judge's chambers while the judge and Iacovetta's lawyer sat in the jury box in the courtroom.

After the meeting, Iacovetta convened with Alfieri and Lewis Knowles and confirmed Knowles's worst fears.

Iacovetta said, "McCormick's son is running for president. Ben wants us to help."

Specifically, Ben McCormick wanted their help in getting the unions, local law, alderman, and precinct captains to deliver Chicago's vote to Danny McCormick. They wanted Illinois wrapped up.

Sam Iacovetta said, "Look, it's either going to be Dan McCormick or that son of a bitch Lundy. You want him as your president?"

Knowles said, "At least with Lundy, you know where you stand. I'd take him over a McCormick."

Alfieri said, "You got something against a Catholic president?"

"It ain't the Pope I'm worried about," Knowles said. "It's the Pop."

"Ah, Ben's not a bad guy," Alfieri said.

"The man supported the goddamn Germans during the war. When they were bombing England. He's a very bad guy."

"Ah, that's hearsay," Iacovetta said.

"It's not hearsay," Knowles said, who understood the rules of hearsay better than most trial lawyers. "It's on the record. The man made speeches, for heaven's sake. Why do you think Roosevelt dumped him?"

"Water under the bridge," Iacovetta said.

"Lewis," Alfieri said, "I don't trust the Old Man either. But I think his son's a good man. He's a war hero. He's good-looking. He's charming. He'll be good for the country."

Knowles said, "You want a president or a

65

movie star? You guys are falling for a sun-tan."

Iacovetta said, "The boys in L.A. love him."

"That's my point," Knowles said.

"Lewis," Alfieri said. "Even if you're right, even if Dan McCormick's just as dirty as Lundy . . ."

"I never said Lundy was dirty."

"Even if that's true," Alfieri said, "McCormick can do things for us Lundy can't."

"Let me guess," Knowles said. "He promised you that if we deliver Chicago, they'll lay off of us."

After a moment, Iacovetta said, "Yeah, that's about the size of it."

"Sam," Knowles said, "with respect, I've done more business with Ben McCormick than you have. Believe me when I tell you he is a double-dealing liar. This is a man who cannot be trusted."

"Well now, wait a minute," Alfieri said, "the Old Man also promised to give us Cuba. We'll get our casinos and hotels back."

Lewis Knowles said, "Really? They're going to overthrow Castro? Is that what McCormick told you?"

Alfieri shrugged. He wanted to believe it.

"It would mean millions for us," Iacovetta

66

said. "Think about that, Lewis."

"I have thought about it," Knowles said. "I thought about it when Castro took over. Go look at a map of Cuba. You know how long it is, one end to the other? Almost eight hundred miles. That's approximately the distance between Chicago and Philadelphia. It's a lot of land. Do you know how long it took the United States Marines to take Iwo Jima? You know how big Iwo Jima is? About eight square miles. Do you know how many men it took to take that tiny little place? About thirty thousand, with over twenty thousand casualties. Iwo Jima was a dot. Cuba is a country. Anyone says taking Cuba is a cakewalk is lying to you."

It set them back. It was funny how much Lewis knew. They spent time gambling and chasing women. Lewis Knowles read. But it didn't set them back for long.

They discussed it for another hour. Knowles told them how Ben McCormick had hijacked a truckload of whiskey after selling it to him. But it didn't matter. Iacovetta and Alfieri had come under the spell of beauty and glamour like everyone else. They voted at the end of the discussion and Knowles lost two to one.

Dan McCormick won the Chicago vote in 1964 by a stunning 78 percent margin. Even the mayor was embarrassed by it. They delivered Illinois to the McCormick family.

They never did get Cuba in return. Even after Castro was assassinated.

Lewis told his associates they would regret it. He was right. But he didn't want to still be right nine years later.

Bob Davidson said, "We met in Vegas. Remember? You were there with your wife and Don Rickles came up to the table and flirted with her. You remember that?"

Lewis Knowles studied the man for a moment. "We did?"

"Yeah. And he made some machine-gunning joke to you. Like you were gonna have him cut down. You don't remember?"

"Vaguely," Knowles said, smiling. He did not want to give this man too much.

They were seated at the back of an Irish pub in the Bridgeport section of Chicago. It was a cold afternoon and the windows were fogged up. The place was empty except for Davidson and Knowles and the bartender.

Knowles had placed his hat on the table but left his topcoat on.

"Ah, well," Davidson said. "I want you to know how grateful I am that you agreed to meet with me."

"You're a respected man," Knowles said.

It wasn't the same thing as saying that he respected him. And they both knew that.

Knowles said, "I was sorry to hear about Jeffords."

Davidson nodded. He wondered if that was another slight — Knowles reminding him that he had once been Jeffords's boy. He decided it shouldn't matter.

Davidson said, "Ah, he was a . . . he was a complicated man. He was sore at you guys for not buying his casino."

"He wanted too much."

"It's for sale now," Davidson said. "At about half the price. That is, if you're interested."

"You sure about that? I hear the man's estate is pretty tied up. What did he leave, about three different wills?"

Davidson laughed. "There may be a fourth. But I'm not associated with him anymore. Or his estate."

"So you're not here to shop a casino."

"No," Davidson said. "And I think you know that. In fact, I think you know a lot more about what goes on in Vegas than I do."

Knowles made a gesture. He was not a man who liked to be flattered. He'd heard it all before. *Chicago's brilliant gangster, the Mastermind of the Outfit,* and so forth. He

69

didn't need to hear it from this man.

Knowles said, "Who are you here for?"

Davidson leaned back in his seat. "I suppose I can't really tell you directly. What I can tell you is that I'm here to discuss a very serious matter. More serious than anything I've ever been involved in. More important than money, even."

"More important than that, huh?" Lewis Knowles suppressed a smile.

"Yes. National security."

"I see," Knowles said. After a moment, Knowles said, "The last time you approached us, it had something to do with national security. As I remember it, you wanted us to kill Fidel Castro. Except you didn't use the word kill. You said 'eliminate.' Which I guess was somehow supposed to make it different."

"I wasn't involved in that."

"Ah, don't try to fool an old man, Mr. Davidson. You discussed that with Sam yourself. And our pretty boy in Los Angeles. And how well did that work out?"

"It didn't work," Davidson said. "No, it didn't work. But we got lucky, I guess. Castro dying from a heart attack five years later."

"Natural causes, huh? And I suppose your people had nothing to do with that."

"No more than your people."

"And then what happened? Fidel's brother took over and Cuba remained a communist country."

"Well . . ."

"Yeah, well." Knowles shook his head and smiled. "Haven't you guys figured out that it doesn't work?"

"What doesn't work?"

"What you call 'elimination.' You kill a country's leader and you think the masses will embrace hot dogs and apple pie. Doesn't work that way."

"So you guys didn't get your casinos back."

"I didn't want them back."

"So now you're going to lecture me about killing."

"No, I'm quite aware of who I am and what I am. I've never tried to tell myself that what I do is for the greater good."

"There's a world beyond yours, Mr. Knowles. A world beyond Sam Iacovetta's and, yeah, beyond Dan McMormick's. The Soviets aren't interested in taking over the local pubs and pipefitters union. They want to take over Europe. Asia. The world. That's what's at stake here. We're both Americans here."

"So now you're appealing to my patriotism?"

"Yes."

"And ask me what I can do for my country."

"Our country."

Lewis Knowles grunted.

Davidson said, "There's a man who used to work for the Pentagon. We've learned he's working for the Soviets. A spy. He's taken a very important report that we believe he's going to give to them. He's disappeared with that report. And we need to find him."

"So find him."

"It's not that simple."

"Well, I would think that if you have the FBI and the CIA and that new intelligence outfit Terry McCormick put together at your disposal, you could find him and arrest him for treason."

"It's not that simple."

"I would think it would be very simple," Knowles said. "If you want to arrest him."

Davidson was quiet.

Knowles said, "But you don't want to arrest him, do you?"

"No, we don't."

"You want to have him killed."

After a moment, Davidson said, "Yes, we think that's the best thing."

72

Knowles shook his head again. "Mr. Davidson, I know something about your background. Your work at the FBI, your contracting work with the CIA. But let me ask you a personal question. Have you ever killed a man yourself?"

"I don't see how that's relevant."

"No, I suppose you wouldn't."

"I've given orders to have men killed. In war."

"This is not war."

"It's a cold war, Mr. Knowles. And the stakes are just as important as if there were troops on the ground. You disapprove of me because I ask you to end a man's life. But this man's death will save lives. Thousands, maybe hundreds of thousands, of lives."

"You say."

"It isn't just me."

"Who sent you?"

"I'm not at liberty to say."

"Well, I know it's not Jonathan Jeffords. You know what I think? I think the McCormicks sent you."

"Who I'm working for is not pertinent. I'm just an emissary."

"In my world, we would use the word bagman." Knowles smiled again. "Oh, don't take offense. We're just discussing business here."

"Yes," Davidson said, his tone not as smooth as before. "Business. That's something I think you could understand."

"Well, I'm afraid I can't help you, Mr. Davidson."

Davidson stood up.

"Mr. Knowles, I suggest you give it some thought. Good day."

Knowles was not surprised when things began to turn against him. He had expected some blowback. But he had underestimated how much. And how soon.

A week after his meeting with Bob Davidson, Lewis Knowles received word from his accountants that all of his Chicago-based businesses were being audited. It was not the first time they had been audited. But Knowles's accountants said the Internal Revenue Service was being particularly aggressive this time. They said it was, of course, possible that an audit could be done and nothing would come of it. But that possibility was slim.

A week after that, Knowles was informed that the Secretary of Commerce was reviewing a contract his auto parts company had with American Motors Corporation (AMC). Knowles asked his man in Detroit, "What does what we're doing have to do with the stream of commerce?" His man in Detroit said he had asked Commerce the same thing and they hadn't told him.

The day after that, Sam Iacovetta called him and hit him with the worst news of all. Iacovetta said he'd gotten a call from their man running their casinos in Vegas.

Iacovetta said, "Lefty's scared. I mean, he's really worried."

"What is it?" Knowles said.

"Lefty says someone from the Nevada state legislature told him the State is considering passing something called a Corporate Gaming Act. Lefty says it's gonna fuck us out of everything."

Knowles had a good idea of what Lefty meant, even though Iacovetta hadn't fully understood it.

"Let me call Lefty and check it out," Knowles said.

Knowles called Lefty and found out it was as bad as he feared.

The proposed Nevada legislation, if passed, would remove barriers against the direct involvement of corporations in the casino industry. It would allow legitimate public corporations to acquire casinos. It would also expand what the legislators called "transparency" on casino operations. Information on the profitability and ownership would be made public. Loans, financing, management — all of it put out in the open.

The proposed legislation also said something about making Las Vegas a more "family-friendly environment."

Lefty said, "I don't understand it. People come here to gamble and get laid. They want family friendly, they should go to fucking Disneyland."

They could have put a Ferris wheel in the front of the Golden Nugget and Lewis Knowles wouldn't have cared. Lefty was missing the point. The danger was corporate takeovers of the casinos.

Knowles had known what a corporate gaming act would do to the Outfit's operations in Vegas for years. He had foreseen the danger and had taken steps to prevent it. He had paid a few well-placed legislators in Washington and Nevada for the express purpose of preventing such laws from being made.

He discussed it later with Sam Iacovetta at his ranch house.

Iacovetta said, "So we find out who these guys are that are proposing the law and we pay them off."

"We can give it a try," Knowles said.

They tried and they failed. Phone calls

were not returned. The Nevada governor and state majority leader were out of town. It was what Knowles had expected.

Iacovetta suggested they get tough. Maybe pay a visit to the state congressmen sponsoring the legislation.

Knowles said, "We can't do that, Sam. They're watching us. Closer now than they ever have."

For perhaps the first time, Lewis Knowles began to feel old. He had always prided himself on knowing himself and the times in which he lived. He had always prided himself on knowing that nothing was permanent. Prohibition had ended and he had adapted. He had been threatened by the IRS before, but he had persevered and paid his sums and gotten out of it. He had even once been jailed for three months for contempt of court when he refused to answer questions before a grand jury. But now they were coming at him from all directions. The IRS, the Department of Commerce, the Nevada state legislature.

It did not go unnoticed by Knowles that the FBI was more or less leaving him alone. But then he knew that the FBI had always maintained its independence from the McCormick family. Hoover had always been a prick, but he had never allowed the

McCormicks to tell him what to do. Knowles knew about the time Terry McCormick had attempted to order Hoover to have FBI agents escort black civil rights leaders on a bus ride into Selma, Alabama, to protest discrimination. Hoover told Terry that FBI agents were not in the business of driving buses. Terry had backed down because he knew Hoover had too much on the McCormicks for them to push him.

Knowles wondered about Hoover now. Hoover was dead, but his legacy — such as it was — lived on at the FBI. Knowles didn't think that was such a bad thing. Hoover's paranoia stemmed from fear of commies and black revolutionaries, not gangsters running unions and casinos. Hoover hadn't cared who was selling bed sheets in Chicago and who was getting rich because of it. He had other things on his mind. Now the McCormicks had Knowles nostalgic for J. Edgar Hoover. If Hoover were alive now, maybe Knowles could arrange to have a cup of coffee with him and see just what Hoover had in his McCormick files.

But it was foolish to think about such things. Hoover was dead and even if he were alive he would not sit at a table with Knowles to discuss anything.

Knowles talked it out with Sam Iacovetta. Near the end of the discussion, Iacovetta said, "Well, Lewis, you warned us it was a mistake to back the McCormicks. It seems you were right."

"I appreciate that, Sam. But you and I have always known it's no use talking about what we should have done."

Iacovetta said, "So we're going to give them what they want. And after that, they'll leave us alone."

Knowles sighed. For he knew they would never leave them alone. Terry McCormick would be elected and there would be another eight years of a McCormick administration. And maybe another eight after that if Andrew McCormick got elected. It was going to be the political dynasty Ben McCormick had worked so hard to build. Ben McCormick's dreams realized.

No, it was no use talking about what they should have done years ago. Even so . . . Knowles found himself thinking about the time Ben McCormick had screwed him on that whiskey shipment. It had been over thirty years ago, at a time when Knowles was still capable of doing his own killing. He had debated killing Ben McCormick then. But he had decided not to because by that time he had developed his belief that killing should only be done as a last resort. And he had believed that killing purely for the sake of vengeance was bad business and bad medicine. It was the practice of an undisciplined man and Knowles had never liked the undisciplined.

He would have never guessed that Ben McCormick would become so powerful. Bootleggers simply didn't become presidents. Bootleggers didn't raise sons who became presidents. But this bootlegger had. Knowles had underestimated Ben McCormick and now he was in service to his spawn.

Bob Davidson stood on a corner on State Street. A black Lincoln stopped at the corner and Davidson got into the backseat.

Knowles said, "If you don't mind, I'm going to check you over."

Davidson said, "Come on, Lewis. I'm not wearing a wire."

"Let's be sure, huh?"

Knowles checked him and found nothing. Davidson frowned, but endured it.

Davidson said, "I hope you appreciate the fact that I'm not asking the same of you."

"Yeah, I'll remember that," Knowles said.

The car pulled onto Lakeshore Drive. A strong south wind pushed against the car.

White caps appeared on Lake Michigan.

Knowles said, "Well, it seems that your people want this man killed pretty badly."

Davidson said, "What do you mean?"

"I'm talking about the IRS, the Department of Commerce, and certain legislation being proposed in the State of Nevada." Knowles turned to him. "If we're going to be discussing business, let's at least discuss it honestly."

Davidson said, "Look, it wasn't my call."

"Right. You're just the messenger. All right, then. Tell the McCormicks they got a deal."

"I never said I was working for them."

"Of course not. Your people have got themselves a problem and they want us to take care of it. We'll do it then. Call off the dogs and we'll put it in motion."

"And not until?"

"Not until."

After a moment, Davidson said, "Okay." He tried to hide his pleasure in the victory. "I want you to know, this service is going to be much appreciated."

Knowles raised a hand. It had been years since he had hit a man in anger and he didn't want to do it now.

"Don't," Knowles said. Meaning, don't insult me.

"All right," Davidson said. "Can you tell me who's going to do it?"

Knowles said, "That's my business."

CHAPTER SEVEN

Kegan got to his shop at around nine forty-five in the morning. He swept the floor and put on his smock and opened the door for business at ten a.m.

He was a barber and he had been cutting hair for almost fifteen years. He had learned the trade after he got out of the Army. He was a dues-paying member of the Master Barbers Association. After paying his overhead, he took home about $180.00 a week.

Kegan was a good barber. He took pride in giving a good cut and a clean shave for a fair price. Many of the customers would talk to him while he did his work and if they wanted quiet, he would give them that too.

He turned the radio on during business hours. Classical music if he was alone, but when the customers were in, he would switch to a station playing a baseball game if one was on.

About a half-hour passed this morning

when his bookie came in.

The bookie's name was Tim McGinnis. He was a short little Irishman who had a day job supplying paper towels and toilet paper to restaurants. He was another Bridgeport boy.

Tim said hello and asked if he could get a shave. He wouldn't ask Kegan for the money. He knew Kegan was good for it.

Kegan gave him the fifteen hundred in fifties. Kegan had lost again, this time betting on the Jets. Namath had played injured.

Tim took off his jacket and took a seat in the green chair. He put the money in his pants pocket.

"Tough break, Vince." He seemed to mean it.

Kegan shrugged as he turned on the hot water at the sink. When the water got hot enough, he soaked a fresh towel with it and wrapped it around Tim's face. Let it sit there for a while and then took it off. Then he applied the shaving cream. After that, he went to work with the straight razor.

Tim talked about the game for a while. Tim thought Broadway Joe needed to start thinking about retirement. Then Tim started talking about college football, which interested him more than the NFL. He was big on Oklahoma. He told Kegan that Chuck

Fairbanks was leaving Oklahoma to coach the Patriots and he predicted that assistant coach Barry Switzer would take over. Tim said that the wishbone offense had been Switzer's idea, not Fairbanks'. Tim thought that Switzer had a big future ahead of him.

Kegan finished the shave and applied some aftershave lotion to hydrate the skin.

Tim put his coat on and handed Kegan a twenty-dollar bill. Kegan went to the cash register to get change.

"Keep it, Vince."

Kegan said, "You don't have to do that, Tim. I'm a big boy."

"It ain't sympathy, Vince. You give the best shave in Chicago."

"The sign says five dollars, not twenty."

"You earned it. Just do me a favor and don't consider it house money."

Kegan's assistant came in a half-hour later. His assistant was named Mackie Redd. Business picked up around lunchtime but slacked off around three o'clock. Mackie sat in one of the chairs and read the newspaper.

It was about four when Lewis Knowles dropped in.

Mackie got out of his chair. He knew who Knowles was and greeted him respectfully. Knowles asked Mackie how his family was doing and Mackie said they were doing fine, thank you. Knowles took his hat off and he and Kegan went to the back office.

Kegan sat down as Knowles placed an eight by eleven manila envelope on Kegan's desk. The envelope was sealed in cellophane.

Knowles said, "Go ahead and open it."

The sealed packet was something new. Right away, that made Kegan uneasy. Something too corporate about it. Knowles seemed to sense this.

"Don't worry," Knowles said. "I'm the one who prepared it."

Kegan opened the envelope. In it was a short typed memo listing a man's name, profession, and last known address. It gave a short history of the target's life. Place of birth, schools, university, military service, post-graduate education, and then public service.

Kegan said, "Lewis . . . this guy's a civilian."

"I know," Knowles said.

Kegan said, "Harvard University, post-graduate studies at MIT. He was a 'whiz kid.' What does that mean?"

"The whiz kids were part of an operation for the Army who did what they called 'statistical control.' They were the guys the Army had doing a lot of the coordination and logistical work during the war. Placement of troops, weapon production, that sort of thing. They were put together for the Second World War. And then a couple of wars after that."

"Korea?"

"And Vietnam."

"This guy's a military analyst?"

"Yeah. A lot of them ended up working for Ford Motor Company. This one didn't, though."

"This one didn't work for Ford?"

"No."

"This one worked for the Pentagon?"

"Yeah, mostly."

Kegan shook his head.

One time, the head of one of the New York families sent a man to Kegan's barber shop to hire him to kill a hood in Philadelphia. Kegan politely but firmly escorted him to the door. He told the messenger he had the wrong man. Then Kegan called Lewis to tell him about it. Lewis was very upset. No one from New York ever tried to contact Kegan directly again.

The way it worked was, Kegan only took his assignments from Lewis Knowles. That was the way it had always been.

Now Kegan said, "Do you remember what you told me? When I first got into this business, do you remember what you told me?"

"I remember."

"You told me we don't kill civilians. You told me we didn't work for civilians who wanted another civilian hit."

"I remember, Vince."

"You also told me never to trust a civilian."

"I remember all of it."

"And now you're asking me to hit a civilian. This guy's a civilian, not a mobster."

Vince Kegan knew what he was. A killer of men, yes, but his role in the Outfit was that of an enforcer. *Within* the mob, not outside of it. A sort of policeman for the Outfit, taking out those who had crossed lines or otherwise fucked up.

Kegan said, "Lewis, you know I make it a point not to ask you why or what for."

"I know that. But this is different."

"Yeah," Kegan said. "Very different. You want me to hit someone who's not a hood. We always stick to our own. I don't think this request is coming from New York or Chicago. Someone outside the Outfit wants this done."

"The Outfit wants this done."

"Ah, come on Lewis. Since when does the Outfit care about some guy working for the Pentagon?"

Knowles said, "You're uncomfortable, I see that. For what it's worth, I'm uncomfortable with it too. You know about Cuba, don't you?"

"I heard rumors."

"You heard that people in Washington wanted Sam to kill Castro. Sam was dumb enough to let them talk him into it. I was dead set against that, but they didn't listen to me. Fortunately, Sam never got anywhere with it. Sam was . . . Sam was charmed by those people. Taken in by the McCormick glamour. And he wanted to do something patriotic."

"This guy's not Castro. This guy's an American citizen."

"But he's betrayed his country. He's got some sort of report, something called the Pentagon Report, and they seem to think he's going to sell it to the Russians. That's why they want him dead."

"Why can't they do it, then?"

"Because they want to be removed from it. Distanced."

Kegan didn't say anything.

"You disappointed in me?" Knowles said.

"I didn't say that."

"It's all right, I can see it. No, don't apologize. I don't blame you. What I can tell you is these guys are squeezing us. Bad.

89

If we don't do this, they're going to shut us down in Vegas. Not temporarily, permanently. And they'll come after us for tax evasion."

"Like they did Capone?"

"Yeah. They won't send me to Alcatraz because they've shut that place down. But I could end up in Leavenworth or someplace worse. And not just for ten, eleven months. We're talking about until I die."

"But you've got friends in Washington and Springfield. You've always taken steps to protect yourself."

"I didn't take enough." Lewis Knowles sighed. He was looking old in that moment, older than Kegan had ever seen him.

Knowles said, "You're young, Vince. You look at me and you think I'm some sort of criminal genius. But these guys are tied to a power I can't even fully comprehend. I've spent my whole life trying to outsmart people and now I've reached the age where I realized the smartest thing I could have done was walk away from this life when I had the chance. Been an accountant or a lawyer. A modest house in Winnetka and my own law practice should have been enough for me. But I had ambitions beyond that. Too proud to be straight. I've spent my whole life building an empire and I realize now it was all a mistake."

"Lewis . . ."

"But forget all that. It's too late for me. If you do this, if you agree to this, Vince, take my advice and get out of this business after it's done. Permanently."

"I never said I wanted out."

"*I* want you out. Listen to me, you do this one last thing for me, and I'll pay you a hundred grand. Twenty now and the rest after. If you're careful with it, you should be able to find some other trade and not look back. Get some help for that gambling addiction you have so you don't get yourself in another hole."

Kegan put his hands on the desk. The most he'd ever been paid for any job was twenty thousand. This was a hundred thousand dollars tax free. He thought about Gerri. A decent apartment in Evanston for her and her baby, Gerri being free from the fear and anxiety that comes with being poor. Gerri not having to smile uneasily when some rich old jerk-off pawed her.

Kegan said, "You're offering me early retirement."

"In a way."

"What about Sam? Alfieri?"

"They'll leave you alone."

"I don't know, Vince. A civilian . . ."

"Well . . . these guys tell me he's a traitor and that we'd be doing our country a service. Maybe they're telling the truth, maybe they're selling me a line. I don't know. Maybe it's not for us to know. I can tell you that we'd be crossing a line, going outside the world we know. But then maybe it's too late for us to be asking questions after the things we've done."

"Yeah, maybe."

And Kegan was thinking of his childhood. His mom and dad fighting, his dad slapping his mom. His mother crying and making a phone call. Lewis Knowles coming to the apartment later and putting the fear of God into Kegan's father. The hitting stopped after that.

Another memory: Kegan at his father's funeral. Not crying when he thought he should be. Relieved that the old man was dead. Lewis at the funeral comforting his mother.

Years later, coming home from Korea, broke and without any prospects. His mother telling him Lewis wanted him to see him. Lewis taking him under his wing.

Kegan was in his late twenties when he realized that people envied him for the respect and patronage he received from Knowles. Knowles treated him like a white man, maybe even treated him like he was smarter than he was. Kegan knew he could never have been a lawyer or an accountant like Lewis could have been. He didn't have the brain and he didn't have the ambition. He certainly didn't have the drive. More to the point, he did not have the innate leadership skills Lewis had. Kegan realized later that, unlike a lot of hoods, he had never envied Lewis. He had never wanted that kind of responsibility.

Now Knowles said, "One more thing. You understand that if you do this, I won't be able to protect you. You get caught, you'll be on your own."

"I understand that."

And Kegan knew then that his decision would remove him from a life he had grown accustomed to. Maybe too accustomed to. Good or bad, it would be a permanent change.

Kegan said, "Why me? Why choose me for this?"

"You're the best I have. And I say that not because you're the best shot I know. It's nothing like that. Something more important. You're quiet. You don't look for fights. There aren't many understated men in our gang. You've got no arrest record. Not even a speeding ticket. You're not in any criminal database in the FBI or any other law enforcement agency's database. You don't look like a gangster. You can ask questions and people will forget who you are. That's a necessary requirement for this job."

"Okay," Kegan said.

"Okay, you'll do it?"

"Yeah, I'll do it."

Knowles placed another envelope on the desk. Inside the envelope was twenty thousand dollars.

CHAPTER EIGHT

Terry McCormick sat in the study of his Virginia house studying the map of the 1968 presidential election results. The blue states carried by his brother, the red states carried by the Republican candidate. There was a lot of blue. Dan had won forty-four states, the opponent had won six. Dan had won the popular vote by 63%, the highest percentage since James Monroe's re-election in 1820.

The Republican had won his own state of Nevada and five states in the south.

Terry thought of all the work he had done for that campaign. The money he had spread around to sheriffs and precinct captains, the threats he had delivered to committeemen who spoke of defection, the nights he had gotten two or three hours of sleep.

When it was done, Dan told Terry it was as much his victory as it was Dan's. Dan even told Terry that he'd worked harder than Dan had.

Which was true. Dan had not cut back on the women during the campaign. Terry had also been unfaithful to his wife over the years. But he could count the number of women on two hands. That was the number Dan had in an average week. One time, a Secret Service agent wrote a letter to the head of the White House detail complaining about what he called the president's "recklessness." The agent said his chief concern was not immorality, but security: the hookers and starlets being brought to the president were rarely if ever checked for weapons and there was, of course, the possibility that one of them could be an agent for the Soviet Union or even Cuba. The letter was brought to Terry's attention. Terry did not discuss it with his brother. The agent was reassigned to Independence, Missouri, guarding Bess Truman.

The agent was a Catholic boy from Duluth. To a degree, Terry could understand his discomfort, if not outright disgust. Dan's attendance at mass was sporadic, whereas Terry's was daily. But Terry believed that the agent had lost his perspective. The agent had not understood the importance of loyalty. When you worked for the man, you owed that man absolute fealty. Otherwise you didn't take the job. You were either on the bus or you were off the bus. Once the agent spoke out, he had removed himself from the bus. Terry felt he had been generous by not terminating the agent.

Terry's loyalty to his brother was unquestioned. Still . . . when he looked at the map of the 1968 results, he wondered if he could beat Dan. Or even match him. Would he be able to win forty-four states? Would he be able to beat James Monroe in the popular vote?

In 1967, Dan was almost killed. A man in Indianapolis had taken three shots at the president as he stepped out of a car in front of a hotel. The third bullet had hit Dan in the shoulder and gone out his back. The Secret Service swarmed the shooter and quickly disarmed him.

The shooter was no one of consequence. A misfit who had never succeeded at anything and had never been liked by anyone, not even his family. No foreign power or criminal organization had sponsored him. Like many would-be loser assassins, he had hoped to become someone important by killing someone important. Investigators would later learn that he knew very little about Dan McCormick's politics. They would also learn that he had previously attempted to shoot a well-known right-wing general and had even considered killing Tony Curtis. The shooter wanted to be famous. After he was convicted, he was put in a penitentiary with the general population and within three weeks was beaten to death by another inmate.

After the shooting, Dan was rushed to a hospital. He had lost a lot of blood. For three long days, the nation feared that he would die, ending an era.

But he didn't die. He survived and became more popular than ever.

Something Terry knew that very few others did: Before the shooting, Dan's wife Nicky had threatened to divorce him. It was, of course, over a woman. Dan had stranded her at a party and left with the wife of a French diplomat. It had been an especially public humiliation. Terry and his father spent days trying to persuade Nicky not to end the marriage. The Old Man had been uncharacteristically tender with Nicky, even to the point of telling her that he agreed she deserved something better. The Old Man even promised to give her her own separate bank account in Switzerland.

The negotiations, such as they were, were still ongoing when Dan was shot. After that,

Nicky surprised them both by flying to Indianapolis immediately. That was when Terry realized that Nicky was still in love with Dan.

Terry also realized then that he was bothered by this, maybe even hurt by it. And then he had to admit to himself that he was a little in love with Nicky himself.

He would admit this to no one. Certainly not to his wife, who was mother to their seven children. And certainly not to his brother.

A funny thing happened after the shooting. Not only did Nicky decide to stay with her husband, she also began to work harder than anyone to build and sustain the McCormick myth. Photos of her and her husband with the children were carefully selected and distributed to the press. Tightly controlled interviews were arranged with magazines that longed to be associated with the First Family who were as beautiful as movie stars. Nicky knew the power of the myth. Knew that sales of magazines tripled or even quadrupled when the covers were graced with pictures of her and her husband. Knew that a country without a Royal Family would seek out and create its own. Nicky McCormick had become a princess. And she wasn't about to give that up over something as inconsequential as adultery.

Terry's assistant knocked on the door of his study.

"Yes?"

"Mr. Mayville is here to see you."

They sat in the red leather chairs in front of the fireplace. The children were upstairs asleep.

Mayville said, "Well, it seems to have worked. Davidson told me that they've agreed to play ball."

Terry said, "I thought they'd come around. These gangster types, they're pussies at the end of the day. All you got to do is take away some of their toys."

"Bob said Knowles didn't make it easy." Mayville laughed. "Said Knowles called him a bagman."

"He said that?"

"Yeah."

"Knowles always was a bastard. But he's not as smart as he thinks he is. Pop used to do business with him. He said the man always overestimated himself. I'm glad it was Knowles we leaned on instead of Iacovetta."

"How come?"

"Ah . . . we asked those guys to help us out years ago with Castro. Iacovetta was willing, even enthusiastic. You know the Italians. But Knowles wouldn't go along with it. He said it was a bad idea. Can you believe that? A hood telling us we shouldn't be in the killing business."

"What was his problem?"

"Who knows? He's British, you know."

"Knowles?"

"Yeah, he was born in Wales or Scotland or someplace like that. That's partly why Pop never liked him. He always thought Knowles looked down on him because he was Irish."

"Really? I was told that Knowles never put much stock in a guy's race."

Terry McCormick looked at his assistant.

Mayville seemed to shrink a little in his chair. "I mean, that's just what I was told."

"You were told wrong."

"Of course," Mayville said. "Davidson promised him we would call off the dogs. Shall I contact our people in Nevada? Tell them to pull their bills?"

"Yeah. Tell them . . . tell them it's on hold for now."

After a moment, Mayville said, "On hold?"

"You heard me."

"But I thought we were going to call it off entirely. I mean, that's what we agreed to."

"I know what we agreed to. After it's done,

we may want to still go through with it."

"Are you . . . that's . . . ah . . . I mean we agreed to . . ."

"Lewis Knowles is a gangster. Are you suggesting we make deals with people like that?"

Mayville thought, *we already have.* Mayville had read the file on Knowles, both the FBI's and the one put together by Terry's own intelligence agency. Both of the files made it clear that Knowles was a man who would kill if pushed hard enough. Now Mayville wondered if Davidson had told Knowles who *he* was. If Knowles had written Mike Mayville's name down in some sort of book.

Terry smiled and said, "What's the matter, Mike? You nervous?"

And there it was. The McCormick display of Irish machismo. It had gotten the country into the quagmire that was Vietnam and the decade-long mess that was Cuba. They gave speeches, here and there, about the importance of peace and defending freedom around the world, but it always came down to a fight. McCormicks never backed down. Anyone counseling restraint or patience was branded a chicken-shit bastard. If they persisted, they were cut out of the loop. Shunned. Mayville had worked most of his life to be in the inner ring. And he knew all it took to be shoved out of that ring was one wrong word, one small gesture indicating disloyalty or cowardice.

Still, Mayville said, "Oh, maybe a little. I mean, this guy's a criminal. Who knows what he's capable of?"

"You can't let these guys intimidate you, Mikey. Hoffa, Iacovetta, Knowles, they go through life thinking they're untouchable. They're not."

Mayville was relieved by Terry's smile. Terry could do that. Belittle you one moment, comfort you the next. Mayville was still in the ring.

Terry said, "Lewis Knowles's time has passed. He just hasn't figured it out yet. He will, though. I'll make sure of that."

■ ■ ■ ■

PART 2

■ ■ ■ ■

CHAPTER NINE

Kegan had a set of rules, some of which had been handed down to him and some of which he had developed on his own. They were:

1. You do not kill a man in his house.
2. You do not kill a man in front of his family.
3. You do not harm the man's family.
4. You do not kill a man when he is in church or when he is near a church.
5. You do not torture a man before killing him.
6. You do not steal from a man you've killed or are about to.

Kegan was not a deep thinker like Lewis Knowles. Still, he had a sense of why a man in his business needed some guidelines. To a degree, the rules were there so as not to offend the local gods or perhaps God himself, presuming He existed. It was silly, because if there was a hell, he would surely be going there no matter what he did. God wouldn't give a murderer a pass simply because he took care not to commit murder near a church. Nor would there be leniency because he didn't kill a man in his home. It didn't matter, really.

And yet it did. It mattered to people like Lewis Knowles. Some people in New York had killed Joey Gallo a few months back. It had been done in an Italian restaurant near the intersection of Mulberry and Hester. No one was sorry about it because no one liked Crazy Joey. Crazy Joey was vicious and a showboat and was vain enough to believe that Richard Widmark had modeled his character in *Kiss of Death* after him when it was actually the other way around. Crazy Joey was a smartass. When Terry McCormick had been counsel on the labor racketeering committee, Joey had gone into Terry's office and said, "Nice carpet you got here, kid. Just right for putting." Very funny. Joey not caring that Terry McCormick was essentially a humorless man and that he would make the entire Outfit pay for Joey's disrespect in the committee hearings. Joey hadn't cared. All he cared about was himself, selfish even by a hood's standards. The

108

only people who mourned the death of Joey Gallo were a handful of actors in the New York theater district who were stupid enough to think that Joey was some sort of charming "character." Lewis Knowles shed no tears over Joey Gallo's death, but Lewis was angry that the killers had shot Joey in front of Joey's wife and ten-year-old daughter. "It's not how you do it," Lewis said.

How you did it was to isolate the target. And that usually meant planning and patience. They had been in a hurry to kill Joey, though, probably because Joe Colombo wanted it done quickly.

Kegan considered the contract that was now in front of him. A man named Albert Hirsch. A military analyst working for the Pentagon. A man who had been in hiding now for seventeen days. A man who had never met Joey Gallo or Joe Colombo or Lewis Knowles. A man who was not in any way associated with narcotics, casinos, prostitution, labor racketeering, or any of the Five Families. A civilian, not a gangster. A buttoned-down type, a high-powered government clerk.

Why?

Lewis had said they told him the guy was a spy, about to sell some sort of secret document to the Russians. But Lewis himself didn't seem convinced of that. And Lewis was the type who could convince you of anything. Maybe Lewis thought the guy had something on the McCormicks, something that would embarrass them or maybe even get them prosecuted for some kind of crime.

But that didn't make sense. The McCormicks were the guys in charge of the law. They were at the top. Lewis had told Kegan there was a fair chance the McCormicks were lying to him, but Lewis said it didn't matter because they had been in the business too long to make judgments.

Kegan couldn't argue with that. He had killed men in Korea and he had killed men in the States. He had done what he had done and he was not vain enough to try to persuade himself it had all been for some sort of greater good or that it was justified at all. Killing Joey Gallo wouldn't have bothered him and killing Mickey Gold had cost him no sleep at all. Gallo and Gold had chosen their lives just as Vince Kegan had chosen his. He shouldn't be bothering himself asking what life Albert Hirsch had chosen.

What Hirsch *had* chosen to do was disappear. Kegan would have to find him before he could kill him.

Lewis's memorandum said that Hirsch

had last been seen in Santa Monica, California. He had lunch with a man named Murray Holcombe. Lewis said he believed the man was a screenwriter.

Murray Holcombe did not look like Kegan thought he would. Kegan had expected to meet a short Jewish man with little hair. But Murray Holcombe was tall and patrician, with a full mane of hair. He wore jeans and a denim shirt and had a yellow scarf knotted about his neck. He did not look the least bit effeminate.

Kegan had put a little dye in his hair. A little more gray to give him another ten years. He also wore glasses.

Holcombe met Kegan at an office he was temporarily keeping at one of the bigger Hollywood studios. Kegan gave him a false name and Holcombe didn't question him about it. The screenwriter saw a big man in a suit.

Holcombe said, "You with the FBI? I already talked with them."

"No."

"Oh, I see. An OGA."

Kegan said, "Pardon?"

"OGA. Other Government Agency. Come on, you don't need to play games with me. I'm hip to it all."

Kegan said, "Okay."

"Well, that's all right. I don't mind going through it all again. You seem like a nice guy. For a fed."

Kegan sighed, but didn't say anything.

Holcombe said, "Listen, I don't mind talking to you. But I've got to meet Warren for lunch to discuss a project. You mind riding with me while we talk?"

"No."

"You'll have to find your way back from Beverly Hills. Do you mind?"

"I'll get a cab."

Kegan rode in the passenger seat of the screenwriter's yellow Ferrari Daytona. The twelve-cylinder engine thrummed a nice bass line as the screenwriter talked about his work. Holcombe told Kegan about how he was doctoring some piece a shit vehicle that Goldman had written for Jane because Jane was hot now but it was hard to say how long she would remain hot and he wouldn't get the credit of course, but the money was too good to turn down and he knew how the business worked. Kegan nodded even though he didn't know what or who the man was talking about.

Holcombe said, "You ever do any private work? I mean, you know, off the clock?"

"You mean work as a private investigator?"

"Yeah."

"Not yet."

"Too bad. You've got the look, you know. The suit, the quiet tough demeanor. You see *Harper*?"

"Who?"

"The movie. You know, the one with Paul Newman?"

"Oh, yeah. I saw it."

"Was it real? For you, I mean?"

"I wouldn't know," Kegan said. "I thought he did a good job."

"That movie was an homage, you know. Everything is an homage of something else. Newman was doing Bogart, *The Big Sleep*. That's why they had Betty Bacall in it. An homage to Bogie. Paul's great. He's not Bogie, of course, but he wasn't trying to be. He chewed gum instead of smoking, that sort of stuff. But he nailed the part."

Kegan nodded.

"The thing about Paul, he's not intimidated by talent. Other people's talent. He loves to surround himself with talent. He figures it makes him better. Not many actors would have the balls to share the screen with someone like Strother Martin. But Paul loves working with him. Loves it."

"Sure."

"But everything's always changing. You can't make *Harper* today. It's all past. They want stories that are more real. It has to be real."

"Right."

"They want higher stakes. That story, all Newman had to do was find a rich man who was missing. It was about the detective and the people in the man's family. That's not enough today. They want larger issues. For Newman's character, it was just about the job. No greater cause than that for him. You understand?"

"I do."

After a moment, the screenwriter said, "Well, you're not like the other guys."

"What other guys?"

"The feds. They came on pretty strong. Leaned on me, said I wasn't telling them everything. Suggested I was guilty of something called misprision of a felony. Do you know what that is?"

"Yeah. It's a failure to report a felony."

"What felony did I fail to report?"

"I haven't the slightest idea."

"Neither have I. Those guys were fascists."

"How did you come to meet Hirsch?"

"His wife's from L.A. You know about her, don't you?"

"No."

The screenwriter seemed surprised. "Jennifer Hirsch's maiden name is Stewart. Her father is a real estate developer. He developed most of Palm Springs and Newport Beach. Millions of dollars there. Anyway, I thought there might be a project there."

"A project?"

"A story. A film."

"Albert Hirsch wanted to make a movie?"

"No, not make a movie. We were just discussing a project." The screenwriter looked at Kegan like he was a bit thick.

Kegan said, "What would the movie — what would the project have been about?"

"Oh, we didn't get that far. He seemed like he didn't want to be there. Like he was doing something his wife wanted."

"He didn't tell you much?"

"I wanted him to tell me *his* story. But he wouldn't tell me. Which surprised me."

"Why did it surprise you?"

"Because this is Hollywood. Everyone's got an idea for a script. Everyone. I was at a party once where I met the mayor. The mayor of Los Angeles, mind you. And *he* told he me he had an idea for a script. It never ends. Everyone wants in."

"Did Hirsch want in?"

"No. . . . I don't know. Maybe he wanted

115

to think about it. But he wouldn't tell me anything."

"Did he tell you what he did?"

"He told me he was an analyst for the Pentagon. He asked me if I would be interested in making a movie about Vietnam. He said that and I just about shut down. I mean, you saw *The Green Berets,* didn't you?"

"Yeah, I saw it."

"Please don't tell me you liked it."

"I like John Wayne."

"We all like the Duke, but . . . come on."

"Isn't that what Hollywood wanted? A good war film?"

The screenwriter looked at him again. "It's what they wanted ten years ago, not now. Duke's a good man, a funny guy actually, but he lets his vanity and his politics get the better of him sometimes. He should stick with the westerns, but that time's sort of passed too."

"Did Hirsch want to make a movie like *The Green Berets*?"

"I don't think so. He wasn't the John Wayne type. He seemed like an egghead to me."

"He was a Marine, actually."

"He was?"

"Yeah."

"Hmmm."

Which was more than could be said for John Wayne, Kegan thought. Though he still liked him.

"I don't know," Holcombe said. "In this business, there are always a thousand projects. You got to learn to listen to your inner ear because you can't do them all."

"So you didn't like his pitch?"

"I'm not sure he wanted to pitch a story to me. Like I said, I think he was there because his wife wanted him to be. His heart didn't seem to be in it. And you can't back a project if you're not in it."

"Did he seem . . . troubled to you?"

"Troubled? What, you mean like he was having a nervous breakdown or something?"

"Something like that."

"I don't know. No, I don't think so. He seemed pretty even-keeled to me. Although you never know when someone's been to HST."

"HST?"

"You never heard of that?"

"No."

"Oh. I guess you're not from here, are you?"

"No."

"It's a training program. Based in San Francisco."

"A military training program?"

The screenwriter laughed. "Almost. . . . No, it's not military training. It's Hocheim Seminars Training. HST."

"Hocheim?"

"Gerhard Hocheim. He's the leader, the trainer of this program. A lot of people are doing it. A lot of actors. I mean, A-list actors."

"Training . . . what's he training them for?"

"Self-awareness."

After a moment, Kegan said, "That's it?"

"Well, I haven't done the training myself. I know some people who have. They all had to sign a contract promising not to reveal what goes on in the training. So unless you've done it, it's hard to say what goes on."

"Hirsch went to this training?"

"Yeah."

"How come?"

"I don't know. People are always looking for answers. Simple answers. And it's a prestigious thing in Southern California."

"Was he interested in prestige?"

"I wouldn't have thought so. But I only met him the one time."

"How long does this . . . training last?"

"Seven days. They do it at the Shamrock

118

Spring Hotel in San Francisco."

"When did he do it?"

"Oh . . . I guess about a month or two ago."

"You tell the feds about this?"

"No. I guess it never came up. They didn't ask and, to be frank, I didn't much like those guys."

"What did they bring up?"

"They did more talking than asking. Little guys with skinny ties and attitude. They asked a lot of questions about communism. Asked me if I was one. Asked why I wrote scripts that had the word 'fuck' in it and had what they called 'subversive themes.' I didn't like the places they were going to, so I only answered what they asked."

"They threaten you?"

"I thought so. Oh, don't get me wrong. I wasn't scared of them or anything. They kind of seemed like clowns to me. One of them said I should be making another *FBI Story*. You know, the one that had Jimmy Stewart. That was the one where Hoover had to approve every scene."

"I didn't see it."

"You didn't miss anything. I thought the guy was trying to make a joke. I mean . . . Jimmy Stewart? But he was serious."

"I thought it was Efrem Zimbalist."

119

"Pardon me?"

"I thought he played the federal agent in the movie."

"You mean Efrem Zimbalist *Junior.* No, that was the television show, not the movie." Holcombe shook his head. "A friend of mine wrote some scripts for the show. He said it was a pain in the ass, but writing for any television show is a pain. Hoover had control over the TV show too. He personally had right of approval over every actor who played an FBI agent. Hoover's dead now, isn't he?"

"Yeah. He died a few months ago."

"Thank God. . . . Yeah, these guys started out under Hoover."

"But you didn't tell them about this H . . ."

"HST. No, I didn't tell them. Say, you don't think the Russians had an agent at the HST seminar, do you? You know, like recruited him?"

Kegan suppressed a smile. He liked the screenwriter and didn't want to hurt his feelings.

"Anything's possible," Kegan said.

"Make a hell of a movie," Holcombe said.

CHAPTER TEN

Holcombe offered to let Kegan drive his Ferrari back to the studio, saying he could catch a ride home with Warren. Kegan thanked him but said no, he would get a taxi back to the studio. He wondered who Warren was but decided it wasn't important.

He paid the cabbie at the studio and got into the car he'd rented, an orange 1972 Camaro with a white vinyl top.

He had memorized the key facts of Lewis's memo on Hirsch. Lewis was not comfortable putting things in writing and he had told Kegan to burn the memo after reading it. Like *Mission Impossible.* The memo made a reference to Hirsch's wife, Jennifer. Formerly Jennifer Stewart. Lewis had made no mention of the woman's father.

The father's name was Jack Stewart, not James. Kegan went to the Malibu library and spent a couple of hours looking at newspaper clips about him. Jack Stewart was born Jack Shamforoff in 1913, the son of a dry goods merchant. He changed his name to Stewart after his service in the Second World War. After the war, he began selling real estate. By 1960, he was one of the ten richest men in Southern California.

He had two children, the daughter named Jennifer and a son named Hunter. There were photos of the grown kids in the *L.A. Times.* The son looked nothing like the father. Blond haired, tanned like a surfer, more Troy Donahue than the latest in a line of Shamforoffs. Maybe it had something to do with the California climate.

Kegan found Hunter Stewart at a beach house in Malibu.

He answered the door in tight swim trunks and no shirt. His hair was messed up and he looked like he'd just been surfing.

Kegan gave him a name that wasn't his and told him he was looking for his brother-in-law.

Hunter Stewart pushed his hair back and said, "What makes you think he'd be here?"

Kegan said, "I didn't think he would be. I thought maybe you could help."

"Are you a cop?"

"No."

"A fed?"

"Not quite."

122

"Maybe you work for the Pentagon?"

"Maybe."

Kegan let it sit out there and the guy named Hunter Stewart said, "Well, at least you're not a reporter. I just made some coffee. You want some?"

They sat on the back deck. Hunter Stewart in a light blue bathrobe, his feet up on the rail. Stretched out before them were the empty beach and the waves rolling in from the ocean.

Hunter Stewart said, "How come you haven't talked to my father?"

"I couldn't get an appointment with him."

"Yeah, I can understand that. He's a very busy man. He's sixty-nine now and still twisting his melon, looking for the next dollar. You know where he is now?"

"No."

"In Macau. He's looking into casinos there. He says it's the next gold mine."

"You work for him?"

"No. I tried to, when I first got out of college. But it didn't work out. He said I didn't have the right ethic for it. It wasn't for me. I decided to get into the business."

"What business?"

The blond man looked at Kegan like he was from way out of town.

123

"The entertainment business. What else is there in Southern California?"

"Oh."

"Lot of shit to go through, I know. But I got a pilot."

"A pilot?"

"Yeah. Something in the works. A Quinn Martin production. If it flies, I'll be playing one of these three agents who work for an international spy organization. It's called *Probe.* The other two guys in the rotation are Tony Franciosa and the third will either be Clu Gulager or Mitchell Ryan. A mixture of science fiction and private detective story. Not as realistic as, you know, whatever it is you do. But it's television."

"Right," Kegan said. He thought the guy had been taking about an airplane pilot.

"Anyway," Stewart said, "it's probably good you couldn't see my father. He'd have given you an earful."

"How come?"

"Aww, he doesn't like Albert very much. He said he was a traitor."

"Why would he call him that?"

"You don't know my dad. A fierce anti-communist. He's a good friend of Lundy's, the sleazeball. He thinks we should be dropping nukes on North Vietnam. He thinks

124

everyone to the left of Goldwater is a commie."

"Including the McCormicks?"

"Oh, yeah. He thinks they're way too soft. I guess the last time Albert and Jen saw him, Albert told him he didn't know what he was talking about. Albert's like that. Not afraid to speak his mind."

"Were you there for this discussion?"

"For a while. It was last Thanksgiving."

"Do you think your brother-in-law's a communist?"

"God, no. He just did this sort of Socratic thing with dad. Asking him questions. Dad was saying that any kid who dodged the draft should be shot for treason. Dad fought the Nazis in the war and Albert knew about that. So Albert asked him, 'If a young German soldier made the decision not to kill Jews, would that be treason?' And 'If a German soldier refused to fight for the Nazis, would that make him immoral? Wouldn't we say that refusal was a moral decision?' And so on. Sent my dad through the roof. He told Albert Americans weren't Nazis. Then he told him to leave."

"And then what?"

"He left."

"And went where?"

"Back to Washington, I guess. We haven't

125

heard from him since."

"What about Jennifer?"

"I don't know where she is. We sort of lost touch over the years. But . . . truth be told, we were never that close."

"Why not?"

"Ah, I don't really relate to her either. She's always sort of looked down on me. She's never said that, but I can tell. Thinks I'm a beach bum, freeloading off the old man. She calls me every few weeks or so to check in on me. Asks how I'm doing, how my career is going. She does that because she feels guilty and dutiful. Bleeding heart. You know the type."

"Does she work?"

"Sort of. She was working for some left-wing peacenik outfit in D.C. She met Albert at a protest at the Washington mall."

After a moment, Kegan said, "What was he doing there?"

"He went there because she was there. I guess it was their first date."

"Their first date was a peace march?"

"My sister's a good-looking woman. Albert . . . well, Albert's kind of a more character actor–looking guy, but no leading man."

Kegan turned his head away. He didn't want blondie to catch him rolling his eyes.

"You said you don't know where your sister is."

"No. I don't know where Albert is either. Isn't he in Washington?"

"I really don't know." Kegan realized then that Hunter Stewart, Jewish son turned Troy Donahue really didn't know anything about his brother-in-law and little about his sister. His world was pilots and movie studios and scripts that would hopefully make him a star. He wasn't interested in much beyond that.

Kegan said, "You know anything about his discussion with the screenwriter?"

"Which one?"

"A guy named Murray Holcombe."

"Albert met with Murray Holcombe? I didn't know that. Christ, that guy wouldn't give me the time of day."

"Is he a big deal?"

"A big deal? The man's a close personal friend of Dustin. Out here, everybody says that Dustin's a close personal friend. But Holcombe's actually telling the truth. You gotta watch yourself if you want to work in this business. People will Dustin you to death."

Kegan didn't know who Dustin was. He decided not to ask.

Hunter Stewart said, "I guess he met with

127

more than one."

"What do you mean?" Kegan said.

"Well, I'd heard Jen had set him up with Miltie Donchin."

"Who's that?"

"He's a writer. He does a lot of stuff for *Playboy.* Human-interest stories."

"Have you read him?"

"No. But I hear he's good. He's doing screenplays now. Word is, he's working on something for Hal Ashby's next film. He's hot now."

"Albert met with him?"

"Yeah. But I don't know if that was to discuss a movie. It may have been for something else."

"A story?"

"Yeah, maybe a story. Maybe even an interview for *Playboy.* Donchin does those too."

"Albert was thinking of doing an interview with *Playboy*?"

"Yeah. I can tell you, he wasn't after pussy. Albert's a choirboy."

CHAPTER ELEVEN

Kegan got Miltie Donchin's telephone number from Hunter Stewart. He called and got an answering service. Kegan said Donchin was expecting an important call from him and gave a name.

Thirty minutes later, Kegan pulled the Camaro up the drive of a mansion in Brentwood. A black man in a butler's uniform answered the door and Kegan felt unreal. Kegan told the butler he was there to see Milt Donchin and the butler led him through the mansion.

There were beautiful young girls walking around the mansion, some of them in bikinis, some of them in white T-shirts with no underwear.

Kegan figured he was in a whorehouse. Half-naked girls were nothing new to him. He'd been in some of the best cathouses in Chicago. None of them had been located in mansions though. This place was big. With a lot of marble statues and some high-dollar art on the walls. An expensive pad to be sure, yet somehow dirty and distasteful, even by whorehouse standards. There was a faint smell of dog urine in the air. The girls wore the same empty, lifeless expressions you saw in a lot of whorehouses.

Kegan said to the butler, "Mr. Donchin lives here?"

"Temporarily," the butler said. "He is a guest."

They reached the grounds behind the mansion. Kegan saw the biggest swimming pool he'd ever seen. The pool was in the shape of a "T." He realized that it was two Olympic-sized pools joined together. A couple of girls sat by the pool in lounge chairs. More girls were swimming naked in the pool.

Kegan saw three men sitting at a table. One of them was in a silk bathrobe over silk pajamas. He had a can of Pepsi in his hand. Another man was someone Kegan had seen in the movies. A Very Big Star. The third man was explaining some sort of concept to them with his hands. This one Kegan figured was Miltie Donchin. The man in the pajamas got up from the table and the Big Star followed him. They walked past Kegan and the butler as if they were invisible.

The butler said, "You can see him now."

It was the first time Kegan had felt dismissed by a butler. Maybe it was progress.

Donchin stood to shake his hand and introduced himself. He gestured Kegan into a chair.

Miltie Donchin was a tall man with dark hair going gray and thick sideburns. He wore wraparound sunglasses and a silk shirt open to his naval. He wore a heavy watch and held a thin cigar.

Donchin said, "So you're a private detective?"

Kegan said politely, "I didn't say that."

"Yeah, and you didn't say you were working for Jack Stewart either. So we'll pretend you're not."

Kegan said, "If you say so."

Donchin laughed. Kegan didn't see how it was funny, but decided to go with it. Sometimes it helped to let the other people believe they had it figured out. Particularly in Southern California.

Donchin threw a big hairy hand out toward the pool and the naked girls and said, "You ever seen anything like this?"

A whorehouse? Kegan thought. But said, "I guess not."

"There are a lot of people who'd kill to get inside the Playboy mansion. You got in by making a phone call. Pretty terrific, huh?"

"Sure."

"Is it everything you thought it'd be?"

"I think it could use a good wash."

Donchin laughed again. "Well, I guess it's not the most hygienic of places. But look at the goodies."

Kegan looked at Donchin. "This your home?"

"For a while," Donchin said. "My old lady and I are splitting up. Hef said I could stay here while I get it sorted out."

"I understand you met with Albert Hirsch."

"Is that what Jack Stewart told you?"

Kegan shrugged.

Donchin said, "Yeah, I met with him. We were considering doing a story on him. But frankly, I didn't find his story that interesting."

"Why not?"

"All he wanted to talk about was Vietnam. The power structure, something he kept calling 'bureaucratic homicide.' Not to brag, but I get ten thousand dollars per story these days. And his wasn't a ten-thousand-dollar story."

"How come?"

"It's all been done before. Listen, I've met

132

with retired CIA agents, generals, soldiers of fortune, all of them telling me they've got the 'real story' on Vietnam. It's been done to death."

"Albert say he had something new?"

"He claimed to. But he wouldn't tell me what. Sorry, but I just don't have time for that sort of shit."

"Did he leave you a number? Some way to get in touch with him?"

"No. Not that I asked him, of course."

Kegan said, "I heard he was mixed up in the HST movement."

"Oh, Christ, him too?"

Kegan said, "Too?"

"My old lady went to that seminar. In San Francisco. Said she 'got it' and said it made her aware that our marriage was not real. She came back from that charade and filed against me that week. That HST crap is what made her leave me."

Donchin was now staring at one of Hef's naked girls coming out of the pool. If the writer had been a character in an *Archie* comic book, there would have been a dotted line going directly from his eyes to the girl's damp pubic hair.

Kegan said, "Was that her only reason?"

"Huh? . . . Oh, well, yeah there might have been other reasons. I mean, Christ, you can't expect me to resist all temptation, can you?"

Kegan shrugged again.

Donchin said, "You only live once, huh? Hi, Marcie."

The girl gave them a look, but only a brief one, before she walked away. Kegan remembered the Hollywood joke about the Polish actress who slept with the writer because she thought it would get her a part in a movie.

Donchin said, "Huh. . . . Maybe I got her name wrong. It's hard to remember all their names here."

"When you met with Hirsch, did he seem all right?"

"What do you mean?"

"I mean, did it seem like he was having some sort of breakdown?"

"A nervous breakdown? I don't think so. He said he was disillusioned, but this is Hollywood. Everybody says that. Disillusion sells."

"You think he was feigning it?"

"He might have been. You got cats out here trying to pitch a story, they try to tell you what they think you want to hear. The guy took a look at me, my beard and long hair, he thinks, yeah, tell him I was always against the war. But this guy was your typi-

134

cal Washington poindexter. He was working for the Pentagon when it served his interests, now he thinks it serves his interests to make some sort of anti-establishment picture. It ain't real, man. It's got to be real."

"Did he say anything about this HST movement?"

"Not to me."

"You know his wife, Jennifer?"

"I know about her. She's kinda cute, but she's not leading woman material."

Kegan said, "She wanted to be in the movies?"

"They all do. These people, they work with the McCormicks, they think some of that magic rubs off on them."

"Did Hirsch say anything about the Mc-Cormicks to you?"

"No."

"Nothing?"

"Nothing. I'll give him for credit that. He didn't name-drop them. But you know, he probably wasn't in a position to do that. Half the people you meet from Washington these days, they talk as if Dan McCormick was a close personal friend. How charming and attractive he is. In a way, I don't blame them. This town's filled with starfuckers. In Washington, they all want to fuck the president." After a moment, the writer said,

135

"Here too."

"You ever meet the president?"

"No. I almost did once. I was invited to one of his fundraisers, but I was too busy to go. He comes out here fairly often, you know. He's slept with more starlets than Sinatra. He loves Hollywood and Hollywood loves him. They say Washington is Hollywood for ugly people. Only he's not ugly. He's movie-star gorgeous. Anyway, we feed each other."

"Excuse me?"

"Hollywood and Washington. We give them glamour and pussy, they give us what we think is respectability. It's all meaningless, of course. Most of the producers and studio executives and movie stars, they don't even bother to vote. You know Ronald Reagan?"

"He was in a movie with Lee Marvin, wasn't he?"

"Yeah. *The Killers.* He played a bad guy." Donchin shrugged. "He wasn't bad. But that was eight years ago and he hasn't done a movie since. Now he's going to be our next governor."

"You're saying he's going to win?"

"I'm about the only one around here who thinks so. People underestimate him because he was never more than a B-movie actor.

But actually, a B-movie star is much better positioned to succeed in politics than a superstar. Know why?"

"Why?"

"Because they know about survival, man. They've had to fight much harder to make a living than a McQueen or a Brando. Something else too. Reagan's been president of the Screen Actors Guild for almost eight years. I've never met a union president who wasn't tough and smart. Christ, he might even be president someday."

"That would be interesting."

"Yeah, a regular renaissance. As for Hirsch, no, I didn't think he was crazy or anything like that. Tell you the truth, I didn't think much of him at all. Is he supposed to be someone important?"

"Not really," Kegan said.

CHAPTER TWELVE

Kegan left for San Francisco that night. He drove till midnight and stayed at a hotel near Modesto. The next morning he had a breakfast of bacon, eggs, toast, grapefruit, and coffee. He smoked two cigarettes after they cleared his plate and looked out the window and thought.

If he found Hirsch and put him down, he would get another eighty thousand. It would be a lot of money, tax free. He was still smarting at Lewis's assertion that he had some sort of gambling problem. That was something, coming from Lewis. Lewis had made millions from his gambling interests. Lewis sounding like his ex-wife. He wouldn't be in this hole if Green Bay had covered and Joe Namath wasn't injured. Did bad luck mean you had a problem?

Lewis had also told him this should be his last job. Now Kegan vaguely wondered if the two things were related. Did doing the

Outfit's dirty little jobs cause him to gamble? Did it somehow make him feel cleansed to lose money after taking another hood off the Outfit's books? A self-imposed reprimand?

Well . . . he guessed it was possible. Kegan knew a man in his position didn't feel a lot of guilt over killing. He was aware that he was missing something that made him capable of such things. A conscience or the common decency inherent in the average man that makes him hesitate to take another man's life. Kegan had never hesitated, had never held back. Maybe it was because he was a monster. Or maybe it was because he was too dumb to feel anything. Or think about it too much. Maybe that was why Lewis had groomed him for the work in the first place.

When he had done his first job for Lewis, he had taken part of his payment to a church and put ten percent in the basket. He had not taken communion then. Indeed, he had not taken communion since he was a teenager. After giving ten percent to the church, he felt sick. He felt God looking down at him like he was Cain. He couldn't pay God to forgive him. Not with five hundred dollars. He realized then that he probably didn't even believe in God. Yet he

139

was somehow seeking to make it right with money. Dumb and superstitious if you didn't believe. Blasphemous if you did.

Kegan knew several wise guys who went to mass regularly, all of them Italian. Some of them were quite generous to their parishes. In a way, maybe he had tried to emulate them when he put the money in the till. But though his mother was Italian, Kegan had never much indentified with the Italians himself. To the degree he thought about it, he thought of himself as Irish and shanty Irish at that. Another unimaginative, dim-witted potato face who hadn't achieved much in life.

You're a barber, Kegan thought. That was what he often thought of himself. That was what he told people he did when they asked. He had some nice suits, a decent apartment, and maybe the respect of some people in the Outfit because of Lewis's fondness for him. It wasn't much. The older he got, the more he realized that he perhaps didn't fit in with the majority of the wise-guy soldiers. Little things bothered him. Having to laugh at bad jokes to avoid conflict, deferring to mobsters who took offense at perceived slights, remembering who was "made" and who wasn't. Always having to watch yourself. At times, he felt he had no more

freedom than a guy working for a corporation. Maybe no more free than a guy living
in a communist country. That was how it
was if you weren't born with the brains to
build your own thing, build your own business, build your own empire. You ended up
taking orders from a boss one way or the
other. How much easier his life would be if
he were smart.

When he was young, before being in the
Army, he had not been ambitious. Kids he
had grown up with wanted to be gangsters.
They believed it made you someone. They
believed anyone who wasn't a gangster was
a sap and a loser. He had thought that once.
Then he became a gangster. He wore the
nice suits, he received respect from Lewis
and some of Lewis's cronies. But as the
years passed, he realized he was discontent,
maybe even depressed. After his marriage
ended, he began to feel like a failure. And
not just as a husband. After it was over, he
saw that he had placed a burden on his wife
that she could not possibly handle. That was
because he had told himself if he was a good
family man, he would at least have something to be proud of, some accomplishment
he could point to other than being the button man of a powerful mobster. But he and
Gerri had not been able to make a baby and

now he knew that the fault had been his because now Gerri was pregnant with some jerk-off cop's child. He would be forty years old in a few months and he would have nothing to show for all that time.

Lewis had once said to him, "You know why you're good at this? You think about what you need to do, but you don't think too much. You've got focus."

Well, Lewis wasn't wrong about many things. But he was wrong about that. He did think about things and maybe too much. He just didn't tell Lewis about it because he didn't want Lewis to think he was weak and self-pitying or, worse, losing his nerve. As for being focused, that was because he had never formed much of a taste for alcohol, unlike a lot of hoods. You want to ruin a hit man for the Outfit, just start feeding him booze.

The waitress came to his table and asked him if he'd like more coffee.

"No thanks," Kegan said. "Just the check."

She wrote up the bill and tore it out of her booklet and placed it on the table. It was a little under three dollars. Kegan put a five on the table and left.

Kegan had been in San Francisco once before. He remembered it being dirtier and grittier than it appeared in the movies. To him, the city of free love was a dangerous place. On his previous trip, he had an occasion to see someone called the Reverend Jim Jones interviewed on the local news and thought the guy was scarier than any mobster he'd ever known. In Chicago, men like Jim Jones would be relegated to street corners to preach their world vision. In San Francisco, he seemed to have unbridled power. Kegan preferred to live in a city kept in order by hoods than one governed by freaks.

Kegan booked a room at the Hotel Daniels. He stowed his luggage and drove to the Shamrock Springs Hotel. He asked the desk clerk where the HST seminar training was being conducted and the clerk told him it was on the second floor.

He got to the broad hallway and was relieved to see that there were no security guards at the doors of the ballroom. But then he found that the doors were locked from the inside.

He stood back from the locked doors. A bellman walked by carrying a tray.

Kegan said, "Excuse me. My wife's in there and I need to speak to her. Dad — her father — is in the hospital."

The bellman said, "Sorry, but I can't get

you in there. None of the staff are allowed in there once it starts. Sorry."

"When will it end?"

"Tomorrow. It goes for three days."

"What about bathroom breaks? Do they get to the toilet?"

"Yeah," the bellman said. "Twice a day. If they're lucky."

There was a sitting area around the corner from the ballroom with a bar and a piano. The bar was closed. Kegan took the escalator down to the restaurant on the first floor. He ordered a BLT to go and a glass of milk. After he put in the order, he went next door to the gift shop and bought three newspapers and a pack of cigarettes. He returned to the restaurant and picked up his lunch and carried it back up to the second floor. He ate his meal and then began reading the newspapers.

A couple of hours passed and he began working his second crossword puzzle. Then he heard the doors to the ballroom open. Moments later he saw a crowd of people rushing to the doors of the bathrooms.

He put down his paper and walked to the men's room.

The men in the bathroom were not dressed like he was. None of them wore a suit. They wore expensive shirts and leather jackets, jeans and turtleneck sweaters and silk scarves. Some of them had terrible body odor. They all looked tired and worn out. Kegan washed his hands at the sink and listened to them talk about "it."

"I think I'm getting it."

"Gerhard said you'll know when you've got it. It's not a question of thinking you have it."

"But how do you know?"

"You'll know."

"He's a brilliant man. Brilliant. He's a visionary."

One of the toilets flushed.

Some of the men filed out. Kegan loosened his tie and pulled it off. He folded it up and stuck it in the pocket of his jacket. He threw some water on his face and made his hair look disheveled.

When he left the restroom he saw a large crowd of people in the hall. At least a couple of hundred. That was good. He mixed in among them as they filed back into the banquet room.

In the vast room, he saw that the folding chairs had been folded and stacked against the walls. The attendants sat down on the floor. There were six hard-looking men in yellow sport coats and slacks who remained standing. Security guards. They kept them

145

on the inside here. At the front of the room there was a podium. On the podium was a handsome woman of about forty with her hair pulled back in a severe bun. She wore a cold smile and her eyes shone like a zealot's. In the center of the podium was the man they called Gerhard Hocheim.

He was a striking-looking guy with a mane of grayish, blondish hair. Small of stature with a big head, like a rooster's. He wore a dark suit and a black turtleneck sweater. Behind him and to his right was a blackboard with the work "IT" on it.

It smelled worse in this big room than it did in the toilet. Body odor and a slight scent of vomit.

Gerhard Hocheim stood stock still as his followers took their places on the floor. He did not make eye contact with any of them. Unlike most of the people in the room, he looked clean and refreshed.

As if on cue from his own personal will, the people in the room hushed themselves to a whisper and then to complete silence.

And Hocheim said nothing. He simply stood there in stone silence while all the followers gave him their complete attention. And then he continued to say nothing. A minute went by and then another. He was demonstrating his power over them.

Another minute passed. And then he began to speak.

"Yesterday, I told you that you were all assholes. That you were all lost. I told you that all your preconceptions about love and family and success were empty and foolish. That whatever knowledge you presume to have about yourselves was the result of external forces. But standing here now, I believe we've made some progress.

"Let's talk about love.

"We all say we love each other. I love my wife. I love my children. I love the Dodgers."

The people laughed.

"Most of us don't know the first thing about love. It's a word we use to persuade ourselves that our lives have meaning. It's a word we use to gain control over others. The truth is, when we say 'I love you,' what we really mean is 'I love you so long as you do things that please me. So long as you do things that *earn* my love for you.' That's not love, that's tyranny. Loving someone — *really* loving someone — means granting them the space to be who they truly are and who they are not.

"You want to love? Or do you want to be loved? If you're here to be loved, leave now because I don't have time for your shit. I am not here to validate you. Stop saying I

147

want to be loved when what you really mean is, I want to be validated. We are human beings seeking a higher consciousness. We are not pets seeking a comforting pat on the head.

"What we believe is love is actually a trap. If you want to be a real person, you must have the courage to free yourselves from the past. No more mama, no more daddy. No more false notions of who we are. The purpose of life is not to seek love, but rather to *not* seek love. True transformation mean's taking responsibility for your life!

"Are you ready to do that?

"Are you *committed* to doing that?"

Kegan shifted his focus from the little speaker to the woman with the shining eyes. He looked at her and saw those eyes bearing right back at him. She was no longer smiling. She nodded at Kegan. And then he realized she was not nodding at him, but nodding to point out where he was to someone else.

Shit.

Kegan looked up to see two of the yellow-jacketed security guards coming toward him. Then they were next to him.

"Let's go," one said.

Kegan stood up. They walked alongside him. A third guard joined them at the back doors. When they got outside of the banquet room, they grabbed his arms. The third one, the one behind, pushed him in the back hard enough that he stumbled.

"All right," Kegan said. "I'll leave."

"Shut up, asshole."

Kegan realized he was still in character as the buttoned-down government stooge. Still wearing glasses and looking soft. The yellow jackets had pulled him out of room where a little man with a big head had been speaking of love. Kegan believed the yellow jackets planned to beat the shit out of him. He knew the types.

They put him on an elevator and took him up to a room on the seventh floor. They shoved him in the room. He turned around and saw one of the yellow jackets holding a baton with a leather strap through the end.

Kegan said, "Hey, calm down. I was just looking for my girlfriend."

One of them said, "What's her name?"

"Jocelyn. She told me she was going to this seminar. Look, I don't want any trouble."

"You're lying. You a reporter?"

"No. Listen, I made a mistake. Just let me go."

"Sit down. I said, sit down."

Kegan took a seat at the chair in front of

the desk.

Kegan looked at the man in front of him, the one holding the cosh. He could tell the man wanted to use it. Kegan took off his glasses and set them on the desk. He did not want to end up with bits of glass in his eyes.

A couple of minutes passed and there was a knock at the door. One of the yellow jackets answered it. A woman came in, the woman who had stared at him from the podium. The glow gone from her eyes now, replaced by steel determination. She locked the door behind her and put the chain through the slot.

She said, "Who are you?"

Kegan said, "My name's Bill Ryan. I sell insurance. Look, I was only trying to find my girlfriend."

The woman said to the yellow jackets, "Get his identification."

Kegan felt a rough hand on his shoulder. Three men in the room with him, one of them to his left, another behind and the third one with the cosh in front of him. His driver's license would identify him as Vincent Kegan. He guessed it had gone far enough.

"Okay," Kegan said. He stood up slowly. With his right hand, he reached into the left

150

lapel of his jacket. He pulled out his billfold and the man with the cosh seemed to relax. Then Kegan swung his left fist down hard into the genitals of the man on his left. The man bellowed and doubled over and Kegan spun and kneed him in the face. Before the man could go to the ground, Kegan shoved him into the man behind him. The second man used both of his hands to grab the first man, leaving his upper body exposed. Kegan punched him in the throat and both men went to the ground.

The man with the cosh rushed forward, but stopped as Kegan lifted the chair up and held it between them. The man with the cosh stopped and thought about what he would do next.

Kegan said, "You drop that or I'll smash you."

There were two men on the ground behind Kegan. One of them tried to raise himself from the ground, like he was doing a push-up. Kegan back-kicked him in the face and he dropped back down.

The man with the cosh rushed him, bringing down the cosh, but he couldn't get past the chair. He took another swing and Kegan grabbed his wrist and dropped the chair. Kegan tugged him closer and punched him twice in the face. The man dropped the cosh and Kegan punched him up under his ribs. The man doubled over, his breath gone. Kegan grabbed a handful of his hair to hold his head study. Then he punched him in the face again, knocking him to the floor.

The woman was now at the door, fumbling with the lock and chain.

"Hold it, sister," Kegan said. "You and I are going to discuss a higher consciousness."

Kegan took her to a laundry room and motioned her to the back. Kegan dried his face with his handkerchief. He studied the woman. Not a bad-looking broad. Less scary now that she was no longer on the stage. And something else: she didn't seem to be afraid of him. Kegan realized she had a taste for strong men. Whether they were commanding the masses from a stage or beating guys up in a hotel room.

Kegan said, "What's your name?"

"You really handled those guys. Where did you learn to do that?"

"Your name, lady."

"Helen Carmichael."

"Was that always your name?"

The woman smiled. "You're a bright boy. No, it wasn't my birth name. Linda's my real name."

"You a hustler?"

"I've seen things, yeah. Gerhard gave me a better life."

"That guy downstairs?"

The woman nodded.

Kegan said, "He could make a fortune selling cars."

Linda nee Helen laughed. "You are bright. That's exactly what he used to do. One of the best car salesmen in Miami. He was Leonard McGill back then. Lenny. But he always felt he was meant for better things."

Kegan suppressed a smile. On some level, he couldn't help admiring the guy.

Kegan said, "Well, it seems you two have a good gig going. Tell you what. I'll keep quiet about it if you tell me a few things."

"You threatening me?" She seemed turned on.

"Negotiating," Kegan said.

"You can tell anyone you like. It's not going to hurt him. It's not going to hurt what we're doing. People believe in the training. They're not going to care where Gerhard came from. He's not even Lenny anymore, by the way. He *is* Gerhard Hocheim. And not just because he legally changed his name. You think he's a hustler, but I'll tell you something: he believes everything he says. People leave our sessions feeling good about themselves, confident about who they are. Where's the harm in that?"

"Nowhere. But maybe you'll help me anyway."

"Why would I do that?"

"Because while he may have become Gerhard Hocheim, I got a feeling deep down you're still a Linda. Besides, maybe you'll feel better after you talk to me."

The woman smiled.

"Maybe," she said.

Kegan said, "There's a man named Albert Hirsch. I believe he came to your seminar a few weeks ago. Do you remember him?"

"We get two hundred people a session. I can't remember who they all are."

"Do you remember him?"

"What did he do?"

"He's an analyst for the Pentagon."

"He worked for the government?"

"Yeah."

"Jewish guy, glasses?"

"Yeah."

"Yeah, I remember him. He didn't get it."

"It?"

"It. He didn't get it."

Kegan remembered the blackboard, the word "IT" in big letters.

"You mean he didn't get what it was you were selling," Kegan said.

"You don't have to piss on it."

"I don't know what *it* is."

"Well, you haven't had the training."

Christ. Kegan said, "Did he stay all through the training?"

"No, he left after one day. He said Gerhard was a fascist."

"He did?"

"Yes. In front of everyone. He was very rude. He didn't understand what we were about."

Kegan sighed. "Where did he go?"

"I don't know. He was staying with some friends here in the Bay area."

"Who were these friends?"

CHAPTER THIRTEEN

The name he got was Thomas J. Caputo. Caputo turned out to be an attorney.

Kegan parked in front of Caputo's townhouse and followed him to work. Caputo drove a new Cadillac. When Caputo stepped out of his car at his law office, Kegan decided he wasn't going to talk to the man in person. He wasn't sure why; he usually acted on instinct and his instinct told him it would be a bad idea to talk with Caputo face to face. Caputo had the look of a smart criminal defense lawyer. He also looked like the type of man who would quickly size Kegan up as a hood. Kegan did not want to be remembered by a perceptive man.

Kegan followed Caputo to the courthouse and watched him do a preliminary hearing. The man knew his way around a courtroom. Even the judge seemed intimidated by him. Caputo won the hearing, his motion to suppress granted based on a violation of the

Fourth Amendment. After that, Kegan knew his initial impulse to avoid meeting the man was well founded.

That's why Kegan went back to the man's house instead of following him back to his office.

The man's wife was still at home. Kegan parked his car down the street and waited. Mrs. Caputo left for lunch around one o'clock. After she was gone, Kegan went around to the back of the house. He jimmied the back door open using a penknife.

Then he was in the kitchen. He stood there for a moment. Then he heard a skittering coming down the hall. A little West Highland terrier came bounding toward him, barking. His heart jumped and he turned back to the door. The dog was still there, about five feet in front of him, yipping and growling, but not looking like he wanted to bite.

"Okay," Kegan said. "Okay."

Kegan went to the refrigerator and opened it. There were a couple of steaks in there. He debated using them, but then thought that the steaks would be missed. They might even harm the dog. The dog kept barking. Kegan went to the cupboard and found the dog food. He opened up a can of Strongheart and spooned it into a bowl. Then he set the bowl on the kitchen floor. The dog stopped growling and began to eat the food.

"Good boy," Kegan said.

He went through the house. He checked all the bedrooms. He did not find any sign of children living there. There was a guest bedroom that was clean and unused. If Hirsch had been here, he was gone by now. Which was more or less what Kegan expected. He went back downstairs. He looked in the lawyer's study. On the lawyer's desk was a yellow legal pad. Kegan went through it. He didn't find anything that helped him.

He walked back into the hall. At the side of the stairway was a little desk with a telephone on it. He saw a bill from Pacific Bell. A separate sheet detailing the long-distance calls. He put the bill in his pocket. The dog wagged his tail as Kegan went out the back door.

Kegan returned to his hotel room and studied the long-distance numbers on the bill. Two of the calls were to a number in Malibu. He knew that Jennifer Hirsch had a home in Malibu. He called the number. No one answered. There were two calls to a number in Seattle, Washington.

Kegan called the Seattle number.

A woman answered.

"Hello?"

Kegan said, "Jennifer?"

"Who is this?"

"This is Jim Ryan. I'm an assistant working for Mr. Caputo."

Kegan bit his lip. A moment passed.

Then he heard the woman say, "Oh. Okay. What's going on?"

"Well, he just asked me to check in with you."

"We're fine. The trial's been continued until Thursday. We still don't know if Albert's going to testify. I know Tom doesn't want him to do it, but . . . you know Al."

"Yeah. Okay. Well, give us a call if you need anything."

"Okay."

Kegan hung up the phone. He wrote down the number on a separate piece of paper. Then he dialed the operator.

"Can I help you?"

"Yes, operator, I have a number here, but I don't have an address. I can't seem to reach this person and I need to mail them a very important letter. Can you give me that address?"

"You have the number?"

"Yes." Kegan gave it to her.

"Yes," the operator said. "It's listed."

"Great. What's the address?"

"I'm afraid I can't give you that information, sir."

"Ah, please. This letter is very important."

"Sorry."

Kegan looked at the number he had. "You sure?"

"Yes, sir. Is there anything else I can do for you?"

"No, ma'am."

Kegan looked at the last four digits of the number. 4806. He dialed another number, but this time the last four digits he dialed were 4800.

"Biltmore Hotel."

Kegan said, "Biltmore Seattle?"

"Yes, sir. Can I help you?"

"Yes, I'm coming from out of town. Can I get some directions?"

CHAPTER FOURTEEN

Kegan caught a red-eye flight to Seattle. The plane landed a little after midnight. He rented a green Plymouth Satellite and drove to the Biltmore Hotel. Took it in and then drove down the street and booked a room at a Ramada Inn. The clerk at the desk told him there was no room service after ten o'clock, but there was an all-night diner two blocks away. Kegan put his bags in his room and walked down to the diner. A fine misting rain made halos on the street lights.

At the diner, he ordered ham and eggs and a tall glass of milk. He saw a Seattle newspaper on the counter and pulled it toward him. He read the sports page first. A story about Mean Joe Greene spitting in Dick Butkus's face and challenging him to a fight. The sportswriter praised Greene for his aggressiveness and predicted he would win Defensive Player of the Year. Joe Frazier had easily beaten someone called Terry

Daniels in the boxing ring. The Miami Dolphins had won another game. And then there was another story about the massacre at Munich, the city that had hosted the 1972 Olympics. Israeli Prime Minister Golda Meir appealed to the international community to "save our citizens and condemn the unspeakable criminal acts committed." There was a photo of Ms. Meir. She wore an expression that made Kegan think that if the international community didn't do something about the terrorists, she would.

Kegan turned to the local news section. Halfway through his meal, he found something that made him stop.

It was a story about a group of young men called "The Seattle Seven." A group of college activists opposed to the Vietnam War had broken into a post office and destroyed thousands of draft records. About a hundred FBI agents had converged on Seattle to track them down. They were caught and arrested for attempting to "sabotage the national defense." Kegan wondered if that was a crime. Then he read the story further and learned that the judge hearing the case had had the same reservations and had reduced the charges to attempted burglary and willful destruction of property.

162

The defendants were briefly profiled, all of them what the newspaper dubbed "The Sons of the Establishment." One of them, indeed, the son of a prominent judge. Another defendant was president of the University of Washington student council. If convicted, they could each face up to five years in prison.

"Stupid," Kegan said.

It wasn't something Kegan could understand. Risking a prison sentence not for theft or assault, but for setting fire to draft records. Kids. They had a chance at a future he had never had. An education and a career. Thrown away for some principle he could not understand. Trying to stop a war they had no chance of ending. For what? Where were these kids' parents? Why didn't they stop them from ruining their lives? Why hadn't they given them a kick in the ass?

There was a photo of the kids marching in a protest at the college campus. They held signs that said "Peace Now!" and "RESIST."

But that wasn't what drew his attention. What drew Kegan's attention was a line in the newspaper article that said, "Trial is set to resume Thursday."

Hirsch's wife had said the trial had been continued to Thursday. . . . Surely, surely, she wasn't talking about this trial. Was Hirsch going to watch the trial? Or was he going to be so dumb as to *testify* at it? Testify on behalf of a bunch of misguided rich kids who'd gotten their dumb asses in a crack?

No. Not with a hundred FBI agents involved. Hirsch would have to be crazy to get involved in something like this. Presuming he was still here.

As it turned out, he was.

Kegan was up at seven a.m. and in the lobby of the Biltmore Hotel at eight. He sipped coffee in the lobby and read the newspaper. At eight-thirty, Hirsch and his wife stepped off the elevator and moved to the front desk. They were carrying their bags.

The man at the desk looked like the man Kegan had seen in the photo. Kegan couldn't believe it. He had found him. Then he heard the desk clerk distinctly say, "Everything to your satisfaction, Mr. Hirsch?"

Christ, the guy was even using his real name. Was it possible he didn't know federal agents were looking for him?

Kegan lowered his newspaper to get a better look at him.

He was shorter than Kegan had thought

he would be. He was slight of stature, with a wiry build. He wore horn-rimmed glasses and had a receding hairline. His wife was about half a head taller than him. A very good-looking lady with an aristocratic pedigree. She brushed something off the shoulder of her husband's suit and Kegan believed she was in love with him.

Hirsch pulled some cash out of his wallet. He was paying his bill. He was checking out.

Kegan realized if he had not taken a flight, he would have missed them.

The desk clerk said, "Shall I have your car brought round, sir?"

"Please," Hirsch said and handed him the keys.

Kegan put his newspaper down. He walked the long way around to avoid them. When he got outside he hurried to his car. He got the car started and pulled it out of the lot and had it parked across the street. It was close. Only a minute or so later, he saw a bellman pull up to the front step of the hotel in an International Harvester jeep with California tags. Hirsch and his wife came out with their bags. The bellman loaded the bags into the back of Hirsch's vehicle. Hirsch tipped him a dollar and got in the vehicle. His wife got into the pas-

senger side and they drove away.
   Kegan followed them.

CHAPTER FIFTEEN

When they stopped, it was at the county courthouse.

Outside of the courthouse were a couple of news vans. They were there to cover the trial of the Seattle Seven. Kegan parked his car and put his gun and silencer into the glove compartment. Then he followed the Hirschs into the courthouse. Hirsch was carrying a big suitcase. Kegan watched the Hirschs step into the elevator. Kegan hung back and watched the lights of the elevator. It stopped on the fifth floor. Kegan took the next elevator.

When he stepped off the elevator he saw Hirsch talking with a big man with long gray hair. The big man wore a hat and a western suit. Kegan guessed the big man was a lawyer. He was telling Hirsch something that seemed to disappoint him.

Kegan got closer by going to the water fountain to get a drink.

He heard the lawyer tell Hirsch, "I'm with you. I tried, Albert. But the judge isn't going to let you testify."

Hirsch said, "He can't say it's not relevant. It's relevant."

"I agree with you, Al. But Costanza is dead set against letting in evidence that gives these kids any justification for what they did. He said he's not going to allow this trial to become a venue to protest the war."

"But it's central to their defense. And they *were* justified." Hirsch patted his suitcase. "What I have here will prove that."

"I know that. But what you've got there is about 5,000 pages of documentation. And there's no way Judge Costanza is going to let us put all that into the record."

"It needs to be in the record. This is history."

"Al, listen to me. Costanza's not a bad guy. We could have drawn someone much worse. He's reduced the charges to burglary and destruction of property. The State wanted to charge these boys with treason and Costanza said no. Now I know what you've got there is powerful, but I don't want to press my luck with this judge."

"Did you tell him what I have?"

The lawyer sighed. "Not fully. Listen to

me, Al. I tell Costanza what you've got there, he may alert the FBI and have you arrested."

"For what?"

"I don't know and I don't want to find out."

"But we have an opportunity here."

"Al, I'm as disgusted by it as you are. *But now's not the time.* My job is to get these kids acquitted. Or barring that, as little jail time as possible. If it comes down to helping them or helping you put a stop to the war, I'm going to choose them. I'm sorry, but that's the way it is."

After a moment, Hirsch said, "I understand. I really did want to help."

"I know you did. And you have. Listen, it's really for the best."

"Why?"

"Because I haven't disclosed your identity to the State."

"I don't care if you do. I'm not ashamed."

"I care. These pricks, they find out your name, they'll try to have you arrested. These are the people who wanted to give these kids life sentences."

"Those kids are heroes. They've got more courage than most of us."

"I hear you," the lawyer said. "But now's not the time. We'll get there."

Hirsch said, "I wish I could believe that."

The lawyer said, "Listen, will you do me a huge favor? And get out of here."

Hirsch smiled and said, "Am I a distraction?"

"Very much so. I don't want to defend *you* for treason." The lawyer smiled. "Not yet, anyway."

The Hirschs got into their International Harvester and left the courthouse. Kegan followed them.

They did not return to the hotel. Nor did they drive south toward California. What they did was go north and then west into the mountains.

After an hour, Kegan began to wonder how long they would go. Would they continue all the way west to Montana? He had left his luggage in his hotel room in Seattle. Maybe that was a minor concern. Clothes, suits could be replaced. But he was on a narrow winding mountain road. If he got too close to Hirsch, Hirsch might look in the rearview mirror and wonder why the Plymouth was following him. Maybe pull over and call the cops. It wasn't like going after one of the made guys. Gangsters were, by and large, predictable. They'd go to their homes, their favorite restaurants and bars, the apartments of their mistresses. Hoods were not hard to find, not hard to track. Most of them didn't like to leave things that were familiar to them. Most people didn't, actually. But Hirsch wasn't like that. He was in California one day, Seattle another, then out in the mountains. Again, Kegan was annoyed with Lewis for giving him this hit. Hirsch was not a gangster. He was a civilian the U.S. government wanted put down. The Outfit should have left this one alone, should have left it to someone else.

And something else. The contractor had told Lewis that Hirsch was a traitor who was going over to the Soviets. But that didn't make sense. The man had tried to talk a lawyer into letting him testify at the trial of a bunch of war protestors. Why would a guy who was going to defect to the Soviet Union hang around Seattle, Washington, to help a group of misguided American college students? Why would he do that when even a lawyer who was defending the kids tried to discourage him from doing it?

Well . . . even Lewis had said he was skeptical of the claim that Hirsch was a commie. He could have told Kegan he believed it with all his heart and Kegan would have probably believed him. To

Lewis's credit, he had not lied about that. Maybe.

Now Kegan was wondering if he was starting to think too much. Any hit had to be planned carefully. You couldn't move too quickly, you needed to be patient while you stalked your man and learned his habits. You had to train yourself to sort of move with him, to get your rhythm in sync with his. At the same time, you couldn't hesitate for too long because overthinking it could fuck you up. If another week passed, or worse, two, Lewis would begin to fear that Kegan had lost his nerve. Kegan himself might start to have doubts.

To begin with, he was out of his element. Driving up a mountain road in the Pacific Northwest. Kegan realized he was probably no better than most of the mooks he went after. Nervous and uneasy when taken out of the city environment he was familiar with.

A song came on the radio that made him feel a little better. Connie Francis singing "If I Didn't Care." He had seen Connie singing in Vegas a few years back and had sort of fallen in love with her. Her anglicized name and Patsy Cline intonations couldn't hide the fact that she was a nice Italian girl from Jersey. They had tried to make a movie star out of her by putting her in films with

George Hamilton and some other teeny-boppers, but it didn't fit her. Kegan thought she was too good for the screen. They had tried to make a movie star out of Elvis and it had ruined him.

It had only been a few years since he had seen Connie on the stage. Yet hearing her voice now made him feel old, aware that her time had passed and maybe his too. The kids who burned draft records probably had no appreciation for a talent like Connie's. They would think she was a square.

For his part, Kegan was glad she had not tried to change with the times. Kegan had seen Sinatra on television a year ago — Sinatra trying to be hip in a Nehru jacket and love beads. Sinatra doing his modern "thing" and looking ridiculous. At least Kegan knew he was dated.

Kegan had never met Sinatra. Lewis had, though. Lewis liked Sinatra and had tried to talk him out of campaigning for Dan McCormick when McCormick first ran for president. Lewis had warned Sinatra that the McCormicks would use him while they could but would dump him after the election because of Frankie's "associations." Lewis had been right about that.

Kegan looked at his gas gauge. He was on about an eighth of a tank. If he stopped for gas, he would lose Hirsch. Maybe they would stop for gas too and then Kegan could stop too. But then they would make him. Hirsch saying to him, "Who are you? Are you following me?" Kegan would have to plug him then — in front of his wife, maybe in front of a gas station attendant — and that would be too risky. He wasn't going to go to prison for Lewis or anyone else. He would have to look back at Hirsch and say he was mistaken and get back in the Plymouth and drive back to Seattle.

Would that be so bad?

What would Lewis do?

Kegan could tell him that the mark saw him, that his wife saw him and that there was too much heat for him to finish the job. He hadn't signed on to kill the man's wife. They would just have to find someone else to do it. Would it be enough for Lewis that Kegan had found out where the man was?

The road leveled off and then started to slowly rise again. The International Harvester crested the rise and disappeared over the other side.

Kegan drove to the crest and saw the International Harvester's brake lights come on. Hirsch was slowing. There was a curve ahead that was almost a full left turn. Only Hirsch did not make the turn, but kept go-

174

ing straight onto a dirt road that peeled off into a heavily wooded area.

Kegan slowed the car. Then he stopped the car and pulled it over to the side of the road.

In the distance he saw the International Harvester make a left turn.

Kegan waited a few moments before he pulled his car back out onto the road. The International Harvester was now out of sight. Kegan drove down the dirt road. When he reached the place where Hirsch had turned left, he turned right. The light was dimmer now, the dirt roads surrounded by tall trees.

In his rearview mirror, he saw the utility vehicle parked in front of a cabin, Hirsch and his wife opening the back hatch to take out their luggage.

Kegan pulled the car ahead and pulled it off into a space between the trees. Slowly, he edged the car forward so that it would not be visible to someone driving down the dirt road. He saw a gap in the trees that made him nervous. He stopped the car and shut off the engine. Then he got out and walked to the front of the car.

Christ. He was on the edge of what could almost be called a cliff. A deep ravine below. Another few feet and the front wheels would have gone over the rocky edge and probably taken him down into the abyss. Kegan shook his head.

Yeah, Lewis would have liked that. *I sent Kegan to hit a guy and the dumb cluck drives off a cliff and gets himself killed.*

Kegan went to the back of the car and looked off to the east. Or what he thought was east. He was still wearing a suit and a pair of high-dollar Florsheim shoes. It was cold and rocky and muddy out here. He didn't have a warm coat or a pair of boots. He hadn't been prepared to hike through heavy woods. He didn't even have a raincoat.

Well . . . hell. He could get the suit cleaned later. And shoes could be replaced. He had another eighty grand coming to him.

He opened the trunk of the car. He lifted the cover on top of the spare tire. There were three tubes around the spare tire wrapped in brown paper. He took out the tubes and removed the paper. Under the paper was a clear plastic wrapping. The three sections, when put together, would comprise an M4 Survival Rifle.

The M4 rifle was developed during the Second World War as part of the survival gear to be stored underneath the seat of an aircraft pilot. It used a .22 Hornet round and had a clip for four bullets. Its purpose was to let the downed pilot shoot wild game so he could eat. But the .22 round could kill a man at three hundred yards if the pilot aimed for the head. When United States Air Force aircraft were decommissioned in the 1950s, their M4 rifles were initially sold on the surplus gun market, but were recalled when it was determined that the barrels were shorter than the legal limit of length mandated by the 1934 National Firearms Act.

Kegan put the sections of the rifle into a rucksack. Then he slung the rucksack over his shoulder and began walking east. He crossed the dirt road and then stepped over into the woods. If he heard a car coming, he would retreat further into the woods so that he would not be seen from the road. A man in a suit carrying a rucksack would arouse the suspicion of a country cop. Still, he did not want to get too far from the road because he believed if he got too deep into the woods, he could get lost.

He reached the dirt road that he had first seen Hirsch drive down. He looked north to see where the dirt road connected back to the paved state road. No vehicles were out there and he crossed over and went back into the woods.

He became a little more confident the further he went. He believed this was a good thing. He thought back to the survival training he had received when he was in the army. They had taught him a lot. He had not known how to swim until he joined the army. They taught him how. They taught him other things too: tracking, evading capture, how to live off the land. Whatever that meant. They told him not to eat insects that were brightly colored because they would poison you quicker than the black or brown ones. It hadn't come in handy in Korea where it seemed to be twenty degrees below zero most of the time. They had told him the main thing was not to panic. That was something he could understand.

When he was in Korea, he thought the war would last forever. MacArthur had said they were going to drive the commies out and take the fight into China. Even as a young man, Kegan couldn't see the practicality in that. He feared it would lead to a nuclear war. But then MacArthur was relieved of command and later President Eisenhower basically called the thing a draw and pulled the American troops out. Ike had let the commies keep North Korea. Kegan knew only a president who was both a Republican and a war hero could get away with that. He wondered why President McCormick couldn't do the same thing in Vietnam. Pull out the Americans and let the commies have North Vietnam. What was there that was worth having anyway?

Then Kegan wondered if he was getting soft or something. A few years ago, every establishment figure in American politics — Democrat and Republican — supported the Vietnam War. Anyone suggesting a pull out would be branded a communist sympathizer or a traitor. Now college students were going to jail protesting it. Everything had changed so quickly. In 1964, most male college students had crewcuts. Four, five years later most of them were long-haired hippies dressed like construction workers. And now Frank Sinatra was wearing love beads, no longer singing "Come Fly With Me," but "Here's to You, Mrs. Robinson." Who would have predicted such things ten years ago?

And Kegan was thinking of Eisenhower pulling out of Korea and wondering why McCormick couldn't do the same thing in Vietnam. No one had accused Eisenhower of being soft. Why should Kegan care? It couldn't be that the thought of college students going to prison would make him think such things, could it? Why should he care about them? They had fucked up and

179

now they would go to prison.

But he thought of some of the people in his business. Gangsters taking over dry cleaning stores and vending machine companies with threats and beatings. Once in a while, the hoods would get arrested and maybe even convicted of racketeering. But few of them did more than a few months' stretch in prison. While dumbass college kids were looking at three four-year sentences for burning paper.

Well, it wasn't his fault the hoods got away with muscling in on legitimate businesses. Power and fear and the use of force were the tools of any businessman. That's what Lewis had always said. Lewis said he didn't make the world. It was what it was.

Kegan found himself facing an incline. Again he wished he had a pair of boots. At the bottom of the slope was a narrow trail. Beyond the trail and up the other end of the slope were three cabins, spaced about fifty yards apart. Kegan felt better. He climbed up the slope, grabbing rocks and trees to pull himself further up. It was not an easy task. He was a smoker and he was in a higher altitude than Chicago's.

It took him a while but he found a place he thought would work. A good-sized boulder he could crouch behind, nestled nicely

180

between some trees. He knelt and felt the dampness come through his pants and cool his knees. He sighed. If the suit couldn't be cleaned, it could be replaced.

He opened the rucksack and pulled out the smallest tube. He took the plastic off and opened up the tube and turned it on its end. A scope fell out. He took the scope and peered out over the boulder to the cabins.

The cabins were on the other side of the ravine, about two hundred fifty yards away. He panned left to right. Each cabin had a back porch looking out at the wilderness. The first and third cabins had no light emanating from them. Kegan took his time and decided that the first and third cabins were unoccupied. That was good.

He saw movement in the window of the second cabin. A man. Albert Hirsch.

Kegan crouched back down behind the boulder and began to piece together the rifle. The stock, the barrel, and then the scope. He slid the scope into its place and then tightened it down using a small screwdriver. When he was done with that, he took the four rounds out of a small plastic bag and loaded them into the box magazine. Then he slid the magazine into place.

He looked up at the sky after that. It was

181

overcast and gray. That was good. There would be no sunlight reflecting off the glass of the scope. Not that Hirsch would be expecting such a thing or looking for it.

Kegan got on one knee and lifted himself up over the boulder. He put the rifle over the boulder and looked through the scope.

Hirsch was now on the back porch. Sitting in a chair reading some papers. He was actually facing the place where Kegan was.

Kegan hesitated then. He told himself that Hirsch would not be able to see him at that distance. Not without a scope or a pair of binoculars. Not a man mostly hidden by a boulder and woods.

Do it quickly, Kegan thought. *Do it before he sees you.*

Kegan put his eye back on the scope. Hirsch's head was now in the cross hairs. A spot on his forehead. Kegan put his finger on the trigger . . .

The woman came out of the cabin. She was carrying a bottle of beer. She moved in front of Hirsch.

Kegan took his finger off the trigger.

Move, he thought.

Move out of the way. He was almost there.

But Jennifer Hirsch did not move. She remained standing in front of her husband. Her hand on her hip, her hip cocked.

Christ, teasing the man in front of her as if he were a recently discovered lover.

Move, Kegan thought.

And she did.

But what she did was sit down in her husband's lap. Taking the papers from his hand and setting them on a table next to the chair. The woman putting her arms around Hirsch's neck and kissing him. Hirsch smiling now as his wife said things to him that made him relax and tip his beer to his mouth.

"Christ," Kegan whispered.

He had a shot now. The woman was sitting across Hirsch's lap, not straddling him. And now Hirsch's forehead was open and exposed. Kegan could put a bullet there and put an end to it. The woman would see the hole and hear the short hiss of a shot coming from the wild and it would be over. She would scream and go into shock and it would all be done.

But the rules were still in place. You don't hit a man in front of his family. Just like you don't hit a man coming out of church. As Lewis said after they hit Crazy Joey in front of his wife and daughter, "It's not the way you do it."

And now Kegan thought, why not? The woman was going to lose her husband one way or another. If she were inside the cabin and Kegan killed her husband, it would be the same. She would come out to the deck and find him dead and the horror would still be the same. What difference would it make?

"Go inside," Kegan said. Get another beer. Go check the stove. Do *something*, but just get your pretty little ass off the deck and leave Hirsch alone.

But she didn't seem to be going anywhere. She was still on Hirsch's lap, chatting with him. Hirsch still smiling as he patted his wife on her thigh. Man, they weren't even going to fool around. They were just enjoying each other's company. Lady, *move.*

"Shit," Kegan said, this time not whispering.

He pulled the rifle off the boulder and crouched back down behind.

Kegan sighed again. It would have to be another time.

He began to disassemble the rifle.

He returned to the car and put the wrapped sections of the rifle back around the spare tire. He placed the cover back over the tire and dropped the empty rucksack on top. He shut the trunk of the car. After that, he used a stick to wipe off most of the mud

184

from his shoes. It didn't make him feel any better.

As he drove the car back to the state road, he reminded himself to be patient. It had never done him any good to rush a job. He reminded himself that the rules were there for a reason. And maybe the reasons didn't make sense because a hit was a hit and a woman was going to lose her husband whether or not she was there when it happened, but it was bad medicine to ignore the rules just because you'd put in a lot of time and effort and got a lot of mud on your shoes. And in any event, at least he knew where Hirsch was.

He stopped the car at the intersection of the dirt road and the paved state road. He had seen a town about fifteen miles down the road. He would go there and fill up the gas tank and get something to eat. He would have time to think and plan and get clothes more suitable for the work.

He pulled the Plymouth onto the state road and began climbing the incline. He would later think he had been maybe a hundred yards from the crest of the hill when the two cars came over the top.

Two cars, muscle cars, a Pontiac GTO and a Chevelle with a hood scoop, the cars abreast of each other, and he could hear the engines screaming and for a split second he thought he saw the face of one of the drivers, a kid behind the wheel. They were drag racing, two cars side by side, and there wasn't any time for either car to pass the other.

Kegan jerked the steering wheel to the right and heard the impact of the Chevelle smacking into the rear of the Plymouth and then the Plymouth was airborne as it left the road and hurtled into the craggy ditch below. A gray boulder coming into view . . .

That was all Kegan would remember before he lost consciousness.

CHAPTER SIXTEEN

When he was in the army, Kegan had had his wisdom teeth removed. He hadn't known that it would require surgery. He had gone to his sergeant because the pain in his mouth had been bad enough that he couldn't sleep at night. Two days later, he went to the base oral surgeon to have his wisdom teeth cut out. They gave him an anesthetic and told him to count backward from 100. He reached 97 and went to sleep. Then he woke up on a cot in the next room with a mouth full of blood.

That's how it had seemed. Counting to 97 then waking up on a cot. He was later told that the surgery took about an hour. But for him, time hadn't passed. He had gone to sleep and woken up.

That's how it was this time. He was thrown forward when his car hit a boulder and had spider-webbed the windshield with his head. Lights out.

Then lights on. A finite passage of time missing. Waking up on a couch in a cabin. A wetness on his forehead, blood and water seeping down onto his temples and into his hair.

Kegan opened his eyes to see a woman bending over him.

"Al," the woman said. "He's waking up."

It took Kegan a moment to piece it together. The pretty woman straightening up now. She looked like the woman he had viewed through the cross hairs of a rifle scope not long ago. The woman who had handed the beer to her husband and sat on his lap.

It *was* the same woman.

Kegan wondered if he was in some sort of purgatory. Would the woman bring a broken beer bottle over to him and start poking holes in his face? Punish him for what he had been contemplating not long ago? Kegan's head hurt.

Albert Hirsch came into view, Hirsch bending over him now.

Hirsch said, "You all right, friend?"

Friend?

Jennifer Hirsch said, "For God's sake, Al. He could be brain-damaged."

"Cool it, will you?" Hirsch said. "I'm trying to find out if he's in shock." To Kegan,

Hirsch said, "Is your vision blurring?"

After a moment, Kegan said, "No."

Hirsch said to his wife, "His pupils aren't dilated. His skin isn't gray."

"Albert," the woman said, "we need to get him to a hospital. I don't care what color his skin is."

"The nearest hospital is fifty miles. He might have died before we got him there." Hirsch looked at his wife. "We did the right thing bringing him here."

It was then that Kegan began to take in the surroundings. He was on a couch in their cabin. . . . How?

Kegan said, "Where am I?"

"You're in a cabin in the mountains," Hirsch said. "You know that, right?"

"Yes. I know that."

"Are you from here?" Hirsch asked.

Jesus, Kegan thought. "No. I'm on vacation. I was looking for a place to stay for a couple of days."

"What's your name?"

Christ. Had they checked his wallet? If they had, it was all over anyway.

"Carson," Kegan said. "Bill Carson."

"Where are you from?"

"Chicago."

Hirsch turned to his wife again. "He seems lucid enough. And he's not hyperventilating."

Kegan said, "I'm not . . . I'm not in a state of shock."

Hirsch said, "Well, you're not in a position to judge. Would you like some water?"

"Please."

Jennifer Hirsch went to the kitchen to get him a glass of water. Outside a light rain began to fall. Kegan thought about how easy it would be for them to kill him. Put a pillow over his face and suffocate him. He wouldn't have the strength to fight them. His head was pounding.

Hirsch said, "Do you remember what happened?"

Kegan said, "I was driving . . . I was driving up the road and a couple of cars came over the hill. Side by side. I think they were racing. I had to drive off into the ditch to avoid a head-on collision. That's all I remember."

Hirsch said, "You've got a hell of a goose egg on your head. No, don't touch it."

Kegan took Hirsch in. A slight man with a receding hairline and horn-rimmed glasses, but he seemed comfortable with authority. And Kegan remembered that he had been a Marine.

"Listen," Hirsch said, "I don't want you to panic, but you've got a pretty nasty cut

190

on your head. It needs to be stitched. Now we can put you in the back of our car and get you to a hospital, but it's a long way from here. I have medical training from my time in the service. I'm a certified medic. I can stitch it myself."

"*Albert,*" Jennifer said.

"Sweetie, he's still bleeding. We've got to stop the bleeding."

"You're not a goddamned doctor. He needs . . ."

"It's all right," Kegan said. "It's all right. Go ahead and stitch it."

"You sure?" Hirsch said.

"Yeah. Just make sure you keep it clean."

"We've got rubbing alcohol. We can keep it clean. But we don't have any anesthetic."

"Do you have any whiskey?"

"We have vodka."

"That'll work."

"It'll hurt."

"No worse than it does now."

Kegan looked at the woman standing behind her husband. She looked frightened.

Kegan said, "Ma'am. It's all right. Really."

Hirsch nodded to his wife and she went outside to get the essentials.

Kegan said, "I'm sorry."

Hirsch said, "For what?"

After a moment, Kegan said, "For putting

191

your wife through this." He didn't know what else to say.

"It's okay," Hirsch said. "My name's Hirsch, by the way. Albert Hirsch."

Kegan wondered about Albert Hirsch. He seemed to be taking steps to avoid being seen at a local hospital. And yet earlier he had been willing to testify in open court to help a bunch of draft dodgers. Was he on the run? Was he hiding or not?

Kegan said, "How did you find me?"

"We were going into town for groceries and we saw your car by the road. You gave my wife a scare, man."

"Sorry."

"It's all right."

"Did you call the police?"

"No."

Kegan almost thanked him. But then realized the man had his own reasons for not calling the police.

Kegan said, "I guess it would be a while before they got to a place as remote as this." Helping the man, for chrissake.

"Maybe," Hirsch said. "We wanted to make sure you didn't bleed to death out there."

"Is the car still there?"

"Yeah." Hirsch frowned. Like, where else would it be?

Kegan was thinking the smart play would have been to take the car and dump it in a lake. Then they could kill him and bury him and no one would ever know where he was. Kegan thought, *stop thinking like a gangster.*

Hirsch said, "I wouldn't worry about it now. It's not like anyone can drive it away. The radiator's busted."

"Oh," Kegan said.

"Look, if you're that concerned about it, we can tow it here. I've got a winch on my Jeep. But right now, I think we should stop you from bleeding all over the furniture."

Mrs. Hirsch returned with a first aid kit. Hirsch told her to set it down and get Kegan a glass of vodka. She did as he asked. Kegan downed the vodka in two gulps. He almost fainted then.

Hirsch frowned. "Yikes. I should have seen that coming. With the blood you've lost."

Kegan said, "It's all right. I'm ready when you are."

"It's going to hurt," Hirsch said.

"I know."

Kegan managed to survive it, grabbing the cushion a couple of times. Sometime later he heard Hirsch say, "I think that'll do it." Then he passed out.

■ ■ ■ ■

The sun had gone down when Kegan woke up. He was in his slacks and shirt. His tie was gone and his jacket hung on a chair. Blood had dried on his shirt. His shoes were on the floor next to the couch. He was alone in the cabin.

He started to lift himself up, felt a wave of nausea, and lay back down. Through the windows he could see the Hirschs on the back deck. Kegan looked at his watch and went back to sleep.

When he awoke the second time, Hirsch and his wife were sitting at the kitchen table. Kegan smelled steak and potatoes. They had eaten their dinner while a bloodied man slept on their couch. Who were these people?

Jennifer saw him and said, "Albert. He's up."

Hirsch came over to him and examined the wound.

"Well," Hirsch said, "the bleeding's stopped. How do you feel?"

"Okay, I guess. Listen, I appreciate what you've done, but I really think I should be going."

Hirsch laughed. "Where are you going to go?"

"I don't know. A hotel."

"Your car's across the road. We towed it here and let it roll back in the space across from ours. The cabin's vacant, so it should be okay for now."

"Thanks."

Hirsch shrugged and said, "The radiator is busted. Even if it weren't, you're in no shape to drive anywhere. Listen, I checked and you can rent the cabin across the road. It's eighteen dollars for the night. If you don't have it, I can pay for it."

"I have the money. But thank you."

"My wife thinks that we should call an ambulance and have you taken to the hospital to be checked out. She's probably right, but it's up to you."

"Thank you, Mrs. Hirsch," Kegan said. "But I think the cabin will be fine."

Jennifer Hirsch said, "That's not quite what I said. I said we could call an ambulance or we could take you ourselves. It's just that the Harvester isn't the most comfortable ride in the world."

Kegan said, "The cabin will be fine."

Jennifer said, "I'm not okay with that. I think you should be checked out."

"Sweetie," Hirsch said, "I treated worse cases than him in Korea."

"This isn't a goddamned battlefield, Al.

We're in civilization now."

To Kegan, Hirsch said, "Well, it's up to you."

Kegan said again, "The cabin will be fine." He paused. "Maybe you can help me walk over there."

"Sure," Hirsch said. "Listen, why don't you eat something first?"

Kegan hesitated.

Hirsch said, "I know. You're afraid you won't be able to keep anything down. I can understand that."

"No, it's not that. I just . . ." He looked down at the blood on his shirt.

"Oh," Hirsch said. "Well, I've seen worse than that. Sweetie, I think my brown sweater should be big enough for Mr. Carson."

"Maybe," Jennifer Hirsch said.

"Would you get it, please?"

Kegan said, "I'm going to try to stand up now."

Hirsch helped him up, taking his arm and then steadying him. Kegan realized Hirsch was not a weak man.

Hirsch said, "I don't know, partner. You don't look good."

Jennifer Hirsch came back with the sweater.

Kegan said, "If you can just help me to the washroom."

They both helped him to the bathroom. Kegan went in alone and closed the door.

He looked in the mirror and saw the stitches on his head, just above the hairline. Christ, he thought, what a fucking comedy. If this ever got back to the Outfit, he would be laughed out of the business. A hood goes to the mountains to do a hit and almost gets himself killed. Potentially saved from bleeding to death by the man he was supposed to put down. As bad as those mooks who blew themselves up trying to rig a bomb for assassination.

He was still very weak. He was glad the car was here instead of out on the road. If Hirsch had been curious enough to check the glove compartment, he would have found a pistol and a silencer. If he had been curious enough to thoroughly inspect the trunk, he would have found a rifle. Maybe Hirsch had done that and was just keeping quiet about it so he could kill him later.

But no. That didn't make sense. Hirsch was no killer. Kegan had been around enough stone killers to know the breed. Hirsch had been a soldier and he had not flinched at the sight of blood. Hirsch had likely killed men in war. But that wasn't murder. Not to Kegan, anyway.

With some effort, Kegan took off his shirt.

There were yellow and purple streaks on his chest and torso. He had been heavily bruised, but there were no signs of internal bleeding. If there was, maybe he would die in his sleep tonight. Maybe that wouldn't be so bad. To die in a cabin in the mountains. It would at least be peaceful. The Hirschs would likely find out later who he really was. Maybe they would be scared then. Scared of what they had been dealing with. Or maybe they would laugh about it. Kegan wouldn't blame them if they did. He was out of it now, feeling weak, stupid, and ashamed.

Kegan pulled the sweater over his head. He felt another wave of nausea then and had to put his hands on the sink to steady himself. It passed after a while and he looked at himself in the mirror again.

He checked his pants to see if his wallet was still there. It was. He checked inside to see if all his money was still there. It was. About four hundred dollars.

He came out of the bathroom. The woman was there alone at the kitchen table. She stood up when she saw him.

Jennifer Hirsch said, "How are you feeling?"

Kegan said, "I'm going to live." He felt stupid for saying it.

Jennifer said, "Albert went to book the cabin across the road. He'll be back soon." She did not seem at all afraid of Kegan, did not seem uncomfortable being alone with him. She came over to him and took his arm. Then she walked him to the kitchen table and helped him sit down. She had prepared a plate of food for him. Next to the food was a tall glass of ice water.

She took the seat across from him and said, "If you don't feel like eating, don't worry. But I do want you to drink the water."

"Yes, ma'am."

"Don't call me ma'am." She smiled. "You'll make me feel old."

She was younger than Kegan. He didn't know why he had called her that. Eating at her table perhaps. Or maybe it was the fact that she came from money and looked it. Kegan was conscious of the class differences. Her a lady of sophistication and breeding, him a mook from the Outfit. He'd eaten dinner with Lewis Knowles before and he didn't know anyone who had as much money as Lewis. He didn't consider Lewis a snob. Maybe Kegan was one himself.

The thing was, she didn't know who or what he was. To her, he was a businessman from Chicago. He had to act the part she had assigned to him. No, that wasn't it. He had to act the part he had assigned to himself. Bill Carson. That's the name he had given to them.

"My name is Jennifer."

"Jennifer," Kegan said. And he looked at her and saw that her eyes were more gray than blue. A very rare, very arresting pair of eyes. He tried to remember when he had seen eyes like that. . . . Dolores Hart. The scene in *Where the Boys Are* where she asked the guy hitchhiking how big his feet were before letting him in the car. He had seen the movie with Gerri because it was what she wanted to see and he had ended up enjoying it more than he thought he would. Gerri told him later that Dolores Hart had become a nun. Kegan hadn't believed it.

Kegan sipped from the glass of the water. Then he downed the whole thing.

Jennifer smiled again.

"I'll get you some more."

"Thank you, Mrs. Hirsch."

"Jennifer."

"Thank you, Jennifer."

He began to eat the steak. It was medium rare and well seasoned. But he ate slowly. She brought him more water.

She sat with him and let him eat. She was a woman who didn't mind silence. This was something Kegan was not used to. Perhaps she sensed he was not much of a talker.

Kegan said, "This is very good."

"We cooked it outside on the grill. Four minutes on one side, then the other. We don't get many opportunities to grill."

Because you're on the run? Kegan thought. But then he said, "It's as good as anything in Chicago."

Jennifer said, "Thank you. What do you do in Chicago? If you don't mind me asking."

"I own a barber shop." It was partially true.

"Oh. That must be interesting."

It wasn't remotely interesting, Kegan thought. But he appreciated her kindness.

He shrugged and said, "It's a living."

"Is this your first time in the Pacific Northwest?"

"I was in Seattle once. After I was in the service." This part actually was true. "We came back through San Francisco and we had some liberty. So I traveled around Oregon and visited Seattle."

"A little too dreary for my tastes," Jennifer Hirsch said. "I'm from California. Used to the sun."

"Do you and your husband come here much?"

"No. This is our first trip here. It's quiet." She said it without much enthusiasm.

"Well, it's nice for a little while," Kegan said. "But I think I'd go crazy if I had to stay out here too long."

"You're a city boy."

"Pretty much."

"I know what you mean. Albert gets antsy when we spend too much time on vacations. He's a workaholic."

Kegan nodded.

Jennifer said, "You said you were in the service. Which branch?"

"The army."

"Were you in Korea?"

"Yes."

"Albert was there too."

"Yes, he mentioned that."

"Oh, that's right. Were you in Vietnam?"

"No. I mustered out after Korea. Vietnam was after my time."

"I guess you and Albert are about the same age. He went to Vietnam too."

"Oh?"

The woman shook her head. "Well, it's a little complicated. He went to Vietnam as a civilian observer. He was working for the Pentagon then. But when he got there, the military got nervous about him not having a weapon when they went out on patrols. So he carried a rifle and wore the military uniform. But . . . you know, he didn't shoot anyone while he was over there."

After a moment, Kegan said, "Well, that's good." It seemed to be what the woman wanted to hear.

Jennifer said, "I should be careful here. People have such strong opinions about the war."

"The Vietnam War?"

"Yes. Are you . . . do you support it? Do you support what we're doing there?"

"I don't know."

"You don't know?"

"Well . . ."

"You must feel one way or another about it."

"I guess I haven't given it much thought."

The woman frowned.

Kegan said, "I guess I don't feel comfortable taking a stance on it because I haven't really studied it."

"Are you reluctant to criticize our government because you're a veteran?"

"Maybe," Kegan said. Though he doubted that was the reason.

After a moment, Jennifer said, "Well, I guess I can understand that. If you don't mind me asking, do you feel . . . good about what you did in Korea?"

"I felt good about getting out of there."

Jennifer laughed. "Well, that's honest."

Kegan wanted to say that he felt it was the only decent thing he'd ever done. But he felt if he said that, he would sound simple-minded. He didn't know why he felt uncomfortable. He'd never been much interested in seeking the good opinion of liberals.

Kegan said, "The way it was told to us was, the communists had taken over all of Korea. We beat them back to the North and then we pulled out and called it a draw." Kegan shrugged.

Jennifer said, "Eisenhower did that. Made the peace. Do you think it was the wrong decision?"

"No."

It was strange because what she was talking about was the same thing he had been thinking before he came to this place to kill the woman's husband. He wondered if it should make him feel better that he and this woman seemed to be on the same page. Maybe they were on the same page. Or maybe he was confused by being knocked unconscious.

And if that wasn't enough, the woman

then said, "I don't see why they can't do the same thing now. Just pull out and let Ho Chi Min have North Vietnam."

Kegan said, "I'm not sure it's that simple."

Jennifer Hirsch smiled and said, "You know that's what Albert used to say to me when we first met. 'It's not that simple, Jennifer.' He was for the war when we met. And I was this liberal peacenik. He thought he could talk sense into me. Turned out the other way."

Kegan thought that might have something to do with her eyes.

Kegan said, "What about the domino theory?"

"Oh, God. The domino theory. Albert used to believe in that too. 'If Vietnam falls to the communists, then Laos and Cambodia and Indonesia will be next.' He doesn't say that anymore."

"What does he say?"

"He says what he knows because he was there. He spent three years in Vietnam and I believe it was the best thing that ever happened to him. He came back and he realized everything his government told him was a pack of lies. The Vietnamese are mostly farmers. They don't know communists from the Knights of Columbus. They just don't want people burning down their villages and killing them. Whether they're Japanese or French or American."

"The French were there before us, right?"

"Yes. And that was after Ho Chi Minh had fought on the American side during the Second World War. We paid him back for that by telling the French they could have Indochina. It was a complete betrayal."

"I didn't know that."

"That's the problem. Most Americans don't know."

"Sweetheart, what are you doing?"

They turned to see Albert Hirsch standing in the doorway. He had apparently heard his wife before coming inside.

Jennifer Hirsch smiled.

"We were just talking, dear."

"Mr. Carson is our guest. I'm sure he doesn't want to discuss politics."

"It's all right," Kegan said.

Hirsch seemed unhappy.

"Really," Kegan said.

"My wife is very passionate about some subjects," Hirsch said. He seemed to relax. He pointed a playful scolding finger at Jennifer. She blew him back a small kiss.

Hirsch said, "How are you feeling?"

"Okay, I think. I think I need some sleep."

Hirsch said, "We've got it all set up. Do you need help with your luggage?"

206

Kegan's luggage was at his hotel room in Seattle. He said, "No, thank you."

"Well at least let me help get you to your room."

"Sure."

Kegan stood. He looked at the woman and said, "Mrs. Hirsch, that was an excellent meal. Thank you."

"You're welcome, Mr. Carson. Please let us know if you need anything."

He followed Hirsch out to the deck. When he got to the steps he clutched the rail to get himself down. When they got to the other side of the cabin, Kegan saw his car parked in front of a cabin across the road. He had to concentrate to focus on the cabin.

Hirsch put an arm around his shoulder.

"Steady," Hirsch said. "I don't think you're quite a hundred percent."

Kegan knew he was right about that. More, he felt humiliated. A man having to almost carry him to his bed. If this got back to Chicago . . . if he lived long enough.

Hirsch opened the door to the cabin. It was clean and well lit. Kegan felt a little better. It had been a long time since he had looked so forward to lying down.

Hirsch stood at the door and said, "Can you make it from here?"

"Yes. Thank you."

Hirsch said, "I'm not sure I like this. We probably should have taken you to the hospital."

Kegan said, "If I was going to die, I probably would have done it by now."

Hirsch laughed. It was a soldier's laugh. "Well, maybe that's true. If it's okay with you, I'll come by in the morning to check on you. But not until ten o'clock or so. I think you need at least twelve hours of sleep."

"Thanks again."

Hirsch left without saying goodnight.

CHAPTER SEVENTEEN

Kegan spent the next two days in his cabin.

He only got out of bed to eat and when he did, he didn't eat much. There were some groceries left behind by the previous occupants. Soup, cereal, milk, and coffee. The milk was curdled and Kegan poured it down the sink. Twice a day, he would warm some soup over the stove and eat it at the table. Then he would climb back in bed. In the evening of the second day, he awoke to find a bottle of Bayer aspirin on the table. The Hirschs had left it there, he believed.

On the third day, he woke up and started to believe that his head injury would not kill him. His fever was gone. He was still weak, but he no longer feared dying.

He showered, dressed, and made a pot of coffee. He stepped outside to drink the coffee.

The Plymouth was still there. He saw it for the first time in daylight in three days.

The grill was punched in and broken. Kegan popped open the hood and saw the place where the radiator was punctured. Hirsch had been right about that.

Well . . . that wasn't so bad. He could get the car towed to the nearest town and get the radiator replaced. After that, he should be able to get the car back to Seattle and settle up his accounts there. Then get a flight back to San Francisco where he had left another rental car that needed to be returned to Los Angeles.

Kegan looked across the road to the Hirschs' cabin. The International Harvester was gone. Maybe they were gone too. Kegan hoped they were.

Stupid, he thought. *The man's wife makes you a meal and lectures you about Vietnam and now you don't want to hit him.* Because he brought you aspirin? Because he didn't let you die in a car in a ditch?

Kegan knew the Outfit was filled with stories about hoods killing hoods they were friends with. Sometimes close friends. Jimmy "the Gent" Burke was known to have killed one of his best friends because the guy had talked too much about the Lufthansa robbery. Friendship rarely if ever made a hood hesitate to kill someone.

And Hirsch wasn't a friend. He was a

210

stranger. A helpful stranger, yes. But even that was subject to question. Had Hirsch taken him in and stitched up his head because he wanted to be kind? Or had he done it because he didn't want the police knowing where he — Hirsch — was? Wasn't it likely that Hirsch had towed Kegan's car back to this isolated place for the same reason? So the police wouldn't find it by the side of the road and then come poking around the cabins, asking questions?

Maybe. But that didn't make much sense. Hirsch had told Kegan his real name. If he was on the run and wary of Kegan, he wouldn't have done that. Hirsch didn't act at all like a wise guy. He acted like a Boy Scout. Earnest and helpful.

And Kegan realized that was the problem. That was *still* the problem and more or less had been from the beginning. Hirsch wasn't a hood. And his not being a hood was what made Kegan hesitate.

For Lewis Knowles and, to some degree, Kegan, contracts on hoods didn't much trouble them. There had always been the unspoken understanding that it was okay to kill a hood because a hood had chosen a life of crime. An assumption of risk. And maybe that was all horseshit. Maybe like most killers who weren't psychopaths, Lewis

211

and Kegan had sought out some justification for what they did. *Hey, these aren't
regular guys, they're criminals. They knew
what they were getting into when they chose
this life.* But even Kegan knew that premise
wouldn't withstand too much scrutiny.
Lewis had taken over — stolen, really —
businesses from hardworking people who
had never committed a crime in their lives.
This was done with threats and muscle.
Maybe not murder, but always the threat of
it.

What made Hirsch any different from
some cluck who owned a bar and grill or a
dry cleaning store? He was no straighter
than they were.

The contractors had told Lewis that
Hirsch was a traitor who was going to sell
classified information to the Russians. More
and more, Kegan was beginning to suspect
that wasn't true. The guy didn't seem to be
in any hurry to defect to the communists.
He was in Washington State, not Berlin. And
the so-called classification information
wasn't being shopped to the KGB, but offered free of charge to a midrange criminal
defense lawyer in Seattle. To help a bunch
of punk dodge drafters, no less.

And there was Hirsch's wife. She came
from a wealthy California family. Kegan

couldn't see a man defecting to the Soviet Union when he had married an American lady with a lot of money. Only someone who was insane would do that. And Hirsch did not seem insane.

Kegan thought it out.

Go back to Chicago and tell Lewis he couldn't find them. Tell part of the truth. That he found a lead that took him to San Francisco but dead-ended there.

Lewis would say, "And what happened to your head?"

"Car wreck. Hit my head on the windshield."

He had never lied to Lewis before. But he wouldn't mind doing it now. Lewis trusted him. Lewis would believe him. Probably.

Or go back and tell Lewis the whole truth. Tell him he found them in Washington State, but then couldn't put the guy down because the man's wife was right next to him. Lewis would probably respect that. Then tell Lewis the people had helped him out after he injured himself in an auto accident. And that after that, he wouldn't be able to kill Hirsch because Hirsch's wife had seen him and would be able to identify him later to the police.

And what would Lewis say?

Kegan wasn't sure.

He knew that Sam Iacovetta would say, "You kill the woman too. Christ, what's the matter with you?"

And maybe Lewis might agree.

And then Sam would be angry at him, maybe angry at Lewis too for sending Kegan out on the job. Lewis would not want to have Kegan hit, but if Sam did, Lewis wouldn't be likely to try to stop him. The best that Kegan could hope for going soft was forgiveness. And the Outfit wasn't known for forgiving. They might forgive an honest-to-goodness fuck-up, but they would not forgive a betrayal or willful disobedience of an order. Even if they were merciful enough to let him live, they'd probably break a limb or two just to send a message about the cost of insubordination.

Well, the hell with that. He owed Lewis plenty, but he didn't owe him his life or a broken arm.

So that was it, then. He would have to lie to Lewis and tell him he just couldn't find them.

"How are you feeling?"

Kegan looked up to see Jennifer Hirsch walking up the road. She wore a pair of capri pants and a sweater and an anorak. Her hair was tucked into a yellow headband.

Her cheeks were ruddy in the gray morning light.

"Fine," Kegan said. "Better."

She came and stood in front of him and looked at his head. She smiled and again Kegan was struck by the thought of her having no idea what he was about.

She said, "Albert went into town for some beer. Would you like some coffee? Oh, I see you've already got some." She smiled. "Well, would you like to come in and have some breakfast?"

Kegan was starved for some solid food. He said, "I'd like that very much."

As they walked to the back of the Hirsch's cabin, she reached out to touch his elbow. Not coming on to him, but to comfort him. Maybe she knew he had been afraid of dying. Hopefully, she'd never know what he was inside.

In the cabin, she gestured him to take a seat at the table. He did and she began to take things out of the refrigerator.

"Bacon and eggs okay with you?"

"It sounds great."

"Orange juice?"

"Please."

"You should always have orange juice after you've lost blood. Orange juice and cookies. That's what they used to give us at the

215

blood drives we did in college. The Gammas used to sponsor them."

Kegan looked at her.

"That's a sorority," she said, seeming embarrassed in that moment.

"Oh."

"If you think that's bad, I was the president of the sorority." She shook her head. "The things I used to care about."

"I don't think it's bad."

Jennifer Hirsch said, "You've got color in your face. You look much better."

"Thanks."

"I think you'll feel even better after a meal. That's yesterday's newspaper, if you want to read it. I'm sure Albert will bring another one back."

She left him alone after that. Kegan read the newspaper. Idi Amin had kicked a bunch of Asians out of Uganda. A dam in West Virginia had collapsed and killed 118 people. General Westmoreland again said that the U.S. was close to victory in Vietnam. And Terry McCormick had appeared at a fundraiser in Los Angeles. There was a photograph of him with Natalie Wood, both of them displaying a lovely set of teeth. Kegan sighed. He knew what Lewis thought of Terry McCormick and his family. It wouldn't matter, though. McCormick's

216

election was guaranteed.

Jennifer said, "Listen, I want to apologize for my behavior the other night."

Kegan looked up from the newspaper.

"What behavior?"

"My antiwar speech."

"Oh. No need. That didn't offend me."

"Well, as Albert correctly pointed out, you had just been severely injured in a car wreck and here I was giving you heat about the war. It was rude of me."

"No, it wasn't."

"I think you're being kind."

Kegan smiled. "I don't often get accused of that."

"You're a veteran," she said. "Veterans usually have strong opinions about war."

"You mean they're for it?"

"Usually."

"Not all of them," Kegan said. "My understanding is, a lot of the people protesting the war are Vietnam veterans."

"Not enough," Jennifer said. Then she realized the sharpness in her voice. "Sorry," she said.

Kegan didn't want to forgive her again. So he said, "Your husband's a veteran."

"Yes."

"Well . . ."

"Yeah, I know," she said. "But he's only

one man."

Kegan wanted to assure her that one man can make a difference. But he didn't really believe that. He never had.

Kegan said, "He's not in the service anymore, is he?"

"No, he's a civilian. He used to work for the Department of Defense. He's on leave now . . . extended leave . . ."

She was stifling a sob. Tears were in her eyes.

Kegan said, "Listen — we don't . . . we don't have to talk about that."

"Sorry," she said. "It's nothing you've said. I guess I'm just tired."

Kegan rose. "Perhaps we can do this another time."

"No," she said. "Please sit down." She wiped the tears from her face.

Kegan, who was a fair detective at times, could read it easily enough. They were running, going from hotels to isolated cabins and never putting down roots. Hiding out and not being able to relax. It could wear down the strongest of people. God, if she knew that a man had been sent after her husband.

Kegan said, "I guess you're anxious to get home."

Too much, he knew. But he'd said it anyway.

Jennifer said, "I'd love to go home. We have a lovely home in Malibu. But that's the funny thing. If he hadn't met me, he probably wouldn't be here anyway. I got him mixed up in this."

Kegan sensed what she was saying, but wasn't sure.

He said, "Mixed up in this protesting business?"

"Oh, more than that. But . . . what am I talking about? I'm taking credit for something I shouldn't be. He's a smart man. He would have figured it out without my help."

Kegan said, "Figured out that the war was wrong?"

"Yes. I'm not responsible for the change in his heart. His time in Vietnam did that. That and other things. If you'd seen what he'd seen, you might . . . Oh, I'm sorry. I promised you I wasn't going to talk about that."

"I don't mind you talking about it."

"I do," she said. "You're a guest."

She set his breakfast before him. Two eggs over easy, bacon, buttered toast. Kegan took his knife and began cutting his toast into strips he could dip into the yolks.

"Soldiers," Jennifer said.

"Pardon?"

"That's what my mother used to call them. The little strips of toast you made."

Kegan said, "I guess I learned it from my mother."

"Is your mother still around?"

"No. She died a few years ago."

"What about your father?"

"I didn't really know him."

"Oh. I'm sorry."

"It's all right. He was not a good man."

She nodded but didn't say anything.

Kegan remembered what Jennifer's brother had told him. That her father thought Albert was a traitor to his country. Then he thought, Jennifer's brother. Who had seen Kegan in person. If a photo were shown to Jennifer and her brother, they would both be able to identify him. Well enough to put him in prison if he killed Albert Hirsch.

It really is over, Kegan thought. He couldn't kill Hirsch and avoid being arrested for it, unless he killed Hirsch's wife too. And he couldn't do that. He would not be able to do that. It was over. He couldn't carry out the contract.

Jennifer said, "Is everything okay?"

"Pardon?" Kegan said.

"Your expression changed."

"Oh? How so?"

"I don't know. It's like you realized where you'd left something you lost. Like you were relieved."

Kegan said, "Probably the food. It's nice to have something solid."

"You smoke?"

"On occasion."

"Let's have a cigarette outside."

They brought their cups of coffee out to the back deck. Kegan took a seat and realized it was the one Hirsch had been sitting in a couple of days ago. The one Hirsch had been sitting in when Kegan sighted him in the cross hairs. Kegan looked out to the woods, for a moment wondering if there was another assassin on the other side of the ravine.

Kegan said, "How long will you stay here?"

Jennifer said, "We may leave tomorrow."

"Back to California?"

"Maybe," she said. "We may go to Washington, though. I'm not sure yet."

Kegan was still thinking of other assassins. The contractor sending another man after the Hirschs after Lewis realized Kegan hadn't got it done.

Kegan said, "Have you thought about leaving the country?"

Jennifer Hirsch smiled. "What a funny thing to say."

"I just meant if you had the time."

"You like traveling?"

"Not really."

"And yet here you are," she said. "Are you running from something, Mr. Carson?"

I will be soon, Kegan thought.

"No," he said. "Just getting old, I guess. A little restless."

She was still smiling at him. Kegan realized she still didn't suspect him of a thing. It made him feel worse. And then he wondered what it would be like to be married to a girl like this. A nice girl from a wealthy family. A girl who didn't associate with hoods or crooked cops who knocked them up and left them stranded. It could have happened in another life, one where he wasn't born to a low-level crook and a woman who hadn't had much opportunity in life. Maybe it could have happened if he'd been born with brains enough to escape working for men like Lewis Knowles and Sam Iacovetta.

Jennifer said, "Albert and I went to Europe once. A week in Paris. I loved it. But he got restless there. He doesn't vacate well. He said he misses this country if he's gone too long."

"And yet he spent three years in Vietnam."

"That was work," she said. "And it was good for him. He found out what he was about there. A renewed sense of purpose, if you will."

The woman pulled on her cigarette.

Then she said, "I know it's a cliché to say you can 'find yourself' on a trip on the other side of the world. But there's something to it. We're all seeking something, I guess."

"Not all of us."

"You're not seeking anything?"

"I never really have."

"I don't believe that. You came out here for a reason."

"Yeah. To park a car in a ditch."

She laughed. "Yeah, there's that. But maybe you were looking for knowledge or peace. Maybe you came here to forget about a woman."

Kegan shook his head.

"That's what I like to think. But I'm a romantic."

Kegan didn't change his expression. Jennifer Hirsch sensed his discomfort.

"Sorry," she said. "I'm just talking. I do that a lot. Talk when I have nothing to say. Albert, he always thinks about everything before he says anything. I just say whatever's on my mind."

223

"Don't apologize," Kegan said. "It's a nice quality."

She said, "How long do *you* plan to stay?"

"Until I get the car ready."

"Wow. That soon?"

"Well, I should be getting home."

"Back to your business, I suppose."

Yeah, Kegan thought, but his business was cutting hair and putting down hoods who angered the wrong people in the Outfit. He wouldn't be able to kill two people who to his mind had nothing to do with the Outfit. He could have done it to this woman's husband a couple of days ago and gone back to collect a lot of money. But now he couldn't do it and this woman would get to keep her husband.

But for how long?

Where would he be when it happened? Shaving one of his customers at his barber shop and maybe it would be on the news on television. Or maybe it would be in the back pages of the newspaper. *Government analyst killed by car bomb.* Or shot in the head by an alleged mugger. Maybe it wouldn't merit any news coverage. A guy who didn't merit much attention outside of Washington D.C. And maybe the next guy they sent wouldn't hesitate to kill Hirsch's wife.

Albert Hirsch walked up the steps to the deck. He carried two bags of groceries.

Jennifer's face brightened. Glad to see her husband.

"Can't leave me alone for a minute," she said.

Hirsch said, "I'll say."

But Kegan could see that Hirsch wasn't the slightest bit concerned. Kegan wished he could be that confident about a woman.

Hirsch kissed his wife and said to Kegan, "Good to see you up. You feeling better?"

"I am, thanks."

To Jennifer, Hirsch said, "Any coffee left?"

"Yes."

"No, stay where you are. I'll get it."

Hirsch took the groceries into the cabin and came back out with a cup of coffee.

Jennifer said, "Mr. Carson says he's going to leave as soon as he can get the car fixed."

"Oh?"

Jennifer said, "I was hoping he would have dinner with us."

"Yeah," Hirsch said. "What's your hurry?"

Kegan touched the bandaged cut on his head. "I think I've had enough vacation."

Hirsch laughed. "I understand."

"As for the car," Kegan said. "I don't think I'm going to bother repairing it. I think what I'm going to do instead is call

225

the rental agency and have them come get it and bring me another one."

After a moment, Hirsch said, "That makes sense."

"I should have called them right after it happened."

"You were in no shape to do that," Hirsch said.

"I did want to ask you a favor, though," Kegan said. "I was hoping you could drive me into town so I could get some new clothes."

Hirsch said, "That's right. You didn't bring any clothes."

"Right," Kegan said.

For a moment the two men regarded each other. Because it was strange, a man driving out to the mountains without any luggage. Kegan had told them he had come from Seattle. He could explain it to Hirsch now, but Kegan felt it would be better to leave it alone. Hirsch was a nice man and a good host, but Kegan suspected Hirsch would be glad to see the back of him.

Hirsch said, "About a half hour?"

"Oh, there's no hurry. I'll go call the agency."

Kegan returned to his cabin and made the call. The rental agent asked him if he had reported the accident to the police. Kegan said he hadn't. The rental agent asked him if he had been injured. Kegan told him he had only been bruised. The rental agent asked if a Chevy Caprice would be okay and Kegan said it would.

Kegan went back out to the car. He took the .38 and the detached silencer out of the glove compartment and put it in the rucksack with the survival rifle.

He returned to the Hirschs' cabin about forty minutes later. Jennifer smiled at him again. If Hirsch had told her anything about Kegan that should frighten her, she didn't show it.

Hirsch and Kegan got into the International Harvester.

As Hirsch put it in gear, his wife waved and said, "Have fun."

CHAPTER EIGHTEEN

They drove the first fifteen minutes in relative silence. The vehicle had little if any soundproofing and it would have been hard to converse much above fifty miles an hour. The sun had come out and Kegan allowed himself to relax and enjoy the sights. He was still feeling out of place, but better about his decision. He had decided to put off thinking about how he would sneak back into Chicago. He would have time to put a story together for Lewis. He again told himself that Lewis would have no way of knowing that he had actually found Hirsch. Still, if Lewis found out, it would likely be the end of him. Lewis didn't like being lied to.

Hirsch slowed the vehicle to negotiate some hairpin turns.

Hirsch said, "We were driving around here one night and a deer jumped out in front of the car. I stopped in time and avoided hitting him. It was a near thing. You gotta be careful up here."

"I would imagine," Kegan said.

"I got attached to this kind of vehicle when I was in Vietnam. There was a man I met there, a retired lieutenant colonel. He had served in Vietnam in the early days, but he spoke his mind too much so they forced him out. He tried to work in the States after that, but he was drawn back to Vietnam. Anyway, he used to drive one of these things all around Vietnam. He said your chances of surviving were much better in one of these things than it was riding in a military convoy. He let me go on these trips with him. He was the guy who began my education. He died a few months ago."

"I'm sorry," Kegan said. "What happened?"

"He was killed in a helicopter crash."

"In Vietnam?"

"Yeah. It wasn't shot down or anything. Just a mechanical failure."

"That's too bad."

"His name was Frank Richardson. Did you ever hear of him?"

"No."

"President McCormick awarded him the Presidential Medal of Freedom last week. Posthumously."

229

Kegan looked at Hirsch.

"You disapprove?" Kegan said.

"Yeah. If Frank were alive, he'd have thrown that medal in the trash."

"I don't understand."

"Frank started out the same way I did. A true believer. The difference was, he grew attached to the Vietnamese people. He liked them. He wanted to help them. At the beginning, he thought we *were* helping them. It took him a few years to realize we were hurting them more than helping. I saw him hit a captain once, an American. Knocked the guy down. The reason he did it is because he heard the captain tell his troops, 'If it's dead and it's Vietnamese, it's Viet Cong.' They would have court-martialed Frank for popping that guy if he were still in the service. See, the captain would not have said that if he hadn't heard it from someone above him in his chain of command. But that's what the mentality had become over there. That's what that patrol captain had been taught. The Vietnamese weren't really human to us. Kill an old man, kill a woman, kill a child. Then tell everyone they were Viet Cong. That's the attitude Frank was trying to change."

"Did he have any success?"

"Oh God, no. Neither did I. Frank got

sick of all the lying. And he let his opinions be heard. He was asked once by McCormick's national security advisor if the worst of the war would be over in six months. Frank said, 'Oh no, sir, I'm optimistic. I think we can last that long.' He said that five years ago and the Vietnamese are still kicking the shit out of us. The brass didn't like hearing stuff like that. Westmoreland would tell them what they wanted to hear. Frank told them the truth. That's why they forced him out."

"But the president gave him a medal."

"The president did that for his own benefit, not Frank's. That's what you do when you have a war that's becoming unpopular. You give out a lot of medals. It was a win-win situation for Dan McCormick. Frank was a war hero and a popular soldier. McCormick got to claim some of that glory for himself."

Kegan said, "I guess it's supposed to keep up morale."

"It's supposed to, but all it does is prolong a very bad situation. More and more people murdered."

"American soldiers have been killed," Kegan said. "Some of them captured and tortured."

Hirsch looked at him.

231

Kegan said, "Yeah, I know about that. It's been in the papers."

"You mistake me," Hirsch said. "I care about the American soldiers. I'm one myself. Sixty thousand dead Americans now and all for a lie. And I know about the torture. I know about the bamboo cages. I know all about the Hanoi Hilton. But for every American killed, there's about twenty Vietnamese. But you're not going to read about them in the American newspapers. They're just numbers to us. As for the Vietnamese, no Vietnamese ever tried to kill an American that wasn't trying to kill them. How would you feel if they were bombing Washington, D.C.? Or Chicago?"

"They're not doing that because they can't. It'd be different if they had the means. If they had the ability."

"No, they don't have the ability. They've got guns and crude weapons. They don't even have the technology we had a hundred years ago. But they've got AK-47s and it's a better gun than what we give our soldiers. And they're *still* beating the shit out of us. But that's not the point. I never met any Vietnamese who had the slightest inkling of invading America. They just want to be left alone. They don't want to be forced out of their villages, out of their homes. They don't want their families burned by napalm or white phosphorus. Americans are good people. If more of them knew what was going on, they'd force the establishment to pull out of that place."

"Are you sure of that?"

"I'm betting on it."

They drove the rest of the way in silence.

When they got to town, Kegan left his rucksack in the International Harvester. If Hirsch had a mind to search it, he would deal with it. Hirsch would be curious about it, maybe even point Kegan's pistol at him while he asked his questions. But he wouldn't shoot Kegan unless he had to. If Hirsch had ever killed before, he'd lost his taste for it since. Kegan wondered about Hirsch again. Telling a relative stranger his personal thoughts about the war. For all he knew, Kegan could be working for the feds and building a case against him for treason. Why didn't he just drop this nonsense? Nothing he did would ever change anything.

They walked into the town's general store. Kegan picked out a pair of Levi's, a shirt, a sweater, a pair of shirts, a pair of boots, and a jacket. He took them to the counter. Behind the counter, he saw shotguns and pistols behind a glass case. Kegan asked the clerk for a pack of cigarettes. Then he paid his bill.

Kegan said to the clerk, "Do you have a room here where I can change?"

"You can do it in the restroom if you like."

"Thanks."

Kegan put on his new clothes in the bathroom. He checked his head wound in the mirror. It was healing nicely. He believed the stitches could be taken out now. Hirsch had done a good job.

Kegan went back outside to find Hirsch talking with one of the locals. Hirsch's expression different now, laughing with the local about something.

Hirsch turned to Kegan.

"Kept your shoes, huh?" Hirsch was smiling.

"They're Florsheims."

Hirsch laughed. "Not fit for hiking."

Kegan had cleaned most of the mud off, but they still looked dirty. Kegan looked forward to getting them shined once he got out of the wilderness.

"You ready?"

"Yeah."

Kegan put the shoes next to the rucksack in the back of the International Harvester. He did not want to open the rucksack in front of Hirsch.

Then they were back on the road, heading back to the cabin. After a few minutes, Hirsch said, "I guess you'll be glad to be heading back to civilization."

Kegan nodded.

A few moments passed and then Hirsch said, "I gave Jennifer heat for lecturing you about Vietnam. And then I went and did it myself. I'm not going to apologize for it, though. I think it's something people should be able to talk about. But . . . you are our guest."

Kegan shook his head. He couldn't do it anymore.

"Hirsch, my name's not Carson. It's Vince Kegan. Some people hired me to kill you."

CHAPTER NINETEEN

Hirsch didn't say anything for a while. He took his foot off the accelerator and turned to look at Kegan.

"Are you putting me on?"

Kegan shook his head.

Hirsch said, "I don't think this is very funny."

"It's not meant to be funny." Kegan shook his head. "Don't worry, I'm not going to do it."

"If you're trying to be funny, it's not working. I think what you're saying is sick."

"I'm not trying to be funny. I'm not putting you on. Someone in Washington wants you dead, Hirsch. They went to the Chicago Outfit and leaned on them and the Outfit contracted me to do it."

"I see. When do you plan to do it, then?"

"I told you, I'm not going to do it."

"Look, Mr. Carson or whatever your name is, up till now, I've taken you for a decent guy. A little elusive, but all right. But what you're doing now is in no way amusing. So knock it off, or I'll pull over and you can walk back."

Kegan took his wallet out and removed his driver's license. He showed it to Hirsch.

"So your name is Kegan," Hirsch said. "So you like to make up names. It doesn't prove anything."

"I'm not interested in proving anything to you. You want to believe I'm some sick crank trying to scare you, fine. But I'm not lying."

"I don't believe you. I'm going to take you back to your cabin and send you on your way. When we get there, you leave my wife alone. You don't go near her. I don't want you scaring her."

"I'll be glad to leave her alone. But you want to protect her, you need to stop this crusade you're on. You need to stop going to courthouses and trying to put government secrets on display. . . . Yeah, I know about that. I'm going to tell you something, the reason I didn't kill you is because your wife was there. If she hadn't been with you, I would have probably done it. It's what I do. But then the two of you saved me from bleeding to death and I met her and you and I realized I couldn't do it anymore. I'm going back to Chicago and I'm going to tell my people I couldn't find you. But they're not going to stop because I failed. They'll find someone else to do it."

"You're lying. You're just trying to upset me because you think I'm wrong about Vietnam."

"That's your cause, Hirsch, not mine."

"How did you know about the trial? The one in Seattle?"

"I followed you there. I found out where you were when I went to San Francisco. I know the two of you went to that seminar there led by that guy who used to sell cars. I know about Jennifer's father thinking you're a traitor. I know about your meetings with people in Hollywood. Mr. Hirsch, I *know.*"

Hirsch was quiet for a while. He made no move to stop the vehicle.

Then he said, "Are you with the CIA?"

Kegan sighed. "No. I'm a gangster. I work for the Outfit. Someone in Washington contracted it out to us. They don't want government fingerprints on it. They told us that you're a traitor and that you're going to defect to the Soviet Union and take this . . . this Pentagon Report to them."

"You know about the Pentagon Report?"

"Yes."

238

"You know what's in it?"

"I haven't the slightest idea. I don't really care."

"But if you read it . . ."

"Hirsch, you're not hearing me. These people want you killed. I've already figured out you're not working for the Soviets. From what I've seen, the Russians would want you to stay here and keep on doing what you're doing."

"And what is that?"

"Embarrassing the United States."

"That's not what I'm about. Maybe you're working for the Soviets. Maybe they sent you here to turn me against my own country."

"Oh, Christ. You've been reading too many spy novels. I'm a hood from Chicago. I'm a nobody. And I don't want you to continue this business of exposing the government secrets to the public."

"Which makes it more likely you're CIA. Or FBI. I know what they did to Martin Luther King."

"They killed him?"

"No, they didn't kill him. Hoover had his man call King and try to talk him into committing suicide."

"I don't know anything about that. I'm not trying to talk you into killing yourself.

What I am telling you is if you don't stop this mission you're on, they're going to kill you."

"What do you suggest I do?"

"Take your wife and leave this country. Go to Europe. Release your secret report there. Do that and maybe they'll call it off. Maybe going public over there will make you safe from them. Though I wouldn't count on it."

"This is my country. I shouldn't have to leave it when they're the ones committing the crimes."

"Crimes . . . it's war, man."

"Civilians are being killed. Not soldiers, human beings who just want to live."

"We killed civilians in Japan and Germany. It's war."

"That's not the same. Germany and Japan declared war on us. Yeah, we killed civilians then and when I was younger, I didn't have any problem with it. But now I don't think even that was right. These people want to 'win' the Vietnam War. Well, I've figured out the only way to 'win' this war is to kill every Vietnamese in Indochina. That's not a victory, that's a holocaust. We do that, we're no better than the Germans."

Kegan sighed. "Okay, Hirsch, you understand it better than I do, so I won't argue with you. But you're wrong if you think you're going to change anything. The Outfit, Washington D.C., there are people in charge and then there's the rest of us. You're not going to win this battle. They're going to kill you."

After a few moments, Hirsch said, "You really work for the Outfit?"

"Yeah." For the time being, Kegan thought.

"So you're a hood."

"That's right."

"You mean, you've actually . . ."

"Yeah. This was going to be my last one."

"Why? You tired of killing?" Hirsch being sarcastic now.

Kegan said, "Maybe. Maybe I'm just tired of taking orders. Hirsch, you're not . . . you're not the type of man they typically send me after. The people I go after are hoods. They've broken mob rules or gotten out of line in some way. We don't go after civilians."

"But you claim they sent you after me?"

"They did. I shouldn't have agreed to it. But they offered a lot of money. They'll offer it to someone else."

"Say you're telling the truth. Say you are a hit man for the Outfit. Why me? Who would want me killed?"

"You'd know better than me."

Now Hirsch shook his head. "I just can't believe it. I can't believe they'd try to have me killed."

"Your government?"

"Yeah."

"They tried to assassinate Castro. Maybe they succeeded. Why not you?"

"I'm an American."

"They killed civilians in Vietnam, like you said. Why not you?"

"Well, I still don't believe you. I think someone in Washington sent you to scare me away. The way they tried to scare King into killing himself. But it's not gonna work, Kegan. I'm not running away."

"You're going to continue with this?"

"Yes."

"Why?"

"Because I can't live with myself if I don't. Do you know what I'm up against? I'm up against an unquestioned belief that we — we the United States — have a *right* to win this war. Not an obligation, but a *right.* Years ago, I believed that myself. I was asked by the president and his brother to write a report, a study, of what it would take to win the war. Do you know why they picked me to do that? Because they were sure, they were absolutely sure, that I was on the same

242

page as they were. And they were right. I was a good American, a good soldier they could rely on. And I was taken in by all that McCormick glamour. The beauty, the charm, the access to power. I was captivated by it just like everyone else. So I studied all the memos, all the orders, all the minutes of the meetings. Not just those of the McCormick administration, but all the way back to the beginning. When Truman authorized aid to the French so they could steal back the Indochinese's country. We aided and abetted the French in that. We helped them violate the Geneva Agreement of 1954. We *chose* to help the bad guys. We *chose* to help the thieves steal. We thought we had the *right* to do that. This was after Ho Chi Minh helped us defeat the Japs. And what for? So the French could feel better about themselves after getting walloped by the Germans. Until I started researching that report, I had believed in Dan McCormick and his brother. I bought all the bullshit. When I was younger, I thought that the president had been the victim of getting bad advice from the wrong people. And then I figured out that wasn't the case at all. The president *was* the one making the bad decisions. You know about the Gulf of Tonkin, don't you?"

243

"Yeah. The Vietnamese attacked our ships."

"Not quite. We were in their waters and we fired the first shots. They shot back. They were defending themselves. That's what really happened. And President McCormick knew that before he submitted the Gulf of Tonkin Resolution to Congress. Dan McCormick lied to us. It's been a crime from the beginning."

"How do you know they fabricated that?"

"It's in the documents. It's on tape. McCormick even joked about it."

"Why would he allow himself to be taped saying such a thing?"

"He set up the tape recordings after he took office. Dan's not as bad as Terry, but he's still very much caught up in that McCormick greatness stuff. He set up the tapings because he thought the workings of his presidency would make great history someday. He believes in the myth that's been created."

"I don't know, Hirsch."

"I know what you're thinking. You look at me and you think you see a man who's had a nervous breakdown. Or maybe lost his sanity."

"I don't think that."

"I have lost something, though. A respect

244

for my country. A belief. I'm trying to get it back. I don't think it's something you can understand."

"I didn't say I didn't understand."

"You said you know about those kids in Seattle?"

"Yes."

"You may look down on them, but to me they're great Americans. I saw another young protestor speak in Michigan. Jennifer and I went together. This kid, this twenty-two-year-old kid, talked about how he knew he would be going to jail for protesting the war, for avoiding the draft. He talked about the mass murder we're engaging in. He asked if we would call a German soldier who deserted the German Army during the Second World War a coward or a traitor. He said we had a duty to our nation not to fight an immoral war. I watched that kid and I realized he was a better American than I was. A braver one, anyway. I watched him and I began to cry. And that was it for me. I promised myself I wasn't going to be part of it anymore. No more lying, no more defending murder, no more covering up the crimes."

"I sympathize with that," Kegan said. "I do. But it's not worth your life."

"So what then? Go to Europe? Hide out

until it's done?"

"Yeah. Until it blows over."

"And how many people will die while I do that? How many more American boys? How many more Asians will be murdered on their own soil?"

"I can't answer that. But you've . . . you've got a wife."

"She didn't marry me to be comfortable."

Hirsch pulled the vehicle up to the cabin. He turned the key and shut off the engine. Then he turned to Kegan and said, "Let's say you are telling the truth. Have you got a gun in that rucksack?"

"Yeah."

"Then I guess you better use it before I reach that door. That way you don't have to do it in front of my wife."

Kegan said, "I already told you, I'm not going to do it. I quit the job."

Kegan reached behind the seat and took the .38 revolver out and put it on the dash.

"Take it," Kegan said. "You stay in this country, you're going to need it."

Hirsch looked at the gun and his expression changed. Kegan thought maybe he was starting to believe him. Hirsch flicked open the chamber and saw that the gun was loaded. Six times. Hirsch closed the chamber and put the gun back on the dash.

"No," Hirsch said. "Jennifer hates guns."

"She likes you, though. She may have married you for your convictions, your courage. But even I know she has no interest in seeing you become a martyr. I'm telling you, they're going to send somebody else after you. You need to be protected. Take it."

"You still don't understand what I'm about," Hirsch said. "I don't want to die. And I have no interest in becoming an assassin."

"Self-defense is not murder."

"I'm fighting this battle my way. With words. With evidence. This isn't the Old West. I'm still fighting for my country, Kegan. But not with violence. Not anymore."

"You won't be able to get your message to anyone if you're dead."

"I'm going to tell you something you won't understand. I'm not even sure Jennifer understands it. A few months ago, I spoke with a bunch of college students who more or less admitted to me they had burned down an ROTC building on their campus. No one was killed or hurt, fortunately. These kids, they thought I'd approve of what they'd done. I made it very clear to them I did not. I told them our military was burning down family huts in Vietnam. And that if they were going to be burning down buildings on American soil, they really weren't much better. They didn't like hearing that, but that's how I feel. I'm going back to the East Coast, to New York, to Washington, and I'm going to show people that Pentagon Report. Because I believe that once people know what their government has done in Vietnam, they won't support it anymore."

Kegan said, "How long is that report?"

"About 5,000 pages."

"No one's going to read that, Hirsch."

"They'll read it."

"Maybe a couple of reporters, maybe even a congressman or two. But even if you get it out there, no one in the general public's going to take the time to read all that. It won't do any good. You're risking your life for nothing."

"Well, I have more faith in the American people than you do. Pardon me if I don't thank you."

Hirsch stepped out of the truck and walked into his cabin.

After a few moments, Kegan took the revolver off the dash and put it back in his rucksack.

■ ■ ■ ■

PART 3

■ ■ ■ ■

CHAPTER TWENTY

Lewis Knowles looked at the packet on top of his desk.

Kegan said, "There's about eight thousand left in there. I'm sorry, but I gave ten thousand of it to Gerri."

Knowles said, "Why?"

"She's pregnant. Some married guy knocked her up and left her. I'll pay you back when I can."

"Why's that your problem?"

"Gerri?"

"Yeah."

"She was my wife."

"Your ex-wife," Knowles said. "You're not responsible for her."

"Well, that's where the money went. And I'm afraid I can't ask her to give it back."

Knowles sighed. "I'm not asking you to do that, Vince. You say you didn't put the money on the horses, I believe you. But you tell me you can't find this guy after ten days, that concerns me."

"I told you I looked for him in California. He was in Los Angeles for a while, but where he is now, I don't know."

"You were gone ten days."

"Yeah?"

"Well, I mean that's quite a while."

"I couldn't find him."

"You always found them before."

"The guys I looked for before were hoods. They're predictable, easy to find. But this guy's not of our world. Besides, in order for me to find him, I'd have to question a lot more people. And then I'd be discovered. And I didn't want that to lead back to you."

"You wouldn't rat on me. That, I know."

"I know it too. But if the feds caught me asking a lot of questions, it would lead back to you. They've got a file on you. Maybe there's something in that file that names me as 'Known Associate.' "

"You never worried about that before."

"You never sent me after a civilian before."

Knowles opened the envelope and looked inside it. He did not count the money. He pushed it back across the desk.

Knowles said, "I want you to keep trying, Vince. If you feel you need to be more subtle, so be it. If you feel you need more time, okay. But we agreed to get this thing done."

"I agreed to try. You agreed to pay me a hundred grand. I'm not asking for the money. So . . ."

"So what you're saying is, you've changed your mind. You don't want to do it."

"No, I don't."

Knowles studied Kegan for a few moments. Kegan had never disobeyed him before. He had always been a loyal soldier. Knowles had dealt with insubordination before. But he had never expected it from Kegan.

Knowles said, "You say you agreed to try. But, see, that's not what *I* remember. I don't remember you saying you were just going to try. But let's put that aside for a moment. What I'm getting from you now is you don't want to do this at all. And that's something different."

"I gave you the money back. I'll pay you the rest later, I promise."

"I'm not talking about the money, Vince. I'm talking about you refusing to do a job."

"I haven't refused. I tried to find the guy, I couldn't find him. I've got to trust my judgment. When the hairs on the back of my neck tell me things are too hot, I'm out."

"I never told you it would be easy. That's

why you're getting paid so much."

"Look, I appreciate the offer. I do. But this isn't something I'm capable of."

"I know what you're capable of. That's why I chose you."

"Well . . ."

"You want me to send someone else? Is that it?"

"No," Kegan said.

"Now you said that rather quickly. Why shouldn't I send someone else?"

For a while Kegan didn't say anything. He had never lied to Lewis before. He didn't like doing it now.

Kegan said, "This isn't our fight, Lewis."

Knowles said, "I don't know whether to be angry with you or disappointed. It's not like you to let me down."

"Well, I'm sorry."

"You're sorry? That's all you have to say?"

"Look, I talked with people in L.A. Guys Hirsch knew, people Hirsch talked to. His brother-in-law. Hirsch isn't a communist. He's just a man who wants the U.S. to pull out of the Vietnam War. He's obsessed with it. I don't think we should kill a man just because he's against the war."

"How do you know that? How do you know that's all he is?"

"You told me yourself you thought the

McCormicks were selling you a line about him being a communist."

"When did I say that?"

"I remember you saying that."

"I remember what I said."

"I remember it too. You said maybe you were being lied to about Hirsch being a communist. I'm just saying now that I think you were right."

"I don't think that's what I said. And I know I didn't say anything about the Mc-Cormicks being behind this."

"Look, I heard about what happened with Castro. That the McCormicks tried to get Iacovetta to assassinate him."

"When did I tell you that?"

"You didn't, but I heard about it."

"That's a rumor."

Kegan said nothing.

"So from that," Knowles said, "you've determined that the McCormicks are behind this contract?"

"That's what I think."

"And what if that were true?" Knowles said. "Does it scare you?"

"Is it true?"

"I didn't say that. I just said, what if it were? Why should that bother you? You're saying you'll kill a man for me, but not for them?"

255

"If it's true, if it's coming from them, they're not going to let me live after doing something like that. So, yeah, I guess I am saying that."

"Why should they know who you are? You think I'd tell them?"

Kegan didn't know the answer to that. He wanted to tell Lewis that he knew Lewis wouldn't sell him out. He wanted to believe it.

Kegan said, "I don't think you would, Lewis. But Sam? Yeah, maybe."

"You let me worry about Sam."

"And what about you, Lewis? You think if you lend yourself to something like this, they're going to leave you alone?"

Knowles sat up. He had never heard Kegan talk to him like this. Questioning his judgment. Questioning *him.*

"What's got into you, Vince? Are you second-guessing me?"

"No. I mean no disrespect."

"I never imagined you would talk to me this way."

"I didn't mean anything by it, Lewis."

"Something's happened to you. You've . . . you've changed. What happened out there?"

"Nothing happened. I just figured out this guy is not someone we should be killing."

"Because you talked to some people?

Because you talked to his brother-in-law?"

"Yeah."

"Vince, I've known you since you were a kid. I've never once thought you lied to me. But now I don't know."

"I'm not lying."

Lewis Knowles was quiet for a long time. Then he said, "This isn't going to go down too well with the boys."

"I figured that."

Knowles's eyes widened. "Did you? And yet you still made this decision to pass?"

"Well, like I said, I couldn't —"

"Yeah, you said you couldn't find him. Whether or not I believe you, I'm going to tell the boys that. I'm going to tell them you couldn't find Hirsch. They'll believe it, coming from me."

"I appreciate that, Lewis."

"Don't appreciate it too much, Vince. Because that's the last favor you get from me. I can't give you anything else, ever. You and I are finished."

"I'm sorry to hear that, but I respect your decision."

Lewis Knowles said, "You're not sorry. I think you should leave now."

Kegan looked at Knowles. Knowles was right. He had changed. But maybe not in the way Lewis thought. Two weeks ago, he had respected Lewis Knowles more than any man on earth. Now he found himself looking at Lewis and thinking, *gangster.* He did not welcome the feeling.

When Kegan got to the door, Lewis stopped him.

"Vince."

"Yeah."

"We're going to put someone else on the job. You know that, don't you? Don't you?"

Kegan said nothing.

Lewis said, "I'm going to try to protect you as best I can. But if the boys find out you had Hirsch in your sights and you let him go . . . there won't be anything I can do."

"I understand that."

"Understanding that, are you sure you don't want to finish it yourself?"

"I'm sure."

Lewis shook his head and Kegan walked out.

When Kegan was on the street, he realized he had done something unforgivable. In sparing Hirsch's life, he had betrayed Lewis. Lewis had told him how Washington was leaning on him. That they had threatened to shut down the Outfit's operations in Vegas. That they had even threatened to imprison Lewis for tax evasion. Now Kegan wondered if Lewis had been telling him the truth.

Christ, what had the Hirschs done to him? He had never allowed himself to think Lewis would lie to him. Now he allowed for the possibility that Lewis had.

Why? So he could feel better about letting Lewis down? So he could feel better about lying to Lewis's face? Why should he believe that Albert Hirsch's cause was more important than Lewis's need to protect himself? It was dumb. If Hirsch's wife hadn't stepped out on that deck and sat on Hirsch's lap, he would have pulled the trigger and ended Hirsch's life and it would have all been over. A tax-free hundred grand and an exit from the Outfit life. And now it was gone and Lewis had warned him that his own life would be at stake if Iacovetta and Alfieri found out he had sold them out.

Sold them out for what? For a woman? For a woman who was pretty and kind? A woman who wouldn't have given him the time of day if she saw him on the street? For a man so misguided about a war that he was willing to ruin his career and risk his life? Why should he have made Hirsch's cause more important than his welfare?

Kegan touched the wound on his head.

The stitches had been removed and the wound was healing well. He would have a scar. Maybe the car wreck had knocked the sense out of him. If the Hirschs hadn't come along, maybe he would have bled to death. But maybe that was just so much sentimental horseshit. Maybe he would have just been fine. Got himself to a hospital and healed on his own. Then he wouldn't have to feel indebted to these high-hats and their dumbass politics.

Kegan remembered a guy he knew in the army who had been an NCO. Years after his service in Korea, Kegan got a letter from another soldier saying the NCO had killed himself after retiring from twenty years in the service. The soldier wrote that the NCO had "lost his identity" when he became a civilian.

Kegan thought of it now. He hadn't much liked the NCO, though he thought he was a good soldier. He understood the thing about losing your identity. If the man was not a soldier, what was he? Was he anything? Kegan was no longer Lewis's reliable enforcer in the Outfit. He was only a man who could give you a cut and a shave. And if the boys in the Outfit found out he'd let Hirsch go, he wouldn't even be that.

CHAPTER TWENTY-ONE

Nicky McCormick never played in the McCormick touch football games. Even before she married Dan, when she was merely Dan's "serious" girlfriend, she stayed out of the games. She would sit in a chair on the sidelines and smoke and sometimes watch. The McCormick sisters and daughters-in-law resented her for not participating, resented her reticence and faux European reserve. A talented politician herself, she knew the benefit of being seen and standing out.

It was a nice, crisp autumn day at Terry's compound. The McCormicks and select guests had had their lunch of smoked salmon and salad and were now on the grass playing touch football. Respected journalists and a couple of congressman in jeans and sweatshirts with Ivy League labels out on the field with the McCormicks, laughing and celebrating the closeness to American royalty. A cheer went up as Terry completed a pass to his teenage son's girlfriend.

Ben McCormick sat with his daughter-in-law, Nicky. The president sat on the other side of her eating an ice cream cone. The president's hand resting briefly on his wife's neck as he looked at his nephew's girlfriend and wondered how old she was.

Terry came off the field and said, "Time for someone else to do the work."

His father and brother smiled at him as he lay down on the grass.

Nicky looking at Terry from behind her sunglasses, her expression giving nothing away.

Nicky said, "It's good to see you relax. You're always so serious."

President Dan McCormick said, "Terry never relaxes. Not even in his sleep."

"How can I?" Terry said. "Having to watch you all the time."

Dan looked at his brother but didn't say anything. He decided that Terry hadn't meant anything by it.

Ben said, "Why couldn't Andy make it today?"

Dan said, "He's at a fundraiser for Chalmers in Arkansas."

"Bill Chalmers? That liberal?"

Terry and Dan exchanged a look. They

were both thinking the same thing. The Old Man already knew where Andy was. The Old Man always knew where his sons were. He telephoned his sons two or three times a day. Why was the Old Man pretending to be surprised that Andy was in Arkansas? Was it to fool Nicky?

Terry said, "He didn't check with me."

"I told you boys," Ben said, "Andy goes his own way."

Terry said, "He should have checked with me."

Nicky said, "Chalmers is a Democrat, isn't he?"

Dan nodded. His eyes still on the teenage girl with blue jeans and the crimson sweatshirt.

"Then what's the problem?"

Terry said, "The problem is he was the sole vote against the Gulf of Tonkin Resolution. He's not on the team."

Nicky said, "But that was a hundred years ago."

Terry McCormick said to his father, "Couldn't you have stopped him?"

The Old Man said, "I didn't know about it."

Terry got to his feet. He looked briefly at Nicky, feeling she had somehow betrayed him in that moment. He looked back at the

Old Man.

"You could have stopped him," Terry said.

The Old Man flashed his McCormick teeth. "War is hell," he said.

Whether he meant actual war or politics was unstated. The Old Man was becoming more cryptic with age. At a dinner last week, he had been overheard saying the Jews spoiled everything they touched. Ben McCormick's anti-Semitism was nothing new to his sons. But since Dan had been in the White House, he'd usually been careful about where he aired his views.

Terry McCormick looked at his father now and wondered if he would die this year. Ben had suffered a minor stroke last year. He had only been in the hospital for about ten days and the family had managed to keep it from the newspapers. Ben McCormick more or less looked the same now as he did before the stroke. Though there were some indications. A tendency to sway sometimes when he stood. Yelling at waiters who put too much ice in his drink or served him from the wrong side. Calling black guys Sambo. His filters breaking down, letting out things he'd always thought. Not so much to indicate illness to an outsider, but clear to those who were close to him.

Terry wondered what they would do

without him. The Old Man had always been there to guide them. He and Dan spoke to people outside the family as if their father was a nuisance to be borne. They only admitted amongst themselves how much they needed him and relied on him. It was no secret that Dan would not have been elected without the Old Man to push him, to help him.

Terry's servant walked across the lawn to tell him there was someone inside the house to see him. Terry asked him who it was.

"Mr. Mayville," the servant said.

Mike Mayville looked out the bay windows of the house to see the family members and guests playing football. He was feeling sorry for himself. Terry had invited him to play touch football before. Why not today? Mayville feeling self-conscious in his suit and tie while the guests wore jeans and sweatshirts.

Terry came in and said, "Hey, Mikey. You doing okay?" Terry flashing the friendly grin and making Mayville feel a little better.

"Fine, sir."

Terry went to the bar and poured himself a tall glass of orange juice. He did not offer Mayville a drink. Mayville remembered being at a policy meeting in the White House once when a servant came in carrying a tureen, serving Dan and Terry clam chowder and ignoring everyone else.

Terry said, "Come on." And Mayville followed Terry into his private study.

They took their seats and Mayville said, "I've heard from Davidson."

"And?"

"They haven't found him."

Terry gulped his orange juice. Set it on his knee and said, "Why not?"

"Davidson isn't sure."

"I would think if they're going to lose their Vegas casinos, they might be a little more sure."

"I'm sorry."

"Don't tell me you're sorry, Mayville. Did I not make myself clear before?"

"You did, but —"

"But what?"

"They said that they couldn't find him."

"Do you believe that?"

"I don't know."

"I don't believe it. I don't believe it for a second. They want one of their boys rubbed out, they find them soon enough. Did Davidson talk to Lewis Knowles?"

"No. He said Knowles was . . . unreceptive."

"Unreceptive? What the fuck does that mean?"

266

"It means that Knowles wouldn't see him. Wouldn't take his calls."

"Did Davidson talk to someone else?"

"Yeah. Sam Iacovetta."

"That's something," Terry said, remembering their earlier dealings with Iacovetta. "What did Iacovetta say?"

"According to Davidson, he's pissed. He wanted the contract fulfilled. He was a little vague, but the message Davidson got was that Knowles was the one who lined up the man to do it, but the man Knowles chose got cold feet."

"Goddammit!" Terry was on his feet now. "What kind of people are these? They can't even kill a fucking worthless defense analyst!"

For a second, Mayville feared Terry McCormick was going to throw his orange juice at him. He had seen Terry's rages before.

Terry said, "You track the fucker down and you shoot him! How hard can that be?"

"Look, it's only been a couple of weeks. Maybe —"

"We don't have the luxury of time, Mike. The election's not far off. Hirsch releases this goddamn report and we could be ruined. I thought you understood that."

"I do understand."

"Maybe I should have put someone else on this."

Mayville's lower lip trembled. He suspected he was about to be fired. He said, "Sir, give me another — let me call Davidson and tell him how urgent — how important this is to you."

"To me? You idiot, can't you see this isn't about me? This affects my entire fucking family. Hirsch is going to take down everything we've worked for."

"People are not going to take the word of a defense analyst over you or Dan. Not the McCormicks. Hirsch is a nobody."

"We've worked very hard to earn our place in history. My father . . . we've all worked very hard."

At that moment, Mayville wondered if Terry's rage had anything at all do with the Vietnam War. The thought surprised him, but it did not horrify him. Mayville was in too deep to begin asking any questions now.

Terry McCormick sat down and put his face in his hands. For a while he didn't say anything.

Then Mayville said, "Would you like me to go?"

"No. Just stay here for a moment."

Terry took his face out of his hands. He said, "I'm sorry, Mikey. Irish temper. Will you forgive me?"

"Absolutely, sir."

"It's not you I'm angry at. It's those fucking hoods in Chicago."

"Of course."

"We tried to tell them how important it is and they didn't want to fucking listen."

"Right."

"And fucking Davidson. We shouldn't have sent him to do the job. He always was a weak little fuck."

"Yes."

"They didn't take him seriously. I should have known he would let us down."

"He . . . he may not have been the best candidate."

"Ten years ago, I would have sent my father to talk with those bastards. They would have listened to him."

"Exactly so."

"You can go now, Mikey."

Mayville hesitated before getting to his feet. He had been hoping to get some face time with President McCormick and his beautiful wife. But it was not to be.

Mayville said, "Do you want me to call Davidson?"

"No. I'll let you know when I need you."

And like that, he was dismissed.

■ ■ ■ ■

At the beginning of his presidency, Dan McCormick had good relations with the Central Intelligence Agency. It didn't last, though. What began the souring of the relationship was the botched invasion of Cuba. President McCormick called off the operation when it started to go south. CIA officials claimed their agents in Cuba had been abandoned and left to die. Dan McCormick saw it as a matter of throwing good money after bad. He would later say he was only guilty of listening to bad advice from the Joint Chiefs of Staff and military commanders left over from the previous administration. The press and the electorate accepted this explanation from their highly popular president.

Inside the White House, however, the failed invasion rankled. Castro made a point of ridiculing the United States in speeches and telling the United Nations that he was a man of peace while the McCormicks were men of violence and recklessness. The fact that the McCormick administration had made a sympathetic hero out of a brutal dictator did not go unnoticed by Dan or Terry. Publicly, they shrugged their shoulders at the embarrassment. They even got the press to laugh at their self-deprecating jokes about it. Privately, though, they were humiliated. Not long after the failed invasion, they became obsessed with killing Castro.

They tried to get the CIA to accomplish the job. They called this plan Operation Ghost Hawk. It all sounded very slick and purposeful, but killing Castro turned out to be more difficult than they thought. Many attempts were made. All of them failed. President McCormick made Terry his chief liaison to the CIA. This turned out to be a mistake. Terry had never had to run for a public office before. So unlike his older brother, he had never learned to cajole or flatter people into giving him what he wanted. Terry just told people what he wanted done and if they didn't deliver, he abused them. Terry was used to having his way. Terry was more than just his brother's trusted aide. He was effectively the Assistant President. An unelected Assistant President, answerable only to his big brother.

The people then running the CIA were not opposed to assassination as a means of foreign policy. And few at the Agency felt much sympathy for a communist like Castro. But they didn't like being bullied by

Americans either. The longer Castro survived, the harsher Terry became. When told by top CIA operatives his demands were unrealistic — that the real world was somewhat more complicated than a James Bond movie — Terry would shout at them and call them chicken-shit bastards and sometimes worse. In time, relations between the CIA and the White House were so bad that the CIA Director quit giving the president intelligence briefings.

Dan McCormick did not want the CIA as an enemy. Nor did he want to alienate the younger brother who was his most loyal ally. So he did not argue with Terry when Terry suggested that as Secretary of Defense, he should have his *own* intelligence agency. One not subject to the authority or interference of the State Department, Congress, the FBI, or the CIA. President Dan McCormick accomplished the creation of this smaller intelligence agency without having to lobby anyone. He did it simply by signing an Executive Order.

When Dan McCormick first ran for president, he said things to placate the liberal Democrats and, to a lesser degree, fiscally minded conservatives. He said he supported civil rights for the Negroes. He was cheered when he said he supported human rights at home *and* abroad. He said he wanted lean, efficient government that was not wasteful or overly bureaucratic. He said that, contrary to the claims of his Republican opponent, he did not support an increase in the size of the federal government. Candidate McCormick believed he meant those things when he said them. But like many men who became president — Republican, Democrat, liberal, conservative — he could not resist the sheer rush and exhilaration of having national police agencies at his disposal. He came to believe that those agencies belonged to him and that expansion of their powers was necessary.

This new intelligence agency was to be run by Secretary of Defense Terry McCormick, a relatively young man who had no experience in law enforcement and had never been in the armed forces.

The agency was officially called the Defense Intelligence Agency. The McCormick brothers referred to it as the Division.

The nominal chief of the Division was a man named Chet Mahoney who had made a fortune on Wall Street as a municipal bond attorney. Mahoney stayed out of Terry's way, allowing him to run the Division. The man Terry discussed his plans with was a former Special Forces colonel and CIA officer named R.C. Cole. Cole was in charge of the Division's Clandestine Services (CS).

R.C. Cole had the kind of background the McCormicks admired. He was a war hero during the Second World War, having parachuted behind enemy lines to blow up railroad lines prior to D-Day. He returned to the States to practice law but left after a couple of years to join the CIA. The McCormicks put him in charge of the Phoenix Program after he told them in a briefing that the key to winning the Vietnam War was "the villages." Under Cole's leadership, American forces collaborated with the South Vietnamese Army to assassinate and torture any known supporters of the North Vietnamese National Liberation Force (NLF). About 40,000 Vietnamese were killed. Critics argued that the Phoenix Program killed more innocent people than bona-fide soldiers of the NLF and only served to galvanize most of the Vietnamese against the Americans. The McCormicks called it an "unqualified success." Terry McCormick saw R.C. Cole as a man who knew how to get things done.

They met at the campus of Georgetown University and walked together outside the Wolfington Hall Jesuit Residence.

R.C. Cole wore a blue suit with a red tie and a Burberry overcoat. Terry wore an overcoat and a hat.

Cole said, "I thought the McCormicks didn't wear hats?"

"I'm traveling incognito," Terry said.

"Hopefully the students don't recognize you," Cole said. "You're a celebrity. Your Secret Service detail isn't even with you."

"I don't trust them."

Cole shook his head. "You guys take too many chances."

"Live brave," Terry McCormick said and seemed to mean it. "How many courses you teaching now?"

"Just the one. International Diplomacy. Senator Jorgenson's son is one of my students."

"Oh, Jesus. He giving you any trouble?"

"He barely shows up. If Jorgenson has any hopes of passing on a political dynasty through that boy, he's going to be sorely disappointed."

"That's a relief," Terry said and meant that too. Terry said, "We've got a problem. Do you remember Albert Hirsch?"

"The defense analyst?"

"Yeah."

"I remember him. I met him at the family compound in Connecticut. He was a pretty good football player, wasn't he?"

"We only invited him once," Terry said. "He's gone off the reservation."

"He left the party?"

Terry sighed. He wondered if Cole had spent too much time in a classroom.

"Not exactly," Terry said. "He's stolen a very important report we entrusted to him. Our mole in Moscow tells us he's been in touch with them. It looks like he's going to cross over."

"Hirsch is going to defect?"

"That's what it looks like."

"Oh, my."

"Yeah. It's bad. He hasn't really left us with a choice."

"So you want him eliminated."

"Yes," Terry said. "Right away."

"Do you know where he is?"

"Last place we know is California. He went underground a couple of weeks ago."

"Where?"

"I don't know. I need him found and killed."

"Okay," Cole said.

"It's a matter of national security."

"I said okay," Cole said.

"I knew I could trust you," Terry said. "How are the boys?"

"Good. Edward's at Gonzaga High now."

"Ah, that's great." Terry put his hand on Cole's shoulder. "Let me know as soon as it's done."

Terry had dinner with his family that night. After dinner, they played Monopoly. Terry landed on the square that sent him directly to jail. His children laughed as it took him four rolls to get the doubles required to get out.

It doesn't mean anything, he thought. He had never been one to believe in omens. Dan had always talked about how easy it would be for someone to shoot him. But then someone had shot him and he had survived and that was the end of it. Omens were for losers.

Still, later that night, he thought about his conversation with Cole. He had not told Cole about his earlier attempt to have Hirsch killed using the Chicago Outfit. He didn't think Cole needed to know about it. The right hand need not know about the left. Maybe the Outfit would still get the job done and then he would let Cole know it had been taken care of. But he had wanted it done outside the regular channels. A killing out of Chicago would be easier to conceal, easier to deny than one done out of Washington. And there was something satisfying about putting the squeeze on Lewis Knowles, the know-it-all gangster who claimed he'd seen through the McCormicks all along. Knowles hadn't delivered, even after they'd threatened him.

Well, there would be time to deal with Knowles after the election.

CHAPTER TWENTY-TWO

Ramsey said, "Get the car."

Bart Jayson, Ramsey's second, got off the bench and dropped his cigarette on the pavement. Crushed it with his foot. Ramsey remained on the bench, feeling his timing was right. At a café across the street he could see Miguel Diego Lopez having lunch with his wife. She was a good-looking piece, fair-skinned and blonde. Chilean aristocracy. Lopez would have been better off not bringing her to Rome. It made him easier to find. Mr. and Mrs. Lopez had drained their cups of espresso and had put their napkins on top of the table. They would leave soon.

They stood up as Jayson brought the black Fiat around the corner. Ramsey got in the passenger side and threw his newspaper in the back seat.

It was a little cool for October in Rome. About fifty-five Fahrenheit in the sun.

Lopez and his wife might keep their windows rolled up. But that would be okay too.

Five minutes later, they were trailing Lopez and his wife in their Alfa Romeo Guilia. Jayson was a solid driver. He knew the vague, unspoken rules of navigating Italian traffic.

Ramsey reached into the back seat of the Fiat. He took a Swedish submachine gun out of a brown sack and racked the slide. He put the gun down between his legs, the barrel pointing toward the floorboards. Then he took a black cap out of the back seat and pulled it tight over his head.

Jayson poked the Fiat around the interposing cars. Soon only a delivery van stood between them and the targets. Then the van shifted to the left and Jayson moved the Fiat into the slot. They began to edge up next to the Alfa.

Ramsey said, "You got a way out of here?"

"Yeah, I've got it."

"Okay, then."

Ramsey rolled down the window.

Lopez had his window rolled up. Well . . . that was how it would be. Ramsey put the barrel of the machine gun out the window, resting it on the sill. He saw Lopez smiling at something his wife said, Lopez's right hand up making a gesture, and Ramsey pulled the trigger and let out a burst, shattering the window of the Alfa and putting rounds into Lopez and his wife. Ramsey saw the man slump over and die.

"All right," Ramsey said. "Go."

Jayson swung the Fiat away from the Alfa and hammered the accelerator. They reached a roundabout in a few seconds and made a series of turns that took them away from the scene.

After they dumped the car and the weapon, they took separate cabs back to their hotel room. Jayson sat in a chair watching Italian television. He didn't see anything about the killing of the former Employment Minister of Chile and his wife. Jayson smoked a joint and let himself relax. They had just killed someone for the Chilean secret police and had a lot of money coming to them.

Ronald Ramsey changed clothes and went outside to make a telephone call. He had received a coded telegram from the States.

Soon there was a voice on the phone he knew well.

Cole said, "Enjoying your vacation?"

Ramsey said, "We're leaving soon."

"Going south?" Cole knew that Ramsey had made a good living doing contract work for the Chileans.

281

"I don't think so. Not for a while anyway."
"Good. I need you here."

Two days later, they met at Bryant Park across the street from the New York City Public Library. All around them signs of decay. A young man with bad skin and stringy hair came up to them and asked them if they'd like to buy some Quaaludes. Ramsey gave him a hard look and told him to beat it. The kid scampered away, frightened.

Cole said, "Bring your crew here, maybe you can clean this place up."

Ramsey said, "I don't think anything can save this town. I walked through Times Square today. It was a disgrace."

"It'll get better," Cole said. "The problem is, they're broke."

"That's not the problem," Ramsey said. "The problem is they let these animals take over the city. What they need to do is send squads out at night to take these people off the streets. Disappear them. Then the decent people can have it back."

"You've been working in South America too long," Cole said. "You can't just make people disappear."

"You can if you've got the will."

"The president's going to give this city a

billion dollars in aid to bail them out. Who knows? Maybe they'll even clean up Times Square."

"That'll be the day."

R.C. Cole regarded Ronald Ramsey. Ramsey was in his early thirties now and completely sure of himself and his place in the world. Cole had recruited him from the Special Forces ten years earlier when Ramsey had been doing work for the CIA in Vietnam. An avid participant in the Phoenix Program, Ramsey had collected the severed ears of the Vietnamese people he had killed. Cole had made him a CIA officer, then reassigned him to green badger contractor status after taking charge of Terry McCormick's Division. Ramsey was ideal agent material. A killer who thought he was a Boy Scout serving his country. It shouldn't take much to convince him.

It didn't.

After Cole outlined it for him, Ramsey said, "Why isn't this creep in prison?"

"They haven't arrested him. He really hasn't committed a crime."

"Treason's not a crime?"

"It's hard to prove." Cole seemed certain when he said it.

Ramsey said, "Yes, I see. Put him on the stand and he'll start revealing the secrets in open court. Or he'll threaten to expose the secrets to cut a deal. Yes."

"We can't have him become a hero," Cole said. "Speaking at college campuses, that sort of thing."

"Yes, he has to be killed before he can spread the cancer."

"You're green now," Cole said, referring to Ramsey's contractor status. "You understand that this cannot be tied in any way to the agency or the administration."

"I've always understood that. I'm a patriot."

"Of course. I can't pay you what the Chileans pay you. Budget cuts and all that."

"This is my country. I'll do it for nothing." Ramsey turned to look at Cole, seeming offended at that moment.

"That won't be necessary. I presume you'll need money for some men, per diem and supplies."

"The minimum will be suitable. Where is he?"

"I'll let you know soon."

It was only a couple of months after Dan McCormick became president that he authorized wiretapping of American citizens. He believed it had started innocently enough. The national security reporter for

284

the *New York Times* had written a story about the Soviets' intercontinental ballistic missile capabilities in Turkey. McCormick believed someone at the Pentagon had leaked the information to the reporter and he wanted to find out who the leaker was. The leak was a particular embarrassment to Terry, who was then Secretary of Defense. McCormick ordered the FBI to wiretap the reporter's telephones and assign agents to follow him. J. Edgar Hoover refused to comply with the order. He claimed it violated the FBI's and the CIA's charter prohibiting spying on American citizens. Terry thought that was rich, coming from a notorious black bag operator like Hoover. But the bottom line was Hoover was not willing to help the McCormicks.

The McCormicks got the CIA to do it. The results weren't effective. They came to the unsatisfying conclusion that the reporter could have obtained his information from any one of about two hundred people working at the Department of Defense.

Still, they kept the wiretaps in place. Their belief was that spying on citizens without benefit of court order was necessary to protect national security. And, as the wise man once said, criminal means once tolerated soon became preferred. In time, wiretaps were placed on many other journalists, not all of them reporting on matters of national security. They expanded the list to include civil rights activists, some of the directors on the board of U.S. Steel, congressmen in both parties, State Department employees, and, in later years, leaders of the college student war protestors.

After Terry's falling-out with the CIA, the wiretapping duties were handed over to R.C. Cole's outfit.

Cole reviewed the file on Albert Hirsch. He assigned the task to men who worked in basement rooms and rarely saw daylight.

It took them two days to come up with something.

A telephone call from the State of Washington to the leader of a war protest movement at the University of Illinois at Urbana–Champaign. The student leader called the man "Albert" and told him he was glad he would be coming to the campus to talk about the war. Albert told the young man to keep the faith.

Reading the report, Cole smiled.

CHAPTER TWENTY-THREE

The Chris-Craft boat skimmed across the smooth water of Lake Geneva, Wisconsin. There were three men in the boat, two of Sam Iacovetta's bodyguards, wearing suits and ties and sunglasses. The third man was Bob Davidson. The bodyguards said very little to Davidson. The wind fluttered one of the bodyguards' jackets open and Davidson saw a revolver holstered under the man's shoulder. They could kill him here, Davidson thought. Tie weights around his legs and throw him overboard and no one would know. . . . Mike Mayville maybe, his line to Terry McCormick, maybe Mayville would figure it out. But he probably wouldn't care. They would find someone else to be the next FBI director.

The yacht came into view and Davidson felt better.

They pulled the Chris-Craft up to the ladder on the side of the yacht. One of the bodyguards gestured to the ladder and said, "You can go on up." The other bodyguard began to secure the boat to the side of the yacht.

Davidson reached the deck. Another man in a silk suit waved to him from the rear of the yacht. Davidson walked there and saw Sam Iacovetta sitting at a table eating his lunch. Iacovetta wearing an overcoat because it was chilly outside, but not wanting to eat in the cabin for some reason. It made Davidson, the former FBI agent, uneasy. He pictured a couple of J. Edgar's men on the shore looking at him through binoculars.

The bodyguard on the deck said to Davidson, "Lift your arms, please." Davidson lifted his arms and the bodyguard checked him for a wire.

Davidson said to Iacovetta, "Is this necessary?"

"We want to remain friends."

"Has it occurred to you that a tape of this conversation would compromise me as much as you?"

"I don't have the McCormicks in my corner."

Davidson sighed. Christ, they had figured it out. Maybe it wasn't hard to figure out.

The bodyguard finished and nodded to Iacovetta. Iacovetta gestured for Davidson to take a seat across from him.

Iacovetta said, "You've been on a yacht before, huh?"

"Sure."

"I'm sure this is nothing compared to what the McCormicks can offer you. Or Jonathan Jeffords."

"You seem to know a lot about me."

"What was it like working for Jeffords?"

"It was a job."

"Coming up through the ranks, I worked for a lot of interesting people. Some of them all right, some of them not. But I never met anyone as nutty as Jeffords."

"He's a visionary."

Iacovetta shrugged that off and said, "You ever been to Monte Carlo?"

"Yeah."

"Then you know this boat is nothing. Do you know what it costs just to rent a slip in their harbor? Five grand a week. You never seen yachts so big. Onassis's playground. I met him once, you know."

"Onassis?"

"Yeah. Big deal. He acted like he was something, hanging around that singer. That guy's no different than us. Just smarter."

Davidson didn't know if "us" meant the men running the Outfit or people like Davidson. Davidson said, "He's anti-

American."

"He is?"

"Yes. He supports the Palestinians."

After a moment, Iacovetta said, "And we support the Israelis?"

"Yes."

Iacovetta shrugged again. "You saw yachts there with open fireplaces, three or four staterooms. I heard of one that had a *swimming pool,* for Christ's sake. And these guys, they're always competing with each other. 'You got a yacht? Okay, how big is your yacht? What's the width? What kind of dock space you got?' Then it's, 'How many crew changes from morning to night? What kind of wood is your dining table made of? 'Cause mine is made of teakwood, see . . .' Guys like Onassis and these fucking Saudis, they keep upping the ante. You never win."

"It's a passion."

"A costly passion." Iacovetta looked around the still waters of this large American lake. "I like it better here."

Iacovetta continued eating his lunch and sipping his wine. He did not offer anything to Davidson.

Iacovetta said, "About that thing you discussed with Lewis."

"Yes?"

"It hasn't been done yet. Lewis sent

someone out to California, but he couldn't find your man."

"That's what I understand."

"Nothing to be upset about," Iacovetta said. "Lewis sent his best man, but he's not used to looking for spooks. He's used to looking for hoods."

"It shouldn't be hard to find him."

Iacovetta looked across the table at Davidson.

"*You* haven't found him."

Davidson said, "We had an agreement."

"I know all about our . . . agreement. We agreed to put this guy down and you agreed to leave us the fuck alone."

"Your operations are still intact. But Albert Hirsch is still alive."

"Don't lean on us, G-man. We're working on it."

"It needs to be done before the election."

Iacovetta smiled. "You mean, it needs to be done so Terry McCormick can *get* elected. Right?"

Davidson looked away and said nothing.

"Hey," Iacovetta said, "it don't mean nothing to me. You say the McCormicks aren't ordering the hit, I'm not going to argue with you. I just don't want you to think you're fooling us or anything."

"You're an intelligent man. We know that."

"We." Iacovetta smiled again. "The New Frontiersmen. Okay, then. Don't worry, I've put another man on it."

"Who?"

"A very capable man. That's all you need to know."

CHAPTER TWENTY-FOUR

Hunter Stewart stepped out of a swimming pool and straightened out his wet trunks. He put a towel around his neck and smiled as he sat down at the breakfast table.

"I'm a Toasties lover as you can see / I love Toasties and I love me."

A few moments passed and the art director said, "Shit. He's got hair on his forehead."

An assistant rushed forward and slicked Hunter's hair back with a comb. Hunter put the towel back on the chair and climbed back into the pool.

The art director waited a few moments, looked again at Hunter's hair, and said, "Action!"

Hunter came out of the pool again, straightened his trunks, and put the towel around his neck. Smiled as he sat down.

"I'm a Toasties lover as you can see / I love Toasties and I love me."

"Cut!"

The art director paused for a few seconds, sighed, and said, "Hunter, it needs to be a little more sing-songy. You don't have to sing it, but a little more sing-songy. Merriment is what we need. Merriment. Okay?"

Hunter nodded and went back into the pool.

They got it on the seventh take. Hunter Stewart put on a bathrobe. He was told Joey Heatherton was supposed to be in this commercial too, but she wasn't on the set today. His agent would later tell him they were shooting her scene at another location.

Hunter got a screwdriver from a table on the set, heavy on the vodka. He sat down to relax.

"That was good."

He turned to see a man who had taken a seat next to him. The man was about forty, well dressed, and handsome. Dark hair that was slicked back. Hunter wondered if he'd seen him in anything.

"You think so?" Hunter said.

"Oh, yeah. People don't understand how hard it is. Something like that."

"Yeah, I know. That water's cold. And they got me in these trunks that don't hide any secrets." Hunter smiled. "Good thing there aren't any good-looking broads on the set."

The well-dressed man smiled back. He had a nice set of capped teeth. He'd paid a lot for them.

The man put his hand out and said, "My name's Carmine."

"Hunter Stewart."

"Who's representing you?"

"Bill Lehr."

"Oh, he's good. He used to represent John Mitchum."

"Bob Mitchum?"

"No, his little brother."

"Oh."

"Yeah, I'd say you're in good hands."

"You an actor?"

"I did some acting when I was younger. I don't have the presence like you. I do some producing."

"You know, I got a pilot I'm working on. It's in development."

"That's great. No shame in this, though. You gotta start somewhere. Hunter Stewart . . . Are you Jack Stewart's boy?"

"Yeah. You know my father?"

"Who doesn't know Jack Stewart?"

Hunter Stewart grunted.

Carmine said, "Well, my people may have something for you."

"Really? A movie?"

"We're still in development. It's about this

guy who was a champion skier, won an Olympic medal but now he's drifting around Colorado and, you know, thinking about whether or not he still wants to compete."

"That sounds great."

"Can you ski?"

"Oh, hell yeah."

"Well, if you can't, we can work around that. It's still in development. But you're with Bill Lehr, right?"

"Yes. Bill Lehr."

"Okay, I'll remember that." The man stood up. "Well, I've gotta go. Say, how's your sister?"

"She's good."

"Haven't seen her around lately. She still in Malibu?"

"No, she's been gone for a while."

"Where did she go?"

"Well, she's been traveling a lot. She called me the other day. She checks in with me here and there. She said she's going to be in Illinois next week."

"Chicago?"

"No. A college town. Urbana."

Carmine smiled. "What's she going there for?"

"I don't know. Some peacenik thing, probably."

Carmine shook Hunter's hand and wished

him luck.

Carmine Forlano was born and raised in Chicago. He began working for Sam Iacovetta when he was a teenager. A few years later, Iacovetta sent him to the West Coast to work for Mickey Gold as a bodyguard. Over time, Iacovetta would call Carmine to check on Gold. Carmine found out that the Outfit didn't trust Mickey and toward the end of Mickey's life, Carmine sensed something bad was going to happen to him.

Carmine did not grieve for Mickey Gold when he found out he'd been killed. He heard the rumors that Mickey had been stealing from the Outfit, but he doubted the rumors were true. He suspected it had something to do with Mickey smacking Chrissy Jennings around. Carmine knew that Chicago had warned Mickey not to hit her anymore. Mickey had been insubordinate.

With Mickey gone, Chrissy Jennings would be fair game. Carmine had always thought she was a nice piece of ass, even though she was a little stuck on herself. He could give her a call now since Mickey wouldn't be around to throw a tantrum and threaten to kill him.

Like Mickey Gold, Carmine had fantasized about being a movie star. Maybe Mickey had been better looking, but he mumbled more than Brando and whatever charisma he may have had in person didn't show up on the screen. Carmine thought he had a nice baritone voice and a better smile. An acting coach had told Carmine you always had to hold something inside, not reveal everything. Mickey hadn't been able to do that.

After Carmine left Hunter Stewart on the set, he drove to his gift shop in Westwood. He asked his sales clerk how business had been that day. They peddled Mexican pottery and wood carvings as fine art.

At the shop, Carmine thought about Hunter Stewart. He was glad Stewart had told him where his sister was without having to be threatened. That was something Mickey would have fucked up. Mickey would have gone straight to the rough stuff. Tying the guy up and threatening to pull toenails if the guy didn't talk. Then they would have had to kill the guy. That would not have bothered Carmine, but it would have meant more mess and more work. Carmine was proud of himself, using charm on Stewart to get what he wanted.

Carmine pictured himself coming out of the pool and singing the Toasties jingle.

How he would have played it differently, his body looking better than Hunter Stewart even though Stewart was younger. He would have given the part more heft than Stewart did. Carmine believed he would have got it right on the first take.

Carmine had once met with a Hollywood producer who told him he had a great look, but he would have to do something about his eyes. "Too hooded," the producer said. Carmine resisted the urge to pop the producer in the mouth because the producer was too connected. Later, he discussed the procedure to get his eyes fixed with a plastic surgeon. The surgeon told him it would cost six grand.

He could call Sam Iacovetta now and tell him he'd got a bead on Jennifer Hirsch and her husband. Tell him they would be in Urbana, Illinois, to talk before a group of college-student punks. Probably some protest bullshit about Vietnam. But if he called Sam, Sam might say thanks and put some Chicago guys on the job and then Carmine would be out ten thousand bucks for a couple of days' work.

Ten grand. Pretty good money, but hadn't Mickey bragged once that the Outfit had paid him twenty grand to put down some squealer in Vegas? Mickey told a lot of lies;

he once said he'd bedded down with Natalie Wood and Carmine knew that never happened. So maybe Mickey had lied about the money too. Ten grand was good, but it wasn't great. Not when you had to pay a mortgage for a house in Brentwood and high rent for a shop in Westwood. Plus another six grand for the eyelid surgery.

And there was something else. Sam had told Carmine that Lewis had put someone else on the job and they couldn't get it done. Sam didn't say who Lewis had put on it, but Carmine had a fair idea of who it was . . . What had they offered to pay him?

CHAPTER TWENTY-FIVE

Kegan began closing the barber shop at five-thirty. He cleaned up the shop and took off his smock and put on his jacket and tie. When he came out of his office he saw a man sitting in the chair holding up a newspaper.

Kegan said, "Sir, we're closed."

Carmine Forlano lowered the newspaper. "Hello, Vince."

After a moment, Kegan said, "Carmine. What are you doing here?"

"I'm in town for a visit. Thought you and I could have a drink."

Kegan looked at Carmine for a few moments. If Lewis had told Iacovetta he had backed out on killing Hirsch, Iacovetta might have sent someone to put him down. It could be Carmine, flown in from the West Coast to do the job.

But Carmine was the sort that would just wait in the back of your car and put one in the back of your head.

"That okay?" Carmine said, smiling his expensive smile.

Kegan had a gun in his desk. Would Carmine let him go back and get it?

Kegan said, "Yeah, it's okay. I'm just surprised to see you."

"Yeah, it's been a while." Carmine was still smiling. "Maybe five years? You and Lewis at the Sands. We met Rich Little."

"A long time ago," Kegan said. Carmine hadn't said much to him then, pretty much treating him like Lewis's muscle and not much more.

Carmine said, "You're wondering if Sam sent me to see you."

"Yeah, kind of."

"Well, don't. It's nothing like that. I just wanted to catch up."

Kegan smiled and said, "You ought to be in pictures, Carmine."

Carmine smiled in a different way, folded the newspaper, and put it down. "Come on. One drink. We'll talk about old times."

"Old times," Kegan said.

They rode in Carmine's rented Cadillac. A red one with a white vinyl roof. Kegan in the passenger seat, unarmed. Carmine looked left at an intersection and Kegan looked down at the right pocket of Carmine's jacket. A bulge there where he had put his gun.

Carmine said, "You the one put Mickey down?"

Kegan shook his head. "I don't know anything about it."

"Everyone knows about it. Mickey was beating the shit out of Chrissy and Lewis and Sam had told him to stop. We all know that. I just want to know if you were the one they sent to do it."

"It wasn't me," Kegan said. "Maybe it was you."

"The night Mickey was killed, I was at the Friar's Club with my wife. You can ask anyone."

Kegan smiled and said, "The Friar's Club, huh?"

"Yeah, I'm a member. I guess you've never been there."

"Nope."

"Not even as a guest, huh?"

Jesus, Kegan thought. "I don't move in your circles, Carmine."

"We're in the same circle, Vince. I just got a little more style than you, that's all."

"Okay, Carmine."

"I know what you do for Lewis, Vince. He sends you out, you whack the bad little

303

boys. In fact, I'm pretty sure you're the one he sent to take care of Mickey Gold." Carmine turned to him. "Don't worry, I'm not wearing a wire or anything."

Carmine held his jacket open, as if that made a shit.

Kegan said, "What do you want?"

"Relax. I'm not here to hardass you about Mickey Gold. He was a fuck stick. Always thought he was such a big fucking deal. I'm glad he's dead, may he rest in peace. No, what I want to talk to you about is Albert Hirsch."

Kegan said, "Who's he?"

Who's he." Carmine laughed. "Come on, Vince, you know who he is."

"Can't say I do."

"Sam hired me to put him down. He said Lewis sent somebody else and they couldn't get it done. Sam didn't say who Lewis sent, but I think it was you."

"You seem pretty sure of yourself."

"It comes with experience," Carmine said. "Now I just told you I'm the one who's going to kill Albert Hirsch, being that you fucked it up. Still worried about whether or not I'm wearing a wire?"

"No, I guess not."

"So did Lewis send you after him?"

Kegan shook his head.

304

"Look," Carmine said. "I'm only asking because I want to know what he offered you."

"You want to know how much for the contract?"

"Exactly."

Kegan said, "I see. Because you're afraid a man of your expertise may be getting short changed?"

"Now you're thinking. Say Sam's giving me, oh I don't know, twenty grand. I'd hate to think you were going to get thirty."

"Uh-huh," Kegan said. "What makes you so sure you can find this guy?"

"Man, I've already found him. Know how long it took me? One day."

After a moment, Kegan said, "So is it finished?"

"No, not yet. He's going to be in Urbana, Illinois, tomorrow night. I think he's speaking at some sort of rally at the university. Against the war, the fucking commie." Carmine shook his head. "For a guy that's supposed to be underground, he doesn't seem too fucking bright."

"Christ," Kegan said, his irritation showing now. Hirsch hadn't listened to him. Now he was going to get himself killed. And probably Jennifer too.

Carmine smiled at him, satisfied. "So you

305

were sent, weren't you? Well, it's like I told Sam, you should always send the A team first."

Kegan saw that Carmine saw that he was angry. He wouldn't be able to hide that now.

Kegan let him see a little more anger and said, "Sam's giving you twenty?"

After a moment, Carmine said, "Ten. What'd they offer you?"

"A hundred."

"A hundred grand! Jesus Christ! That motherfu—"

Kegan grabbed Carmine by the shoulder and hair and slammed his head against the steering wheel. Carmine reeled, woozy, and Kegan took the gun out of Carmine's jacket pocket and shot Carmine in the side of the head.

With some effort, Kegan managed to steer the Cadillac to the side of the street and bring it to a stop. He pushed Carmine to the floor. Kegan looked up and down the street. He didn't see anyone walking around. He decided the best thing was just to get away from the car right now. He regarded Carmine's corpse.

Fuck him, Kegan thought. He had never liked Carmine anyway. Lewis hadn't liked Carmine either. West Coast asshole. Carmine had always overestimated himself. Thank God he was greedy too.

CHAPTER TWENTY-SIX

Once, in Vietnam, Ramsey had sat at the edge of a jungle at night, unsure if Charlie was in the brush. A couple of privates from Company C had happened upon them. They were alone. A couple of green nineteen-year-olds who'd only stepped off the C-9 a few weeks earlier. Ramsey ordered them to walk into the brush to do a recon. They hadn't been there long enough to know any better, so they quickly obeyed him. Within seconds they were cut down by Charlie fire, proving Ramsey's suspicions had been correct. Ramsey didn't think much of the dead boy soldiers afterward. They had helped him expose the enemy. They had served a purpose.

Now Ramsey and Bart Jayson and a third tall, bony-faced man named Roy were in a college town in the middle of Illinois. No brush here, just a few hundred long-haired college students gathering on a quadrangle, waiting for the student protestors to take the stage and say a lot of bad things about their country.

How would you flush Albert Hirsch out of that mob?

Standing at the back of the crowd, Jayson said, "I don't think we're going to know if he's here unless he takes the stage."

"If he's here," Ramsey said, "he'll take the stage."

"Then what? Send Roy up on the roof with a rifle?"

"No," Ramsey said. "We stick with the plan and take him after. As he's leaving, we put him down with a silenced pistol. Then melt into the crowd. If we do it right, they'll think he had a heart attack or something."

Jayson took a slow pan of the student body. Long-haired boys and girls, thin as young jackals.

Jayson said, "Christ, this makes me sick."

"They're lost," Ramsey said. "These kids don't admire generals or astronauts. You know who their heroes are? People like Manson or that singer who exposed his jimmies on stage in Florida."

"You mean Jim Morrison?"

"Is that his name?"

Jayson nodded and said, "I believe he's dead, sir."

"Good."

"His dad's a rear admiral in the Navy."

"Then he's probably relieved," Ramsey said. "These kids are a product of a sick society. Someone just needs to clean it up."

"We'll get there, sir."

Killing Albert Hirsch would be a start, Ramsey thought. He had little doubt that the McCormicks were the ones pulling the strings on this assassination. It gave him some comfort. He had not voted for Dan McCormick because he thought McCormick was too soft on communism. A courageous president would have nuked Hanoi by now. The McCormicks preferred to use the Special Forces and the special little agency they had created for Terry to use at his will. That was okay with Ramsey. He liked the work. But he still thought the McCormicks lacked the will and vision necessary to put the country back on track. The McCormicks didn't understand that half measures don't work.

To Ronald Ramsey, Albert Hirsch was symptomatic of the problem with the McCormick approach. Ramsey had read the file on Hirsch. Like a lot of people from the respected institutions, Hirsch had started out as a loyal McCormick man, charmed by the silver-spooned family and their good looks. And now Hirsch had turned on them. The McCormicks should have seen it coming. Ramsey believed he would have seen it coming. In the sort of administration Ramsey would have preferred, Albert Hirsch would have never received any sort of clearance permitting access to the country's secrets.

The student, whose name was George Hart, was an earnest young man of twenty-two with glasses and frizzy brown hair. He had gotten into the university on a swimming scholarship and was majoring in history. His father had stopped speaking to him a year ago, telling his son he was ashamed of him. Now Hart sat in the back of a Ford step van with Albert Hirsch and his wife.

Hart said, "Again, I appreciate you coming. It means a lot to us, having an Establishment figure speak. You know, an older person."

Albert Hirsch sat on the floorboards with his back against the wall. He smiled and said, "I guess I'll be glad when it's over."

Jennifer said, "What about the police? Are you sure it's safe?"

"They're letting us alone for now," Hart said. "Not because they're being kind. They don't want another Kent State."

Jennifer shivered.

Hirsch put a hand on her arm. "Don't worry," he said. "Nothing like that's gonna happen."

Hart said, "I'm going to go out there and get Larry off the podium. He'll go on for an hour if we let him."

Hart stepped out of the van and closed the door behind him.

Hirsch said, "Everything's going to be fine. Don't be scared."

Jennifer said, "I just have a bad feeling. Don't you ever get those?"

"Sometimes. Not today."

Jennifer smiled, trying to cheer herself up. "That boy," she said. "So young. He must think we're ancient."

Hirsch said, "He lost his scholarship and he's got almost all A's. He was set to go to law school and now they've told him he's no longer got a slot there. I asked him this morning if he was scared of being arrested and going to jail. He said he would handle that when it came. Can you believe that?"

"He's scared too. He's just not going to let you see it."

"Of course he's scared. Don't you see? That's why I have to do this. We can't let kids like him go to jail for speaking out about what's wrong while we sit in our living rooms shaking our heads. We can't let any more boys be sent to Indochina."

"We," she said. "Us old folks?"

Hirsch smiled, but only for a moment. "I don't know how old I was when I figured out I was at the upper end of the generation gap. Part of life's journey, I guess. You know what separates us from them? It's just innocence. They haven't lost their innocence yet and we have. That's all the generation gap is."

"But Kent State . . . those kids."

"That was two years ago. It's not going to happen here."

Jennifer Hirsch took her husband's hand and wished she could believe it.

George Hart introduced Albert Hirsch to the hundreds of students who had never heard of him. Many of the kids were there for the wrong reasons. To get high, to get laid, to be part of something they hadn't fully studied, to be included in something that had seemed to take on a life of its own, to take a stand against their parents who had survived the Depression in the thirties and fought the war in the forties but could not understand that their country could possibly be the bad guys in any arena. Who was Albert Hirsch to them? A balding middle-aged man with horn-rimmed glasses who fought in the Second World War and Korea.

Hirsch thought about all this before he walked to the podium. He told himself it didn't matter. There were kids here for the right reasons. He promised himself he would not talk down to them.

He told them who he was and about his military service. He told them he was a "square" and proud of it. That got a few laughs. He looked at Jennifer. She smiled back at him and he felt he could move mountains.

Then he said, "I'm not here this evening because I believe in revolution. I don't want any more bloodshed. If you're looking to me to seek approval of the burning of buildings or the desecration of soldiers' graves, look elsewhere. I'm not your man. If you're hoping to hear me heap scorn on American soldiers, you're going to be disappointed. Those young men are not so different from you or me. The majority of them are kids, put someplace they don't want to be. Like you, most of them are confused and frightened. They were put there by old men who are too ignorant to know what they got themselves in for and too arrogant to pull out. Too arrogant to admit they've made a

314

terrible mistake.

"What we *do* share is a passionate determination to end U.S. involvement in the Vietnam War. I'm going to quote to you something the late Martin Luther King, Jr. said. 'A time comes when silence is betrayal.' That time is now. We can no longer be silent about the crimes that are being inflicted on the Vietnamese people. I spent three years in Vietnam. Three years listening and learning. For the first two years, I was a true believer. As strongly and as firmly as you now believe the war is wrong, for those two years I thought it was right. I believed we were there to help the Vietnamese. I even believed that the power of Camelot, the beauty of it all, could be extended to Vietnam. I believed that. But I've come to see that Camelot is a myth. And it's very hard to fight a myth. It's very hard to take down a dream. It's like fighting a god.

"What is the dream? The dream is that the United States can change another country's culture and essence through war and fire and pure force of will. That by occupying a country with American troops, we can somehow get them to love us and become Americans like us.

"But it doesn't work that way. No country has ever welcomed an occupying army from

315

another nation. And if they have, they haven't for long. Some ask, well, why not? Why shouldn't they welcome us? Aren't we there to liberate them from the communists?

"If only it were that simple. The average Vietnamese doesn't know a communist from a Rotarian. They're farmers, most of them. Many of them have had their huts burned by American soldiers and forced to relocate to concentration camps that are little better than prisons. Do that to any nation and ask yourselves, 'How can they *not* hate us?' How would you feel if they burned down your home and forced you to move someplace else? If they killed your family because a South Vietnamese councilman with a grudge wrongly identified you as Viet Cong? We drop bombs on them — in both South and North Vietnam — and then we arrogantly demand that they see us as liberators. We support corrupt and brutal dictators and claim that it's being done in the name of freedom.

"I speak not on behalf of North Vietnam or the National Liberation Front. As Dr. King himself noted, they are not paragons of virtue. Anyone who studies the issue, as I have, knows it is absolute nonsense to say that if you're opposed to U.S. involvement in the war, you must then be on the side of the North Vietnamese. I speak — selfishly — for America. It's not about them. It's about us.

"Who are we? What sort of country do we want to have? Do we want to continue to support leaders who support a war that they've long known is a lost cause? Do we want leaders who know deep down the only way we're going to win this war is to exterminate every man, woman, and child in Vietnam? And say we did do that. Say we bombed Indochina into a parking lot, what then will we win? The same sort of 'victory' the Germans had over the Jews?

"Plenty of decent Americans have said, 'But these are good men. Dan McCormick is a good man and his intentions are noble.' Six years ago, I wouldn't have argued with that. But if history has taught us anything, it's that well-intended men can inflict just as much destruction as the man who purposely sets out to do evil. The mindset that led to our invasion of Vietnam is as old as man. We did a great and noble thing when we defeated Germany and Japan twenty-odd years ago. But like all imperial powers, we became arrogant. Power corrupts. Twenty-five years ago, we were the good guys fighting the bad guys. But now we've become the bad guys. And like most bad

317

guys, we don't see that we're bad. We don't want to. But we must. Truth is our power here, not violence.

"I know you've all been told, 'You're young, you don't understand. You're too immature.' I confess I used to think that myself about the young. But I read somewhere — I think it was in *Catcher in the Rye* — that the difference between the mature man and the immature man is that the immature man wants to die nobly for an unworthy cause, while the mature man will live humbly for a worthy one.

"Vietnam is an unworthy cause. It isn't worth the life of one more American boy. It isn't worth the life of one more Vietnamese child. We may well have killed a million Vietnamese already. We know the number of American soldiers killed is now over sixty thousand. For every one of ours they've killed, we've killed twenty of theirs. For what? They haven't invaded our country. They haven't dropped bombs on Washington or New York or central Illinois. We have designated them as our enemies. They haven't done the same to us.

"It's time for us to admit that, no matter how well intended it may have been in the beginning, no matter if decent men mistakenly believed they were doing the right thing eight years ago, no reasonable person *today* can say our intentions in Vietnam remain honorable. We are committing crimes against humanity. By remaining silent in the face of this injustice, by quietly going along with the corruption of what made this country great, we become traitors to this nation. It's time to stop. Thank you."

Hirsch had ended his speech on what he thought was a low note. He had never fancied himself a public speaker. At first the crowd was silent. And then there were cheers that became a roar.

It took a few moments for Jayson to make himself heard. He had to lean close to Ramsey when he spoke.

Jayson said, "Are you all right, sir?"

Ronald Ramsey was not all right. He was almost trembling with anger. He said, "They got to him."

"Pardon?"

"The Soviets," Ramsey said. "They got to him. No real American would say those things."

"Goddamn first amendment," Jayson said. "Let people say such things."

"That's not speech," Ramsey said. "It's treason."

"Well, fuck him. He'll get to die a martyr."
Ramsey said, "Let's get it done."

CHAPTER TWENTY-SEVEN

Hirsch left the podium. Jennifer took his hand and kissed him.

"I'm so glad I married you," she said.

George Hart said, "Man, that was something. You really reached them. Do you want to come to the student union, have a beer?"

"No thanks," Hirsch said. He was still smiling. "We have to get going."

"We've got a place you can stay. Professor Groh has offered his home. Oh, shit."

Hirsch turned to where Hart was looking. A horde of helmeted police officers were pushing into the crowd. The police officers were holding clubs. Hirsch saw a student say something to one of the cops. The cop held up a can of mace and sprayed the student in the face.

Hart said, "You better get out of here."

Hirsch took Jennifer's hand and started moving. Shouts. Pandemonium. The smell of violence and fear began to spread.

"Albert."

"Come on," Hirsch said.

But then another wave of state troopers came from the other direction. Hirsch moved to his right and they both started to run to the university library. It was open and they rushed in.

It was a three-story library. Through the windows they saw cops chasing students. A young man falling, a couple of troopers descending on him.

"Upstairs," Hirsch said.

They ran up the stairs to the third floor. When they reached the top, Hirsch heard footsteps behind them. Hirsch pushed the doors to the stairwell open and they walked onto the third floor. There was no one there.

"Albert."

"It's all right. Maybe they just want to disperse the crowd."

Jennifer said, "I heard someone."

"Probably just another student."

They walked quickly past the shelves of books and periodicals. They passed little private study rooms where the lights had been turned off. They walked north, away from the quad below. It was quiet in the library, unsettling, but he could still hear the crowds outside.

Hirsch said, "I should be down there.

Maybe I could talk to whoever's in charge."

"And put a stop to it?" Jennifer said. "Albert, they'll club you too. And then throw you in jail."

"We shouldn't have run away."

Jennifer said, "Please, *please,* Albert. Don't go back down there. Wait for things to calm down."

They reached a group of empty study tables. Hirsch looked out the large plate glass windows. He saw students running away, cops chasing them.

"Christ," Hirsch said. "Why? They were just peacefully assembling."

Jennifer said, "You know why."

"They weren't hurting anyone. I don't know what's happened to this country."

"Sit down," Jennifer said. "Come sit down."

Jennifer sat down at one of the tables. Hirsch walked over to her and took her hand. He remained standing.

"We'll win," she said. "In the end."

"In the end," Hirsch said, wanting to believe it.

They were quiet for a moment, Hirsch trying to hide his fear from this woman he loved. Thinking of arrest and trials and a long term in prison. Wondering if being scared of such things made him a coward.

They heard footsteps. Someone in hard-soled shoes. Maybe another student, but . . . Jesus.

Quietly, Hirsch said, "Come on."

They left the table and moved into the bookshelves. Into a narrow corridor of stacked research papers no one would ever read.

The footsteps got louder. They waited for the sound of a police officer to call out to them, ordering them to come out and show themselves. They waited for the sound of cops talking to each other. They waited for the sound of college students whispering or crying or even panicking about being beaten or caught. But they didn't hear anything like that. They knew then there was someone there, someone on the floor with them.

Albert and Jennifer stood face to face in the narrow corridor. Jennifer opened her mouth and Hirsch held a finger to his lips to silence her.

The footsteps neared, someone getting closer. Hirsch pushed Jennifer and they started moving further down the aisle. And then they both started moving faster, hearing the footsteps coming from behind.

Hirsch's plan was to get to the end of this corridor and then shift over to the next one, dog-legging it, and then keep moving because whatever survival instinct that had kept him alive in Korea and Vietnam was now telling him they needed to get out of this library, go back out to the quad, and face the state troopers rather than this terrifying unknown.

Because now he could hear the footsteps hurrying, closing . . .

Jennifer saw him first.

She screamed and Hirsch looked ahead to see Kegan step out in front of them, blocking their escape. Hirsch grabbed his wife and they skidded to a stop as Kegan raised his arm and pointed a long-barreled pistol at them, and before Hirsch could cry out, Kegan fired twice and Jennifer screamed again and Hirsch heard a thump behind him.

Hirsch turned around and then Kegan bumped him aside as he walked between Hirsch and his wife, past them to where a bony-faced man lay on the ground with two bullets in him.

Kegan crouched next to the man and slid the man's gun away from him. Kegan made sure the bony-faced man was dead.

Kegan turned to face Hirsch and before Hirsch could say anything, Kegan raised a palm to quiet him.

Kegan walked back to Hirsch and Jennifer.

Hirsch whispered, "What are you doing here?"

"Shut up," Kegan said. "There are two more."

Hirsch, angry and frightened, said, "Are they with you?"

Kegan shook his head, trying to put aside his anger. "Stay behind me," he said.

They began moving, Jennifer behind Kegan, Hirsch behind Jennifer. He didn't want her shot from behind.

Ramsey and Jayson were on the other side of the library. Jayson moved into the corridor and found Roy's corpse.

"Christ," Jayson said. He picked up Roy's gun and put it in his pocket.

Jayson hurried back to Ramsey and said, "Roy's dead. Hirsch must be armed."

Ramsey said, "Cover the stairwell. I'm going to wait downstairs."

Jayson waited to see if Ramsey was going to say anything more about Roy. Ramsey didn't. Apparently, they were just going to leave the man here.

Jayson said, "But he's armed."

"So are you," Ramsey said and went to the elevator.

■ ■ ■ ■

Kegan reached the corner and peered around. The entry to the stairwell was about twenty yards away. They could reach it quickly. But he had seen three men follow the Hirschs into the library. Three men he knew weren't college students or state troopers.

They could reach the stairwell quickly but those two men hadn't just upped and left. Kegan had heard what he believed to be an elevator door open and close, but that could have been a ruse to get them to think they had left.

If they were still here, they would be waiting in the stairwell or somewhere nearby. They would wait.

Where would you hide? Kegan thought.

Kegan looked out over the set of bookshelves south of the stairwell. A magazine rack nearby and a large blockish cabinet holding Dewey Decimal cards. That would be a good place.

Kegan backed away from the corner and edged around to the far south wall. He crept along the back of the bookshelves. Then he stepped into a corridor. The shelves were metal and separated and he crouched down to peek in between.

He could not see behind the Dewey Decimal cabinet. But then he looked toward the window behind it and saw the reflection of a man crouching there. A man with a gun.

It was not a sharply defined reflection, but Kegan saw enough to think the man was not a mook. He didn't have the Outfit look, the Outfit clothes. He doubted the man with the gun was a friend of Carmine's.

Kegan got a couple of aisles closer. He took another look through the crack and saw the man directly. The man wearing a houndstooth jacket and a scarf. Trendy.

Kegan took a book on the shelf and threw it toward the stairwell. It hit the ground and the man stood. Kegan ran around the shelf and got behind the man.

Jayson turned and started to raise his gun and Kegan shot him in the shoulder. The man flipped back and Kegan ran over to him and kicked him in the face. Kegan kicked the gun away and put a knee down on the man's chest. The man gasped.

Kegan said, "Where's the third man?"

Bart Jayson didn't answer. Kegan hit him on the head with his silencer.

"Come on, killer," Kegan said. "Where is he?"

"Fuck you."

Kegan pushed the front of the silencer into Jayson's eye.

"You think I won't kill you, you little turd? I've done it before."

"What are you? . . . KGB?"

"No, I'm not KGB, you fucking fool. I'm going to count to three. One. Two."

"He's downstairs. He's waiting for you to come downstairs."

"You were going to kill an unarmed man. Why?" Kegan pressed the barrel into Jayson's eye socket. *"Why?"*

"He's a traitor. That's what they told us."

"Who told you that?"

"Who do you think? Washington, man. The guy's a fucking spy."

"Washington sent you?"

"Yeah."

"I'm going to let you live. But if I ever see you again, if you ever go near Albert Hirsch again, I'll kill you, you hear me?"

"Yeah."

Kegan smacked Jayson across the temple with his gun. Then he did it again. Kegan picked up Jayson's gun and put it in his pocket. Then he searched Jayson's coat and found the other gun. Kegan took that too as well as the man's wallet.

Kegan got the Hirschs to the bottom floor.

He dropped the two guns he had taken off Jayson into a trash bin. When they got outside, Kegan went to the nearest uniformed cop.

"Officer. Officer!" Kegan pointed back. "There are kids in there setting fire to the library! They're burning it, man!"

The cop called out to a couple of his brother officers and they rushed into the library.

Kegan pushed the Hirschs through the crowd. It was dark out now and that was good. Kegan took a hat off a student and pressed it onto Albert Hirsch's head. Then he pulled Hirsch's sport coat off him and dropped it to the ground. The three of them melted into the crowd.

CHAPTER TWENTY-EIGHT

Kegan parked Hirsch's International Harvester behind the hotel and walked back to the front. The hotel was perched on a bluff overlooking a two-lane state highway in Indiana. The air was cool and wet.

Kegan went to the door of a hotel room and rapped four knocks out in four/four time. Jennifer Hirsch let him in.

Albert Hirsch sat on the bed. The television was on, a black-and-white picture without much of a vertical hold.

Hirsch said, "You can only get one channel. A station out of Indianapolis."

Kegan said, "You wanted to go underground, didn't you?"

"I don't think that's funny," Hirsch said. "Those men were there to kill me."

Kegan said, "You've been shot at before."

"Not by Americans."

Kegan shook his head. "I told you," he said.

"Yeah, you told me. You know what I heard? A crazy man I met in the woods telling me the mob had sent him to kill me. Had put out a contract on me. Would you have believed it in my place?"

Kegan said, "I wouldn't be in your place."

"Yeah, I know," Hirsch said. "You're too smart to mess with the boys at the top. Too wise to antagonize authority. Well, I'm not sorry, Kegan. I'm not sorry for anything."

Kegan looked at Hirsch's wife and said, "That's not what I meant."

Kegan's look did not go unnoticed by Jennifer Hirsch. She knew what he meant.

Jennifer said, "Albert, what Vince is saying is that he wouldn't be in your place because he hasn't . . . he hasn't had the sort of life you had."

For the first time, Kegan saw Hirsch irritated with his wife. Not the mock irritation of a loving husband. A genuine anger.

"I see," Hirsch said. "I was born with advantages he hasn't had. Well, if that's what you think . . ."

"Jesus Christ," Kegan said. "Stop feeling sorry for yourself. You know, for a man with such a big brain, you don't think too much. I heard your speech. It wasn't just those kids you reached. And I saw how pleased you were when you reached them. But . . . I don't think you fully grasp what danger you're in."

After a moment, Hirsch said, "Actually, I do understand. While you were out running errands, I watched the Indianapolis news. Do you know what was on the evening news? A story about the Illinois state police breaking up that rally. Do you know what was *not* on the news? A story about two men shot to death in the university library."

Jennifer said, "Are you sure?"

"Nothing," Hirsch said.

After a moment, Kegan said, "And what does that tell you?"

Hirsch said, "I don't know."

"Yeah, you do."

Jennifer Hirsch looked at Kegan.

Kegan said, "What it means is someone with higher authority than the state police covered that mess up. I sent those cops into that library so they would find those guys. No way they didn't find them. And yet nothing on the news about it. Some higher power stepped in and called the police off. Who could give an order like that?"

Hirsch said, "How do I know they weren't with you?"

Jennifer said, "Oh, Albert, come on."

Kegan had to look at the lady again. She was something, all right.

Kegan said, "The Outfit doesn't have that kind of pull. You were speaking at a college university, not Las Vegas, Albert."

"What?"

"Tell me. I asked you, who could give an order like that?"

Hirsch turned off the television and went to sit at the desk.

"I suppose," he said, "it could have come from Washington."

Kegan said, "Maybe from the McCormicks?"

"Oh, for God's sake. They're not like that."

Kegan said, "Did you listen to your own speech? You said they were war criminals. Murderers."

"That's war. That's . . . that's someplace else. Another country."

"You've brought it home."

"Come on, man," Hirsch said. "They're good men. They're just misguided. I don't work for the same sort of people you do."

"You sound like a man trying to convince himself," Kegan said. "But I know what kind of people *I* work for. Christ, you give noble speeches to kids at a college campus and move them to tears and you feel all proud of yourself for taking a stand. But you don't stop and think about what danger you're putting yourself in. What danger you're putting *her* in."

"Now just a minute."

"In my world, they have rules. You break those rules, they'll kill you. That's how it works."

"I didn't break any rules. I tried to do what's right. All my life, I've tried to do what's right. I'm not like you."

"First of all," Kegan said, "you said I killed two men. I didn't kill them both. The one by the door, I let live. I probably shouldn't have, but I did."

"So now you're a humanitarian."

"Albert," Jennifer said, "stop it."

"You want a prize for that?" Hirsch said. "You want special recognition for not killing a man?"

Kegan said, "The man that's still alive, he wasn't from Chicago. He wasn't a mobster. I know the type. That guy was some sort of soldier. He was sent there to kill you."

"Well, he didn't succeed, did he?"

"Albert," Jennifer said, "what is wrong with you? Vince saved our lives. You're talking as if we got out of there by ourselves."

Kegan exchanged a look with Jennifer, Kegan wanting to nod at her at that moment, as if to thank her, but shaking his head instead, to tell her to stop.

Kegan said, "Albert, the guy said Washington sent him. Okay. Maybe he's just some crank that likes to kill public speakers. But what if he's not? What if he is some sort of agent?"

"If he is, he is."

"If he is, he wasn't alone. They'll send someone else. They always do. Please, take your wife and leave the country. I'll help you leave. But don't stay here. Don't continue this."

"There are things more important than living."

"You said earlier that it was stupid to die for an unworthy cause. Isn't that what you're doing?"

"It's not unworthy."

Kegan sighed and said, "It isn't just about you."

Hirsch didn't get it. He said, "That's what I've been saying all along. People are dying. I have the ability, I have the information that can . . . that can put a stop to this. How can I remain silent?"

Kegan put the keys to the International on top of the television.

He said, "I'm going to bed. If you want to leave, I'm not going to try to stop you. If you're still here in the morning, we'll talk some more. And maybe then you'll tell me who it is who wants to —" Kegan stopped and looked again at Jennifer. "Who it is you've made so angry."

Kegan left the Hirschs' hotel room and walked down four rooms to his own. He unlocked the door to his room and went inside. He took off his jacket and tie and turned on the television. For some reason, he got a better picture than the Hirschs. Johnny Carson was interviewing George Segal. Segal was holding a banjo, picking and talking. Kegan lay down and lighted a cigarette.

An hour later, he still lay there. The television off. He lay there and smoked and listened to the occasional sound of traffic going by.

There were four raps on the door. In four/ four time.

Kegan took the pistol off the nightstand and walked to the door.

"Who is it?"

"It's me."

Kegan opened the door. Jennifer Hirsch stood there in a kimono. Kegan sighed, wishing she were still in street clothes.

"Can I talk to you?"

"Yeah, come in."

Kegan sat on a ragged old chair. Hirsch's wife sat on the bed.

Kegan gestured to the cigarettes on the nightstand and asked her if she'd like one. She nodded and lit her own cigarette.

Jennifer said, "I'm sorry about Albert. His behavior wasn't . . . it wasn't appropriate."

"It's all right. It's not every day that . . ."

"That someone tries to kill you?"

Kegan shrugged.

"It's all right," she said. "I know you were trying to spare me earlier with that 'who's made you angry' business. I appreciate it, but . . . but it's not entirely necessary. I'm not quite the paper doll you think I am."

"I don't think that."

"Albert knows I'm here, in case you're wondering. He trusts me completely."

"Oh."

Jennifer Hirsch was quiet for a moment, aware then that this man was attracted to her. If she had known it before, it hadn't shown.

Jennifer said, "Albert's scared, yes. We're both scared. But it's worse for him. It's worse than just being scared. He's . . . well, he's horrified. He can't believe that his own government would try to have him killed. Believe it or not, he's disappointed. He feels betrayed. He expected to be arrested, yes. But he never imagined something like this. When we met you out west, when you told

Albert who you really were, he didn't believe much of anything you said. He thought you were a lunatic."

"I don't blame him."

"Or he thought you were some sort of government agent yourself. Sent to him to try to scare him into backing down." Jennifer smiled. "He felt a little betrayed then. Because he liked you."

"You were kind and I was grateful."

"Yeah, but . . . he's always prided himself on being a good reader of people. And he misread you, apparently. But maybe he's not so good a reader as he believes he is. He fell in love with the McCormicks. We all did. I mean, how can you not? They're all so beautiful."

"They're just men."

"I know. Capable of heroism and evil. Are you really a gangster?"

"Yes."

"You've . . . you've killed people?"

"I don't want to talk about that."

"Okay. Sorry."

Kegan shook his head, telling her she hadn't offended him.

After a moment, Jennifer said, "There are a couple of questions I'd like to ask. And they're coming from me, not Albert. If you don't want to answer them, okay."

"Okay."

"First, how did you know we would be at the university?"

"Another guy, another Outfit guy, told me. I told you they would send someone else after you."

"He told you?"

"Yeah."

"Where is he now?"

"He's dead."

"Oh . . . so you? . . . All right, I'll leave that alone." Jennifer Hirsch took a breath to relax herself. "How did he know we would be there?"

"I don't know. Really."

"So you have killed two men to protect us. . . . Sorry, I told you I'd leave that alone."

"I'd appreciate it."

"The second question I have is, why?"

Kegan shifted his position in his chair. He regarded the beautiful woman sitting on his bed smoking a cigarette.

"Why?"

"Yes, why. Why did you come to the university? Why didn't you just stay out of it? Why make the effort to save us?"

"I don't know."

"What are we to you, Vince?"

"I don't know, really. You're a couple of squares. Civilians. You're not criminals. I guess I just didn't think the two of you should die over something like this."

"For protesting the war?"

"Or trying to put a stop to it. Albert . . . Albert, he thinks he can put a stop to it. It's something he believes in. I don't think he can. But he believes he can. So . . . I guess I thought he shouldn't be killed for trying."

"Or me?"

"Or you."

The woman looked at him for a while, realizing that was as much as he was going to admit to her.

Jennifer said, "You think the McCormicks are behind it?"

"Yeah, I do."

"But they're not gangsters."

"Anyone can be a gangster given the right opportunity. I think even Albert knows that. He said it himself. We've become the bad guys in this thing. We're the ones doing the killing. We're the ones using muscle to take over someone else's territory. Someone else's country. In my world, we do that sort of thing so we can make money. But I've figured out over the years that money's only a means to power. We do it for power. It takes very little to convince yourself you're entitled to it. I never met any hood who didn't feel entitled to take what he wanted.

341

It's all about power at the end of the day. The guy I work for — the guy I used to work for — he used to do business with Ben McCormick. They're not much different. Old Man McCormick's just a bit smarter and a lot more ambitious."

"And you think they'd kill someone to hold onto their power?"

"Why not?"

"Because . . ."

"Because they're good-looking?"

"No, that's not it. I just can't . . . I just can't imagine them doing that."

"If he's a threat to them, they will. He said himself, today, Camelot was a myth. A false dream. Did you hear him?"

"I heard him."

"He called it a dream. And he said he wants to take down that dream. Those are fighting words."

"But they're just words."

"Words are a strong weapon. Maybe stronger than Albert realizes. I happen to know your movie-star president tried to have the Outfit kill Castro. A little no-account dictator who could never really do any harm to us. Even I knew that. But they tried to kill him. Some stupid people at the Outfit tried to do it for them, but they failed. But someone else got to Castro. I think your president found someone else to do the job."

"Look, he's not my president and that . . . that's crazy."

"Is it?"

"Yes. If what you say is true, Castro was no threat to us. Why would they do it?"

"Because he embarrassed them. They tried to invade that country and they lost. People like that don't like to lose. Is Albert a communist?"

Jennifer Hirsch laughed. "God, no. He's a Boy Scout."

"My people said that someone from Washington said he was. That he was working for the KGB or something. I never believed it. My boss didn't either. But there's a difference, maybe, between the people I work for and people like the McCormicks. In Washington, they want to believe they're innocent. That killing him would be good for the country. For all I know, they've talked themselves into believing Albert is a commie and a traitor. And if that's the case, it only makes them more dangerous."

Jennifer was quiet for a moment. Then she asked Kegan if she could have another cigarette. Kegan nodded.

Jennifer lit that one and said, "Earlier, you said to Albert, 'I wouldn't be in your place.'

He thought you were insulting him, calling him stupid or, as you put it, square. But I know that's not what you meant. And if it wasn't just that, I heard you clearly when you told him it wasn't just about him."

Kegan looked at her for a long time.

Jennifer said, "It's okay if you feel that way about me. I'm not afraid, you know. I could never be afraid of you, Vince."

"I know." In that moment, he did know.

"And I love my husband very much."

"I know that too."

"I think you don't give yourself enough credit. And maybe too much to me. There are good women out there. There is one out there for you."

"No, it's too late for that."

Jennifer Hirsch seemed to stifle a laugh and put her hand to her face. When she took her hand away, Kegan saw a tear on her cheek.

"The irony is," Jennifer said, "Albert's jealous of you. God, after all the things he's accomplished. A decorated soldier with a brilliant career. Maybe the only man in Washington who stood up to that bully Terry McCormick. But he's down on himself because you were the one who saved us from being killed today. He wished it had been him. You men and your silly notions of courage. That's why he was so short with you earlier."

"He's braver than I am," Kegan said. "And he knows how to give a speech."

"That he does."

Kegan stood outside the door and watched her as she walked back to her room. She did not turn back to look at him before she went inside.

CHAPTER TWENTY-NINE

Lewis Knowles drove himself to the bar. He passed the topless go-go girls and the noise and the drunks and went to the back and climbed the stairs. A bodyguard he knew stood at the door at the end of the hall.

"Mr. Knowles," the bodyguard said, his tone respectful as always.

"Hey, Dom. He ready for me?"

"Yeah."

Dom knocked twice and then opened the door. Knowles walked in to see Sam Iacovetta sitting behind a desk. Iacovetta was eating from a box of Chinese takeout. He used chopsticks to eat and he didn't drop anything.

Iacovetta said, "You hungry?"

"No," Knowles said. "I try not to eat after ten o'clock."

"I should have remembered that."

Knowles put his hat on the desk.

Knowles said, "I suppose you saw the news."

"Yeah. I thought it may be our guy, but I wasn't sure. So I called one of my boys who knows a reporter down there. It was Hirsch all right."

"Did the police arrest him?"

"Not to my knowledge. Just busted a lot of hippies on the head and threw them in jail for the night. Teach them a lesson, hopefully."

"You support the war, Sam?"

"Fuck, I don't care about the war. But I sure as fuck ain't gonna take the side of a bunch of long-haired punks bad-mouthing their country."

Knowles smiled and said, "Because they got no respect for the law?"

"Ahhh, don't go mixing us up with them losers. We run a respectable outfit. Those kids, they're just . . . anarchists."

Knowles said, "They're just young."

"Albert Hirsch isn't young," Iacovetta said. "And my sources tell me he was there."

Knowles looked at his old friend and said, "Did you know he would be there?"

Iacovetta thought that over for a few moments and then jammed his chopsticks into his sweet and sour pork.

"Not exactly," Iacovetta said. "You remember Carmine?"

"Forlano? Little C?"

"Yeah."

"He was killed today. Shot in the head."

"Jesus, I didn't know that. In L.A.?"

"No. Chicago."

Knowles said, "Chicago? What was he doing here?"

"He was looking for Albert Hirsch. I sent him after Hirsch after Kegan bungled it."

"You sent Carmine?"

"Yeah."

"When were you going to tell me this?"

"We tried your man, it didn't work. I put Carmine on it. That a problem?"

"No, Sam. We agreed the job would be done. I just think you should have told me first, so we could avoid any conflicts."

"Such as?"

"Nothing in particular."

"Well, you talk about conflicts. Carmine was killed about a mile from Kegan's shop. And no one's seen Kegan since."

Knowles sighed and was quiet for a moment. Then he said, "That may not mean anything."

"Maybe not. But it looks bad. Lewis, how well do you know Vince?"

"I know him well enough to know he wouldn't freelance. Say he did kill Carmine.

Who's to say Carmine didn't come after him? That Vince was defending himself?"

"Maybe it happened that way. But Lewis, they were both sent after Hirsch. Maybe Carmine told Kegan what he was up to and Kegan got sore at him, taking away his lunch money."

"Kegan wouldn't kill someone for something like that."

"Yeah, and you also said Kegan always gets the job done. Only this time he didn't. Is it possible you don't know your boy as well as you think?"

"Vince is loyal to me. He wouldn't do something like that unless he cleared it with me first. So if he did do it, he must have done it to defend himself."

"Maybe," Iacovetta said. "When we find him, I want to ask him myself. Are you going to have a problem with me doing that?"

"No," Knowles said. "But I want to be there when you do it."

"Fair enough."

Knowles was saddened by this. He had always been able to predict Kegan. He wanted to believe now that Kegan had nothing to do with killing Carmine. He didn't want Sam to know he probably agreed with him. Vince had gone off the reservation.

Iacovetta said, "For what it's worth, I

didn't think Kegan would do this sort of thing either. I always liked Kegan."

Now Iacovetta was speaking of Kegan in the past tense. When they found him, maybe they would give him a chance to explain himself. Maybe Kegan would be able to give them a good explanation. Good enough to let him live. But odds weren't high. Knowles never liked Carmine Forlano and did not mourn his passing. But Carmine was popular with the Outfit. Dues would have to be paid.

Knowles said, "Does our man from Washington know about this?"

"Davidson?"

"Yeah."

"He knows part of it. I told him that I had a man in place to hit Hirsch. I *had* to tell him that. And he knows our man got killed in Chicago. I didn't tell him about Kegan."

"How did he take that?"

"He got pissed. Talked about 'inefficiency' or some such shit. I got tough with him. I said that maybe one of his government spooks knocked off Carmine because he was getting in their way."

Knowles smiled. "He buy that?"

"Maybe a little of it. That guy, he wants us to think he knows everything that's going on. But I think they've left him in the dark on a lot of things. These cloak-and-dagger guys, they're always working three or four schemes at the same time and they end up tripping over each other's cranks."

"That's the problem with their outfit," Knowles said. "It's just too damn big."

CHAPTER THIRTY

Senator Bob Mannford, Democrat of Oklahoma, wanted to show Terry where he was born. Terry agreed to see it. Dan had told Terry to do whatever Mannford asked. Dan had said, "Bob ran the U.S. Senate for fifteen years. Oklahoma doesn't have much to give you in way of electoral votes. But don't underestimate Bob's influence." So Terry got into Mannford's new crimson-colored Cadillac and rode with him to a ramshackle lean-to outside of a town called Ada. It was just the two of them in the convertible, no Secret Service, no state troopers.

Terry had lunched with Mannford and the business leaders of the state at the Cattleman's House in Oklahoma City. Sharing sixteen-ounce T-bones with oil men wearing cowboy boots and Stetson hats. They secured a promise from him not to tamper with the oil depletion allowance if he was elected president and then moved on to what he was going to do to win the Vietnam War. They told him that Senator Peter Jorgenson, the state's other senator, had gone red on them. Terry, being cautious, merely said that Jorgenson was misguided.

Senator Mannford, a shrewd and perceptive man, noticed Terry dropping some g's here and there. *"I'm tellin' ya . . ."* And so forth. Trying to fit in with the Okies. It was not something the brother would have done, Mannford thought. The brother was more comfortable in his skin. He had a better set of teeth too.

No one knew quite how big Senator Mannford's fortune was. But he was believed to be the richest man in the Senate. Richer even than Old Man McCormick. Mannford was in his late seventies now.

The cabin was still standing by a dirt road. Mannford parked the Caddy and they got out and Mannford showed him the inside and outside, showing him where he and his brothers had slept. Terry was respectful, nodding and making observations about how far the man had come.

Terry said, "No plumbing, huh?"

"No plumbing," Mannford said. "No electricity. Nothing. People forget that until Roosevelt got elected, you couldn't get electricity in places like this."

"But look how you turned out," Terry said. "Coming from a place like this."

"Yeah, I got lucky. But it didn't happen overnight. And I lost two brothers. One in the flu epidemic of 1918. Another at Flanders field. It was a hard life."

"Flanders field . . ."

"That was the First World War. I was in the army then, a second lieutenant, but they didn't send me overseas because I had an ulcer. I spent all of it in New York coordinating supplies."

"Well," Terry said, "you served."

"I was lucky," Mannford said again. "You know much about that war?"

"Well, I read Tuchman's *The Guns of August*. It's one of Dan's favorite books."

Mannford shook his head. "Did Tuchman write about what a waste it was?"

"Ah . . ."

"I know something about it myself, although I never wrote a book. That war took about twenty million lives. It killed about a third of France's young men. I remember where I was when we got in it. When I first learned that the U.S. was going to fight in it. I was at the dried goods store in Ada. You know what people did when they found out we were going to fight it? They *cheered.*

354

They celebrated. Can you imagine that?"

"Yeah."

"See, back then, there wasn't any television or radio or entertainment. I'm old enough to remember men and women sitting on porches talking about the Civil War. Happy to talk about it because there just wasn't much else to do. So we were happy to get in this new war. But . . . we had no idea what we were getting into. Some third-rate Hungarian prince got shot in Serbia and Europe decided to slaughter each other over it. And Americans called Wilson a coward because he didn't get in it soon enough."

"I don't know if it was that simple, Bob."

"I know enough to know that it could have been avoided if they had wanted to avoid it. And I think I know enough to say that if we hadn't fought that war, Hitler wouldn't have come to power twenty years later."

Terry said, "I didn't figure you for a pacifist, Bob."

It was the wrong thing to say, Terry realized. But he was fearful that the old senator was leading up to something. He wondered if the old man was about to confess his support for Pete Jorgenson, junior senator of Oklahoma.

But if Mannford took offense, he didn't

355

show it. He said, "Don't worry, Terry. I'm not going to support Pete."

"Pete wants to pull out of Vietnam."

"Pete doesn't have a chance of being elected. I know that and the men you met with today know it too."

"Are you sympathetic with his views? Perhaps quietly sympathetic?"

Mannford smiled and Terry saw strength in that smile. He had not been called the King of the Senate for nothing.

"Don't cross-examine me, young fellah. I'm not testifying before one of your sub-committees."

"Sorry, Bob. I didn't mean anything by it."

"I'm sure you didn't," Mannford said. "No, I'm not a pacifist. I voted to support Dan's resolution because I was assured by him personally that the North Vietnamese had been the first aggressors against the United States Navy. But say I didn't believe that it happened the way you guys said it did, even a man with my money and power has to make compromises. That's the cost of being in politics. If I hadn't voted that way, I would have lost my seat and if that happens, the people of my state suffer because, as you and your brother know, no one's in a better position than I am to bring the projects and public works here and build this place up. It's why we're so much better off than Alabama or Mississippi. That's what oil has done for this state. That's what those public works do for my state. I'm a conservative and a public servant. My constituents say don't give rights to the blacks, I go along with it. They want me to support the war, I go along with that too. I don't want my people to live in poverty. I want them to have roads, utilities, jobs. So I've made my bargain. And that's my problem."

"And now you regret it?"

"I don't know. Maybe. Maybe I'd feel different if this thing hadn't dragged out so long."

"It's complicated."

"They said it was complicated in 1917. I voted for that resolution in 1964. It's 1972 now and, despite what you say, it doesn't seem to be getting any better."

"It will."

Mannford shook his head, letting Terry know he wasn't fooled.

Mannford said, "You needn't worry about those men you met with today. They know Pete and they like him. But they'll support you because you told them what they wanted to hear."

"I told them what I believe, Senator."

"I believe you do believe it," Mannford said. "And maybe that's the problem."

Terry couldn't repress a hard sigh. "Listen, are you going to back us or not?"

Mannford took one last look at the cabin. All of it still in place.

Mannford said, "We better get back to town."

The family jet took Terry out of Oklahoma City and deposited him in Wheeling, West Virginia, where he would meet with union leaders for a fish fry dinner. Terry had wanted to sleep on the plane, but the conversation with Mannford had upset him. Christ, an oil man from Oklahoma expressing doubts about the war. And not only that, but suggesting that he and Dan may have lied to him about the Gulf of Tonkin Resolution. They had, of course, just like they had lied to everyone else about it. But it was so long ago. Why should it matter now? Terry decided he would tell Dan about it later. Tell Dan that Bob "King of the Senate" Mannford was getting senile and talking about the First World War. Maybe Dan would find it amusing. And then maybe Dan would get Mannford on the phone and remind him who had final say about what interstates got built in his shitty little state.

R.C. Cole was waiting for him on the tarmac in Wheeling.

Terry waved the Secret Service agents away and walked with Cole.

Cole said, "I wanted to discuss this with you privately."

"Go ahead."

"They found Hirsch yesterday at a university in Illinois. They didn't get him."

CHAPTER THIRTY-ONE

Hirsch knocked on Kegan's door in the morning.

Hirsch said, "We're leaving in a few minutes. Can we drop you somewhere?"

"My car's in Urbana," Kegan said. "You can't go back there."

"Well, then let me take you to the nearest place you can get on a bus."

"Okay."

They were quiet for a moment. Then Hirsch said, "Listen, thank you for what you did for us. For me. I'm sorry I was unpleasant last night. I just . . . I just can't believe all of it."

"You believe me now?"

"That you're a gangster? Yeah, I believe it. But maybe I shouldn't be calling you that anymore."

"It's what I am."

"I don't know many gangsters who'd risk their lives for a stranger. Or who'd turn down money for what you call a hit."

"My decision, not yours. Albert. What are you going to do?"

"I'm going to Washington and I'm going to give a copy of that report to a reporter."

Kegan sighed. "Why?"

"I've already told you why. And don't bother telling me again that it won't do any good."

"You trust this reporter?"

"Yeah." Hirsch laughed. "With my life, if what you believe is true."

"Two men tried to kill you last night. You saw them. Don't you believe it?"

Hirsch was quiet for a moment. Then he said, "I saw them. But it doesn't matter. I have to do what I have to do. Maybe now more than ever. You tell me I should disappear. But where would I disappear to? You say Europe, but they have people in Europe too. They can reach me there. Don't you see, the safest thing for me to do now is to bring this thing out in the open."

"And then you'll be untouchable?"

"That's the hope."

"Albert . . ."

"Listen, I'm not seeking glory here. I'm not trying to be a hero. Circumstances — historical and personal — put me where I am. It's too late for me to go back. I don't

361

really have a choice anymore."

"When did you talk to this reporter?"

"This morning. I called him collect."

"Oh, man."

"What?"

"This reporter, what does he report on?"

"The Pentagon."

"Don't you see, Albert? They've almost surely got that man's phones tapped. And you called him collect."

"Tapped his phones?"

"They tap the Outfit's phones everywhere. My boss jokes about it. No way they're not going to tap people you've been talking to."

"So what if they have?"

"So now they know you're going back to Washington."

"Then they know."

"Christ. You're not taking Jennifer with you, are you?"

"She wants to go."

"Then talk her out of it. Put her on a plane to Los Angeles and tell her to have her family pick her up. Tell her to stay with her father for a while."

"She's not getting along with her father."

"She'll be safe with him, though. Tell her."

"She's not the sort of woman you can tell things to."

"Then talk her into it. You're good at

362

persuasion."

Albert Hirsch smiled. "Oh. Did I reach you last night?"

"It was a good speech," Kegan said. "I hope you have the evidence to back it up."

"I have it, all right. In a suitcase in my room. You see, I've been carrying it all along."

"Your Pentagon Report?"

"Yep." Hirsch seemed proud of himself.

Kegan shook his head. "Jesus. You mean you left that in the car while you made that speech?"

"It was locked. And no one knew it was there except me and Jen."

Kegan said, "If those guys had been smart, they would have just waited for you at the car. Lucky for you, they were impatient. Albert, you can't count on being lucky again. These guys are going to come after you again. The Outfit's going to send someone else. These people don't quit."

"Your people?"

"No. *Your* people. Who is it you made so angry?"

"Oh God, I don't know. Any number of people. Maybe some right-wing general or cabal."

"Or maybe the McCormicks."

"Don't start with that again."

"Jennifer said something last night that's been sticking with me. She said you were the only one in Washington who stood up to Terry McCormick. What happened there?"

"Well . . . she may have exaggerated that."

"She said he was a bully."

"Washington's full of bullies."

"Did you embarrass him? Threaten him in some way? Tell me."

"Terry was always bawling someone out. He had a bad temper. And he was, I don't know, a bit simplistic about things. He's never been in the military, never seen combat. Anyway, after he commissioned me to write that report, he called me to his home to discuss it. Not his office, his home." Hirsch smiled. "I used to be a welcome guest there. Anyway, he said he'd read the report and he said my findings were 'misguided.' He told me that I'd misunderstood what my mission had been. This from a guy who's never set foot in Vietnam. And I guess my mission was to write a report that supported the administration and I had failed to do that. Well, we started arguing and after a while he said I was a chicken shit who was trying to ruin his family. He said I was a traitor. Not to my country, mind you, but to his family. I got mad and told him that there were more important things at stake than the reputation of the almighty McCormicks. I think I may have also said that the country was more important than his family. I was pretty upset. He's Irish and you know how they can be."

"I know," Kegan said. "I'm half Mick myself."

"Oh, I didn't mean . . ."

"It's okay."

"So he comes over to me and actually jabs his finger in my chest. I couldn't believe it. Now, I'm no tough guy or anything, but I was a Marine and we don't take that sort of thing lightly. And I'm reasonably sure I could beat the hell out of Terry McCormick. So here I am, an analyst with a PhD, a born-again pacifist, and I guess I just lost my cool. I told him if he jabbed his finger into my chest one more time, I would break it." Hirsch sighed. "I was ready to do it, too. Isn't that terrible?"

"No. You should have broken it."

"No. That wouldn't have solved anything. But, I hate to admit that I took some pride in this, but I think in that moment, I may have actually scared him. And I was *happy* that I scared him. I mean, truly satisfied. After I threatened him, he backed away.

Then he told me I was to bring the report and all copies to his office the next day. And that if I leaked it to anyone, he would have me put in jail."

"And you didn't take the report to him, did you?"

"No. I couldn't. He was going to bury it. So I took my copy and I went underground."

"And now you're here."

"Now I'm here. And even now I sometimes wonder if I'm doing this for the right reasons. To stop the slaughter in Indochina or to get back at some dumb Irishman who tried to push me around."

"You're not wondering that," Kegan said. "I heard your speech. You know what your reasons are."

"Supporting the cause now, huh, Vince?"

Kegan shook his head.

Hirsch said, "You know the sad thing is, I always liked Terry before that. There were plenty of people who hated him from the beginning of Dan's administration. I wasn't one of them. Yeah, he was a bully and he wasn't as educated in foreign policy as he should have been and, of course, he would have never been Secretary of Defense without his brother being in the White House. But he could be pretty funny and warm at times. His thing would be to yell at you one day and be affectionate with you the next. Include you in a joke or maybe grab you on the shoulder like you were an old pal. I always thought it was his way of apologizing. And it was flattering to be included in that circle. He doesn't have Dan's charisma and he doesn't have Andy's legislative skill, but he can still be very charming. Terry's a Catholic who knew his catechism and he's devoted to his brother and his kids. He didn't start out being a monster. But war corrupts people. Terry said, more than once, 'We can't be the first American administration to lose a war.' He's so caught up in not losing and securing his family's place in history, he's not the same man he was eight years ago."

"Maybe," Kegan said, though not really believing it. He thought creeps were more often born than made. "What do you think his chances are of being elected if that report goes public?"

Hirsch said, "Who knows? You said yourself no one's going to read it."

"Never mind what I said. What do you think?"

After a moment, Hirsch said, "I guess it's possible it could derail his election. I mean, the Gulf of Tonkin fabrication alone is

367

enough to ruin him and his brother."

"Who's the other brother?"

"Andy. He's a senator. The youngest son. I think he's opposed to the war. At least, he's suggested that he's leaning that way in a couple of speeches." Hirsch paused. "That's partly why I don't go along with your theory. Andy's as much a threat to Terry as I am."

"Does Andy have the report?"

"No. I don't think he even knows about it."

"Then he's not a threat. He's the man's brother. You ever meet the father?"

"Ben? Yeah, I met him."

"What did you think?"

"He was . . . ah, he was okay."

"Really? The man I work for says he's one of the meanest, most crooked bastards he's ever known. And you know who I work for."

"Yeah, I've heard that. And I know about the anti-Semitism. He was a little gruff with me, yes. But he's a man from a different generation."

"He once burned a hooker with a cigar because she'd laughed at him," Kegan said. "That's the sort of family you've been working for."

"Look, the son is not the father. Terry's no Jew hater. These are not gangsters."

"Right. They're public servants. Albert, you talk about their charm, but the most charming people I've ever known are hoods. You look at your people, they're not wearing pinkie rings or silk suits, and you think, okay, good enough. But they're the same animal."

Hirsch shook his head and said, "Well, I think you're wrong about them. But let's say you're right. You think that I should run from people like that? Someone's got to take a stand."

Kegan said, "Let someone else do it. If not for your sake, for your wife's."

"I don't want you to talk about her anymore, okay? She's *my* wife. I'll do what you said. I'll put her on a plane to California and make her hole up at her dad's. But I don't want you to talk about her anymore."

"Okay," Kegan said, "But are you still —"

"Yes, I'm still going to Washington."

CHAPTER THIRTY-TWO

Cole had heard the story. A lot of guys in the CIA had heard about it.

After the attempt to invade Cuba had failed, the McCormick administration found out that the planes of two Florida Air National Guard pilots had been shot down. The administration had given express orders that American soldiers were not to be directly involved. But somehow lines got crossed and the pilots had been sent out on some sort of reconnaissance mission.

Terry was livid when he found out about it. He poked a deputy director of the CIA in the chest and said, "You better hope those fucking pilots are dead."

R.C. Cole was mercenary to the core. Loss of life meant little to him, even American life. But even he had been stopped cold by Terry's reaction.

Fortunately, for the administration, the pilots *were* dead and the McCormicks were spared the embarrassment of Castro parading U.S. pilots on Havana television as proof of American imperialism. Working quietly, it took the National Guard six years to persuade the administration to pay a stipend to the widows of the pilots.

Cole was thinking about that story now. He believed that Terry McCormick should never have been exposed to that much detail of the operation. Should never have been put in the position of *knowing* that some well-intended fool had sent a couple of National Guard pilots out to Cuba. But Cole had been warned of McCormick's tendency to micromanage. Cole had been told, "Terry can't resist the cloak-and-dagger stuff. He's convinced he can do it better than we can."

Terry was micromanaging now. He had ordered Cole to let him meet with the men he had sent to Illinois.

So there they were, in the basement of the Division's headquarters, in a soundproof room with the United States Secretary of Defense and likely next president meeting with two green badger assassins. Terry McCormick had even brought one of his toadies with him, a buttoned-down Ivy League type named Mayville.

Cole, the Phoenix Program operative and

collector of kills, took Mike Mayville in. The man in the suit nodding his head as Terry snapped out his questions and demands for action, Mayville happy to be serving his king, happy to be included. One of the green badgers had his arm in a sling, evidence that he had been shot and Cole was looking at McCormick and his flunky assistant, Cole thinking, *you really shouldn't be here.*

But Ronald Ramsey didn't seem to mind talking to the next president. Ramsey didn't hesitate at all.

Ramsey told Terry McCormick what happened in Illinois. Then he ordered Bart Jayson to tell McCormick what he saw.

Terry said, "Are you sure it was him? Are you sure it was Hirsch?"

"Yes, sir," Jayson said. "We saw him enter the library. His wife was with him."

Terry said, "And you followed?"

"Sir, yes. We located the subject on the third floor. Agent Hun—"

"I don't need to know his name."

"Yes, sir. The other agent located them on the third floor. I was on the other side of the building. The agent was killed."

"Hirsch killed him?"

"Sir, I don't think so. I think the man who was with Hirsch killed him. The man who shot me."

After a moment, Terry said, "Well, who was this fucking guy? Was he a cop, a security guard, or what?"

"Sir, I don't know. He didn't tell me his name. I asked him if he was with the KGB."

"What, over tea and crumpets? You had a fucking conversation with him?"

"No, sir. He hit me from behind."

"Looks to me like he shot you from the front."

"Sir, he got the jump on me."

"Mr. Secretary," Ramsey said. "I don't believe the man was a police officer. Or a security guard."

"And why is that?"

"Because he threatened to kill this operative if he ever saw him again. And he used a pistol with a silencer. I think he was some sort of assassin."

"Well, you think he might be available to us? Because he seems to know a lot more about this business than you two."

R.C. Cole turned his head away. He wished he had the guts to ask the next president of the United States to leave the room and let him handle it.

Jayson said, "Sir, I think the guy was a gangster. Someone from organized crime."

"Organized crime," Terry said, like it was

the dumbest thing the man could possibly say. "And what the fuck would you know about that?"

"Not a lot, sir, but the way the man was dressed, the sort of gun he used, the way he talked. He didn't seem like he was a member of law enforcement, sir."

Mike Mayville said, "You mean to say he was a hood?"

"Shut up," Terry said. To Jayson, Terry said, "Hirsch was there to protest the war, wasn't he? You saw him make that bullshit speech, didn't you?"

"Yes, sir."

"And you're telling me this peacenik, this man who thinks we're doing all sorts of horrible things to the Vietnamese, this man had an armed bodyguard with him who killed one of your men and threatened to kill you?"

"Yes, sir."

"And you let this man get away?"

"Sir, he . . ."

"Yeah, I know, he blindsided you." Terry looked at Cole. "Christ, where did you get these guys?"

R.C. Cole cleared his throat and said, "Terry — Mr. Secretary. We can't predict everything. These men did well to even find Hirsch. Locating him was not easy. It was a chaotic situation."

"Christ," Terry said. "You guys always do this. You tell me you're going to get it done and then you come back and tell me there was something *unexpected.* For fuck's sake, *improvise.* Adapt. This shit isn't hard."

"Sir," Ramsey said.

And this time Terry turned to look at this man. Ramsey's *sir* not sounding like the other man's.

"Yes?"

"If I may," Ramsey said, "the mission was my responsibility. If there was a failure, the fault is mine. You tell me what street corner to stand on, I'll stand there."

Terry turned to Cole. "What the hell is he talking about?"

What he was talking about was offering to let himself be killed, Cole realized. That was Ramsey for you.

Cole said, "That won't be necessary."

Cole looked back at Terry and said, "We have something. Something else. We've learned that Hirsch is coming to Washington to meet with a reporter named Simon Jacobs."

Mayville said, "How do you know that?"

"We intercepted a phone call Hirsch made to Jacobs," Cole said. "We believe Hirsch is going to give Jacobs a copy of the Pentagon Report."

Terry smiled. "Really?"

"Yes."

Terry said, "Has Hirsch still got a place at the Watergate?"

"Yes, sir. So we don't have to go looking for him again. He's coming here."

Terry felt better and it showed. His toothy grin was now fully exposed.

Cole wanted to ask Terry to leave then. But before he could say anything to wrap it up, Terry spoke again and again he said too much.

"Okay," Terry said. "Take him as soon as you find him. Before he gets the report to that other sheeny. If the reporter gets a hold of that report, you take him too. And after that, you bring that report to me."

Cole closed his eyes and opened them. Again, he wondered why Terry couldn't have just asked him one on one. As it was now, the future president had just told one staff member and two mercenaries that he wanted a couple of Americans murdered on American soil.

Terry and Mayville drove back to Virginia in Terry's Pontiac convertible. The Pontiac had been a gift to Terry from a dealership in Chicago. Terry drove with the top down. Terry was in a good mood, waving back to people who recognized him and called out to him, "Good luck!" and "Give em' hell, Terry!"

Mayville was more nervous than usual. He looked at the surrounding traffic and up at the windows of the buildings they passed. There were no Secret Service agents with them. They were completely exposed. He had thought that after working for Terry so long, he would have gotten used to Terry's recklessness and bravado, but he hadn't. Dan had become more cautious after the assassination attempt almost killed him, but Terry carried on like he was indestructible. Maybe he was.

Mayville said, "Terry . . ."

"Yeah, Mikey."

"What if they don't get him?"

Terry turned and gave him another one of his hard stares. "What are you talking about?"

"I mean, what if they don't get Hirsch? What then?"

"They'll get him. He can't run forever."

"But he's not running. I mean, it doesn't seem like he's running anymore."

"Right," Terry said. He seemed to think he'd given enough assurances.

"What I mean to say is, aren't you concerned that he's bold enough to come to

Washington?"

"Why should I be? Mikey, he doesn't know we know he's coming here." Terry laughed. "We've had a wire on that Jacobs bastard for years. Not because we thought Albert Hirsch would ever be calling on him. I'll admit, I didn't see that coming. We got taps on so many reporters I can't keep 'em all straight. And now it's paying off."

"So we got lucky," Mayville said. Though he didn't seem too convinced of it.

"It ain't luck," Terry said.

Mayville waited for Terry to add, *It's destiny.* But he didn't. Mayville said, "Listen, about the other man, the bodyguard. I think I may know who it is."

"Yeah?" Terry didn't seem that interested.

"Yeah. I spoke with Davidson about it. That's okay, isn't it?"

"Sure."

"Davidson told me that Lewis Knowles sent a man out to . . . to get Hirsch and that the man didn't succeed. So then Iacovetta sent another man to do it and the second man was killed."

"Really?"

"Yeah. Iacovetta thinks that the man Knowles sent killed the man Iacovetta tried to send. That's what Davidson thinks happened too."

"So what?"

"So maybe the first man, the one Knowles sent, maybe he was the one at the university. Maybe he was the one who killed the agent in the library."

"Mikey, that doesn't make a lot of sense."

"You heard those guys. They said they thought he was a hood."

"So what then? So Knowles is trying to protect Hirsch now?" Terry smiled. It was like the good old days, cross-examining witnesses at the Senate subcommittee.

"No. No, I don't mean that. I don't think Knowles would try to protect Hirsch. I mean that maybe, possibly, this hood has gone, well, has gone rogue and acted on his own."

"Why would he do that?"

"I don't know. Maybe Hirsch befriended him or something. Maybe he hired this guy to protect him."

Terry shook his head, as if he were speaking to a child. "Mike, don't take this wrong, but what you don't know about the gangster mentality is a lot. Those guys are losers. Strictly bottom of the barrel. Yeah, they may have some people with some brains at the top. But their worker bees are dumber than posts. They're fucking savages, every one of them. And something else. Albert Hirsch is

379

an egghead, a goody-goody. He can no more relate to a hood than he can a fucking Zulu."

Mayville offered Terry the laugh that was expected. But even Terry saw that it was forced.

Terry said, "What's the matter, Mikey?"

"I don't know, sir. I just wonder if we could perhaps talk to Hirsch."

"What?"

"I don't mean bargain with him or anything. I mean, just bring him in to talk to him. He respects you. You could talk him out of going public with this thing. Get the report from him and, I don't know, send him somewhere."

"You weren't so hesitant before."

"I know, but . . ."

"But now someone's been killed and you're bothered by it."

Mayville wanted to say, *I didn't sign up for this job to put contracts out on American citizens.* He wanted to say it badly. But he didn't have the courage to say it and he knew he never would. Before, he had gone along with it. Before, it was all discussion and planning, talk and unwritten memoranda. But now he had seen the results of that planning. One man killed at an American university and another one wounded. The one named Ramsey seemed to have a screw loose. Was Mayville mistaken or had Ramsey offered to let himself be assassinated on a street corner? What the hell for? What sort of forces were they unleashing, assigning men like that? Empowering men like that? Mayville had not been troubled by death in Indochina. It was all so many dots on a map to him. But what had happened in Illinois *did* bother him. It suggested something worse than a war on the other side of the world that wasn't going so well. It suggested internal strife that could tear the nation apart. Americans killing Americans. Americans being *ordered* to kill Americans by an American government. Last time that had happened, they had called it the Civil War. Mass prisons had been built at Andersonville and Rock Island where American citizens were penned like livestock and treated worse. For the first time in years, Mayville began to think he was in a place he didn't want to be. He wondered what it would have been like if the McCormicks hadn't seduced him all those years ago. What it would have been like to work for a Wall Street law firm where his profession would have been dull and unglamorous but would have been safer and less corrosive to the soul.

Mayville said, "I don't know." He didn't

know what else to say.

Terry said, "A man died for this mission in Illinois. We call this off, we say he died for nothing. It's the same for Vietnam. Albert says we should pull out and leave it to the commies. And then what do we tell the families of all our boys who were killed over there? That they all died for nothing?"

"No, sir."

"Stick to shuffling papers, Mikey. And leave the big decisions to men who've got the stomachs for it."

CHAPTER THIRTY-THREE

It was late afternoon when Kegan got back to Chicago. He drove to his apartment and parked in the lot in the back. He locked his car and started to walk to the fire escape in the back. Then he saw Mrs. MacGregor pulling her groceries in her handcart. Mrs. MacGregor was a widow of about seventy. She lived one floor below Kegan. Kegan liked her. She was polite and didn't ask too many questions. Kegan looked at her and her groceries and wondered why she didn't move to a building that had an elevator.

Kegan said hello to her and asked if he could help.

"Thank you, Mr. Kegan."

Kegan took three sacks of groceries out of her handcart. Then he folded the handcart and held it in his hand. He began to follow her up the back stairs. They got to the second-floor landing where Mrs. Mac-Gregor kept and watered her flowers. She unlocked her door and Kegan walked inside her kitchen and set the bags on the table.

Mrs. MacGregor said, "I noticed you were gone for a while. Did you have a vacation?"

"Yes. Fishing."

"Catch anything?"

"Just a cold."

She smiled to herself, not giving too much. She'd never been much of a talker.

She said, "You have someone watching your place?"

After a moment, Kegan said, "Well, my ex-wife has a key to my apartment. Was she here?"

"No," Mrs. MacGregor said. "A man came out and went back in. He wore a nice suit."

Kegan said, "When was this?"

"This morning."

Kegan said, "This morning."

"Yeah. He came down these stairs and a few minutes later came back up. I thought he was a friend. He was wearing a suit."

Kegan said nothing.

Mrs. MacGregor turned to him and said, "You knew about it, didn't you? I mean, there's not any trouble, is there?"

"Of course not." Kegan said, "Well, I've gotta get to the shop. Be sure to lock the door behind you. You know about the crime in this city."

"You don't have to tell me," she said.

Kegan went back out to the landing. He looked up. Iacovetta or maybe even Lewis would have sent more than one man. They'd found out about Carmine. Quietly, Kegan went back down the steps and to his car.

He drove to a bar about three blocks away. He ordered an Old Style beer and took it to a table by the window. Then he walked back to the pay phone in the corridor by the bathrooms and called the police.

He told them that he saw a couple of men break into an apartment at his address. He did not tell them his name. He did not tell them that it was his apartment. He said he saw a man carrying a television out of the apartment and he knew the man didn't live there. Then he hung up.

He went back to his table and drank his beer and looked out the window.

It took about eight minutes. Then he saw a blue and white Chicago patrol car rush by the bar. The lights flashing, but no siren.

Kegan walked back to his car and drove by the front of his apartment building. There were two police cars there. Kegan parked the car on the street. A few minutes went by and he saw the uniformed police officers bring two men out the front door.

One of the men was well dressed, wearing a silk suit and cashmere topcoat. That was Paulie DeGorgio. The second was a thick slab of a man wearing a peacoat and jeans and a wool cap. This was Bruno Saimar, a massive Albanian known for his skills with a baseball bat. Both men worked for Sam Iacovetta.

Neither man struggled with the police. They knew they'd be bailed out of jail within hours.

Kegan waited until all the police cars were gone before he went into his apartment. Then he went up and let himself in.

Well, they hadn't made a mess of things. They'd made themselves coffee and watched his television and stubbed out a couple of cigars in the ashtray on his coffee table. They hadn't come here to turn his place over. They'd come here to wait for him.

Kegan went to the bathroom and opened the cabinet under his sink. This was where he kept a safe. He unlocked the safe and took out the cash he kept there. Then he packed a couple of suitcases and left.

Kegan called Lewis from the airport. Lewis got to an untapped phone and Kegan called him again.

Lewis Knowles said, "You in town, Vince?"

386

"Not for long. I just found Paulie and the Albanian at my apartment."

"Oh? They still alive?"

"They're in police custody. They were breaking and entering."

Knowles laughed and said, "I like it."

"Well, they didn't break anything. I guess the Albanian left his bat at home."

Knowles was quiet for a moment. Then he said, "It wasn't my call, Vince. Believe me."

"I believe you."

Knowles said, "You didn't fulfill your contract on the Hirsch thing. I could cover for you on that. But Carmine Forlano's dead and Sam thinks you killed him. Now I'm not saying you did. But Sam's got in his head that you did and I can't talk him out of it."

"I won't ask you to."

"I covered you as much as I could."

"I know," Kegan said. "Listen, Lewis. I'm sorry I couldn't deliver for you. I didn't intend to be . . . I wasn't trying to screw you. Are they still going to come down on you?"

"The feds? Well, Terry McCormick's not known for making idle threats. So, yeah, you've put me in a bind."

"Sorry," Kegan said. "But you should have

asked someone else."

"We did ask someone else. And you took him out."

Kegan said nothing.

Knowles said, "Why, Vince? Why would you risk your action for someone like Hirsch?"

"Carmine was going to —"

"I'm not talking about Carmine. I don't give a fig about him. Carmine was a creep, but he was one of ours. He's one of Sam's boys. You had to know, Vince. You had to know that once you killed him, it would be over for you."

"It was over for me before that," Kegan said.

"Well, I don't know what you mean by that," Knowles said. "You had a good setup. We treated you pretty good. We paid you well."

"Look, maybe McCormick won't be elected. And if that happens, maybe the heat'll be off."

"He's going to be elected as sure as the sun's coming up in the morning. But even if we get that lucky, it's not going to change things for you. Not after what you did." Knowles paused. "Well, don't tell me where you're going, because I don't want to know."

It was something, Kegan thought.

Knowles said, "Take care of yourself, Vince."

CHAPTER THIRTY-FOUR

They called the Watergate complex the Republican Bastille. Hirsch didn't find that out until after he and Jennifer moved in. Jennifer's father had paid for it, so maybe he had known. Bob Dole was a tenant as was Senator John Warner and his lovely wife Elizabeth Taylor. The Democratic National Committee's headquarters were there too.

The complex had been completed five years earlier, in 1967. It had been designed by an Italian architect. There were five buildings in the complex. An office building, one hotel, and three apartment buildings. Hirsch and his wife lived in Watergate East.

Hirsch arrived at his apartment in the evening. It was a nice apartment, with a good view of the Potomac. It had bearskin rugs and modern art. It was empty now and Hirsch felt very alone.

He thought of his wife and of the last time

he saw her . . .

After much persuasion, Hirsch had taken Jennifer to the airport in Indianapolis and put her on a plane for Los Angeles. He had not told her what Kegan had told him. Not all of it. At the gate, Jennifer asked Hirsch if he believed in God.

Hirsch laughed and said, "We already discussed that."

"That was when you were pursuing me," Jennifer said. "Now we're married."

"Okay. The answer is still the same."

"Meaning, 'you think so.' "

"I think so."

Jennifer Hirsch said, "Did you ever think that maybe Vince was sent here to protect us?"

"He was sent for another purpose altogether."

"Don't make fun. Not about that."

"Sorry. . . . What do you mean? Some sort of guardian angel?"

"No, he's hardly that. But . . . well, you know."

"Jen, he's done some things that are . . . they're things I wouldn't be proud of. But I've killed men too. I've been part of a killing machine. I'm no better."

"Don't say that."

"It's all right. If I'm to meet your Maker,

I'd like to try and put it right. If it's not too late. As for Kegan, well, he may be a bad man gone good or he may still be a savage. To tell you the truth, I don't mind having a savage on my side right now."

"I don't mind either. Albert, last night. When I went to his room, you know I didn't —"

Albert Hirsch touched his wife. "Sweetie, you don't have to tell me a thing. I have always trusted you and I always will. I couldn't do what I'm going to do if I didn't feel that."

"But what if Vince is right? What if it won't do any good?"

"Then I'll at least have tried. Would you want anything less from me?"

"I'm not sure," she said quietly. And she began to cry.

"I'm sure," Hirsch said. "Let that be enough."

"But what if you don't come back? What'll I do without you?"

"I'm coming back, I promise. I'll see you in a few days. We'll swim in the ocean together and hold each other. Believe it."

Hirsch waited till she got on the plane and then watched it pull away from the gate. He drove through the day and the night and around three in the morning pulled over at a rest stop somewhere in Pennsylvania.

He woke up with the sunrise. And in those first, still moments of the morning he wished he had never met Jennifer. He thought about the pain that would be inflicted on her if he were killed. If she had not met him, she would not have to feel that pain. Like many men in a crisis, he wished for a time machine that could transport him back to a place where he could have made a left turn instead of a right. Take him back to a place where he would not have met Jennifer and could spare her the pain of this awful ordeal. It was easier for a man to risk his life when he didn't have people close to him. People who relied on him, people who needed him, people he needed. He had no desire to be a martyr. He did not want to die. He wanted to live a long life with the woman he loved. This awful war might take his life too. And if the Chicago mobster was right, it would all be for nothing.

But Hirsch had lived long enough to know that regret was a useless emotion. If he could go back and make a different turn, he might have ended up hit by a bus. Or taken down by a sniper's bullet in Vietnam. If he had not met Jennifer and started to see Vietnam through her perspective, he might been persuaded by the McCormicks that Vietnam was still a worthy effort. And that would have been a different kind of death.

Hirsch started the car and drove east.

He thought about his wife and he thought about Kegan. He thought about the events that brought them together. The man talking himself out of killing him and then, later, saving his life. Saving Jennifer's too. Why should he feel grateful to such a man? Hirsch had no doubt that Kegan was in love with his wife. He was also strong enough to admit to himself that Jennifer felt an affection for Kegan too. Perhaps it was just gratitude, but maybe it was something more. Maybe if she had been born in Chicago to circumstances more humble than her own, she would have ended up with Kegan for a husband. His wife married to a gangster working for the Outfit. Would Kegan have taken good care of her? Would she have persuaded him to give up a life of crime? Or would the fact that he was dangerous attract her in the first place? Or was jealousy just another useless emotion?

He knew Jennifer knew that he had been jealous of Kegan. Not because he feared Kegan would take Jennifer from him, but rather because he had been the one to save her life. But now Hirsch realized the jealousy stemmed from something less primal than that. Now Hirsch realized that Kegan, in some way and on some level, was smarter than he was.

Not book smart. Not analytical smart. But smart enough to know that Terry McCormick was behind all this. Hirsch understood it now and he felt stupid for not seeing it before. Hirsch had been in the room with Terry when the Florida Air National Guard pilots had been reported missing over the sea near Cuba. Had himself heard Terry say, "You better hope those fucking pilots are dead."

At the time, Hirsch had told himself that Terry was just upset. That it had been a bad day for everyone. A humiliating setback for the McCormick administration. Terry said ugly things when he lost his temper. Surely, Hirsch told himself, Terry had not meant that.

President Dan McCormick, always the shrewd politician, later took Hirsch aside and said to him, "Terry's been under a lot of strain. He's heartbroken for those pilots and their families. You know that, don't you?"

And Albert Hirsch had said, "Yes, Mr. President, of course."

And like that, Hirsch had been sold. A few words of understanding from the most glamorous president of the twentieth century and Hirsch was reassured. Not just reassured, but flattered that Dan McCormick had spoken to him personally. Relieved that he was still part of the McCormick team.

You tricked yourself, Hirsch thought. You allowed these men to charm you into believing that lie and a lot of other lies. For now he understood that when Terry McCormick said he hoped those pilots were dead, he genuinely meant it. Those were the sort of men he had given himself over to.

And now it had caught up to him. Now Terry McCormick wanted him dead too. An Irish gangster had sent another Irish gangster to kill him.

Hirsch thought about it again when he was in his apartment at the Watergate. He thought about it when he heard the doorbell.

He locked the door that he realized he should have locked before. Then he looked through the glass peephole. Hirsch unlocked the door and opened it.

Hirsch said, "I shouldn't be surprised."

Then he let Kegan in.

CHAPTER THIRTY-FIVE

Kegan looked at the suitcase next to the couch.

He said, "It's in there?"

"Yeah. All of it."

"That's your only copy?"

"Yeah. It takes a lot of time to copy five thousand pages."

Kegan shook his head.

Hirsch said, "You want some coffee?"

"Sure."

"You flew here, I guess."

"Yeah."

"To try to talk me out of this, I suppose."

"No," Kegan said. "I know I can't do that."

Hirsch said, "So what then? Be my bodyguard?"

"Yeah."

Hirsch turned around from the coffeepot. "I haven't asked you for that."

"I know," Kegan said. "You're too proud

and I'm too stupid. Let's get that thing to your reporter friend and I'll be on my way."

"That suits me," Hirsch said.

Hirsch finished making the coffee and brought two cups over to the kitchen table. Hirsch gestured to Kegan's bag on the coffee table. "I suppose you brought a weapon," Hirsch said.

"Yeah. I didn't carry it on board. They've started to check hand luggage because of all the hijackings."

"Still."

Kegan said, "There weren't any problems. I've done it before."

"I'm sure you have."

Hirsch was quiet for a moment. Then he said, "Sorry. I'm grateful that you're here, Vince. Grateful for everything. I don't have many friends left these days."

Kegan laughed for what seemed the first time in years. "Neither do I," he said.

Hirsch caught his meaning and said, "They kick you out of Chicago?"

"Sort of."

"I'm sorry, Vince."

"It was my decision."

Hirsch said, "Listen, Vince. I've thought about what you said. I think the McCormicks are behind this. Not the president, I don't rate much with him. But I think Terry would be willing to kill me. Don't ask me why I've changed my mind, it would take too long to explain. But I agree with you now. I think he's been behind it all along."

"Well, that's something," Kegan said.

"It's more than something," Hirsch said. "A member of the presidential cabinet wanting to murder an American citizen is more than that. I just . . . I just don't know what's happened to this country that such a thing could . . . Christ, I'm scared. Not just for myself, but . . ."

"It's their outfit," Kegan said.

"One I was part of," Hirsch said. "And now we're both marked."

Kegan said, "This reporter you're going to give this to, you trust him?"

"Yeah. He's a good man. I met him in Vietnam. He was working for a different newspaper then. He was getting a little too critical with his questions over there, so the president called his boss and had him removed from the assignment. Had him taken out of Vietnam, actually."

"The president did that?"

"Yeah."

"Jesus."

"Yeah." Hirsch said, "Anyway, I have to trust him. Once it's published, I should be safe."

Kegan hoped that was true. He said, "When are you supposed to meet him?"

"In about an hour. At a restaurant in Silver Spring. Will you go with me?"

"Sure."

Ramsey had booked a room at the Howard Johnson's Motor Lodge across the street from the Watergate complex. He had Jayson and three other men with him on the assignment. He communicated with the men using a hand-held two-way radio. With his binoculars, Ramsey saw Hirsch go into his apartment. He radioed the men and told them the eagle had landed. He left one of the men in the hotel room to monitor the building.

Ramsey said into his radio, "When the sun goes down. We move when it's dark."

Then he left the hotel to join Jayson and the other two men at the Watergate.

Ronald Ramsey wore the gray uniform and cap of a Watergate security guard. He had a gun holstered at his side.

CHAPTER THIRTY-SIX

Ramsey was near the swimming pool when he got the squelch from his man in the hotel room.

"Sir, another man's entered the apartment."

"Who?"

"I can't identify him. A big man wearing a suit. Hirsch let him in."

"Damn," Ramsey said. "Maintain your position."

Ramsey radioed Jayson and the other two men and told them their hood was now with Hirsch. He told two of them to get on the floor of Hirsch's apartment and wait for his signal.

Hirsch and Kegan had finished their coffee and were moving toward the door when the doorbell rang.

They both stopped.

In a low voice, Kegan said, "Does anyone

else know you're here?"

"They shouldn't."

"What about that reporter?"

"He's waiting for us. I expressly told him not to come here."

Kegan said, "Take your suitcase and get in the bedroom."

Hirsch did as he was told. The doorbell rang again. A pause and then some knocking on the door.

"Sir, it's security! Please open the door!"

The man knocked again.

Kegan took the pistol out of his pocket. He left his silencer in the other pocket. There might not be time. Kegan went to the door and looked in the peephole.

He saw a security guard in uniform.

Kegan said, "What do you want?"

"Mr. Hirsch?"

"What do you want?"

"There's a burglar on the loose in the complex. We're checking all the apartments."

"He's not here," Kegan said.

"Well, sir, I'm afraid I'm going to have to check the premises myself."

"I just told you," Kegan said. "There's no one here but me."

"I have orders to search every apartment on this floor. I'm afraid I'm going to have

to insist. Listen, I'm not trying to be difficult here, but if you don't open up, I have
to call the cops. Now come on."

Kegan didn't like the vibe. But he realized
they weren't going to be able to leave the
apartment without dealing with this guy
first. He stuck the gun into the waistband
of his pants where it was hidden behind his
jacket. Then he unlocked the door and
opened it.

Ramsey came inside.

Kegan took him in. A security guard with
a .38 Smith and Wesson revolver in his gun
belt.

Ramsey said, "I'm sorry to be a nuisance.
But my boss told me I have to check every
apartment on this floor."

"It's all right," Kegan said, backing away
from him. Still not sure about this guy.
"What's your suspect look like?"

"White male. About thirty. He was seen
carrying a stereo."

"Well, there's no one like that here."

"Sir, he could be hiding here and you may
not know it."

Kegan said, "I've been here all day and
that door's been locked the whole time. I'd
know if someone came in."

Ramsey moved into the living room. He
looked at the bedroom door. The door was

closed. He looked back at Kegan who was looking at him, something exchanged in that moment. Kegan now in the kitchen area, the counter bar between them.

Ramsey said, "Do you mind if I look in the bedroom?"

"I do, actually. I've got a lady friend in there who doesn't want to be disturbed."

"Yeah?" Ramsey said. "Well, I think you're lying to me. I don't think there's any lady in there."

Kegan said, "Now how would you know that?"

Ramsey stared at Kegan for a moment. Ramsey's hands were on his waist, posing like a tough cop. But his right hand had twitched and Kegan wondered if he was thinking about it.

Kegan looked at the telephone on the kitchen counter and said, "I've got an idea. Why don't I call the security desk and see if they know anything about this burglar?"

Kegan began to move toward the phone.

That was enough. Ramsey pulled his gun from his holster and Kegan dropped behind the counter. Ramsey fired and his first shot hit the telephone. Ramsey fired a second shot and that one went into the refrigerator. Kegan pulled his gun out of his pants and crawled to the side of the counter.

He's either going to come over the counter or he's going to come around the side.

If he came over the counter, he'd have to jump and hurdle it. And then Kegan looked to the black-and-white photograph of Albert and Jennifer Hirsch framed in glass. If he came over the counter his reflection would appear in the photograph. Maybe. If it didn't appear, that meant the man was going to come around the corner. Hopefully.

Kegan got ready. His arm raised, a pistol at the end of it.

The security guard stepped around the corner, his gun in his right hand when it should have been in his left. His eyes went wide as he tried to shift his aim and Kegan shot him twice in the chest.

Ramsey flipped back and went to the ground. Kegan rushed over to him and took his gun away.

"Albert! Come out! It's okay now."

Hirsch came out of the bedroom. He was still holding the suitcase.

"Jesus Christ."

"It's okay, he's going to be dead soon."

Hirsch looked at Kegan for a moment. Wondering just who this man was.

Kegan said to Ramsey, "Who are you?"

"Who are *you*?" Ramsey said.

"You're going to die soon," Kegan said. "You might just as well tell me who sent you."

Ramsey looked at Hirsch and said, "You're a traitor." Then his head fell to the side. He was dead.

"Jesus Christ," Hirsch said. "You killed a security guard!"

"He wasn't a security guard. He tried to kill me. Albert, have you ever seen this guy before?"

"No. . . ."

"That's because he doesn't work here. He just called you a traitor. Would a security guard do that?"

Hirsch didn't answer him. It had been a few years since he had seen a man die in front of him. Then he realized it hadn't been a few years, it had only been a couple of days ago in a college library.

"Let's go," Kegan said. "Albert, let's *go.*"

When they got to the door, Kegan said, "Stay behind me."

Hirsch said, "You think there are others?"

"I wish I didn't," Kegan said. He put Ramsey's revolver in the jacket of his pocket and moved toward the front door. Then he stopped.

"Is there another way out of here?"

"No," Hirsch said. "Well, there's the

406

balcony. But we'll have to step out on to someone else's place and come back through."

"Then that's what we'll do," Kegan said.

They went through an empty apartment with a lot of modern art and shag carpet. They reached the front door of that apartment and Kegan looked through the peephole. He didn't see anyone. Quietly, Kegan opened the door and peeked out. Kegan saw a man in the hallway dressed in white. He was standing in front of a laundry cart but he held a shotgun. The man in white heard the door creak open and turned around. He began to swing the shotgun around and Kegan fired at him twice, the first shot hitting his head, the second hitting his neck. The man in white went down.

Another door opened and a man stepped out holding a pistol. Kegan whirled on him and the man stepped back and Kegan shot twice through the door. Kegan dropped his revolver, knowing it was out of rounds, and he took Ramsey's pistol out of his pocket and ran toward the door. He opened it and felt weight against it and shoved, the man on the other side now pinned between the door and the wall. Kegan put his arm around the door and fired two more shots.

Kegan hurried Hirsch down the corridor and pressed the button to the elevator. It seemed a long time before the elevator arrived.

When it reached them, it was empty. Kegan pushed Hirsch inside.

The elevator opened in the lobby. Kegan put his gun in his jacket and they moved outside. They turned a corner that led them out to the swimming pool area and that was when Kegan saw a man with his arm in a sling speaking to someone on a two-way radio, the man looking panicked. Bart Jayson looked up and saw Kegan. Jayson began to reach into his coat and Kegan shot him in the thigh.

Jayson flipped forward as if being tripped and then hit the pavement. Kegan closed the distance and took his gun away from him and threw it in the pool.

Kegan grabbed him by the hair and said, "Remember me? Remember what I told you?"

"Jesus! Don't! Don't kill me."

"Didn't you hear what I said?"

"Yes, I heard you. I heard you! It wasn't my idea. They made me come here. *It wasn't my idea.*"

Kegan said, "I told you what would happen if I saw you again. I *told* you."

"Hey."

It was Hirsch who was speaking now. He had put his suitcase down. His hand now on Kegan's shoulder. And then he was in front of Kegan, blocking him from the man on the ground.

"No more," Hirsch said.

They could hear sirens now. Squad cars on their way.

Kegan turned to look at Hirsch and in that moment saw what had made Hirsch a leader of men. Hirsch was giving him an order.

Hirsch said, "Let's go."

CHAPTER THIRTY-SEVEN

The conference was scheduled at Georgetown University. Its stated purpose was to bridge the gap between the students and members of the business community, many of whom were Republicans. Terry McCormick was the keynote speaker. The students who were allowed to attend were carefully screened beforehand. No anti-war activists had been let in. Not that Georgetown didn't have students protesting the war. They did, but those students had been banned. The goal was to convey the idea that Terry was willing to address the young people of America. To convey the idea that he was not afraid to face them.

Terry started with a joke about his family. It got a laugh, particularly from the businessmen's wives. It drew them closer to him, giving them the belief that there was some sort of intimacy there. That they were sharing the magic. Terry then spoke of his own children, one of whom, he said, had asked him why they were still in Vietnam. Terry said, "So I speak to you not just as a public servant, but as a father.

"We are asked why must we travel down this painful road? Why must we sacrifice our young men for people on the other side of the world? I answer that eight years ago, a new president for our time called us to protect freedom, not just here but everywhere. Our role is to defend freedom at the time of maximum danger. That is our task. We shall not shirk away from that task merely because it has become difficult. Or because it has become unpopular.

"We are in Vietnam because we have made a promise to defend freedom. And we are reminded that we were not the ones who started this fight. North Vietnam launched its aggression upon the people of South Vietnam and upon our own United States military forces.

"There are some young people today who don't understand that. They do not constitute the majority of the students in our universities, but they speak as if they do. In America, we welcome a healthy dissent. It is what we are fighting for in Vietnam. But there are boundaries. The tragedy of the student opposition is that too many of them

411

are seeking nothing less than a revolution. Too many seek to tear down rather than build. In their zeal, which may be well intended, they risk destabilizing our nation in its hour of need. Those who know me and my brother know we are men of peace. But we must recognize the distinction between peace and reckless pacifism.

"Mr. Orwell once spoke to the people of Great Britain about the danger of pacifism at a time when Germany was dropping bombs on London. Orwell said, 'In a time of war, pacifism is objectively pro-Fascist. This is elementary common sense. If you hamper the war effort of one side you automatically help that of the other.' Further, 'the idea that you can somehow remain aloof from and superior to the struggle, while living on food which British sailors have to risk their lives to bring you, is a bourgeois illusion bred of money and security.'

"I share the heartbreak of those who have lost their sons to this war. But let me assure you that American casualties are trending down. The war is going well and victory is at hand."

Terry opened the floor to questions.

A student raised his hand and asked why the rate of withdrawal could not occur sooner. Terry handled it deftly, saying that he shared the goal of peaceful withdrawal with honor.

A businessman's wife asked a question about the rumors of President McCormick's use of coarse language. Terry smiled and said, "Well, er, maybe Nicky can get the president to watch his language, but I can't." Much laughter.

"I have a question."

Terry turned to look at a middle-aged man standing in the middle rows. The smile left Terry's face.

It was Hirsch. A man that Terry thought had been killed. Hirsch standing in a room with him now. Albert Hirsch looking at him now.

"Go ahead," Terry said.

Hirsch said, "You spoke earlier about the English pacifists indirectly supporting the Germans during the Second World War while, as you put it, the Germans were dropping bombs on London. My question is, when did the Vietnamese drop bombs on Washington? Or New York?"

"They haven't," Terry said. "But they have been killing American soldiers." Terry peered down at him, feeling a little victory. "Was there something else?"

"Yes," Hirsch said. "You spoke about

American casualties trending down but you failed to mention Indochinese casualties or refugees or destruction of villages, which, as you know, are trending *up.* In both North and *South* Vietnam. So my question for you is, what is your best estimate of the number of Indochinese we will kill under a second McCormick administration?"

The room went silent. For the first time that evening, Terry McCormick seemed to lose his composure. Never in his career had someone condemned him so harshly in public. He waited for someone to hiss at Hirsch or tell him to sit down and shut up. But it didn't happen. All eyes were on him.

Terry said, "That's, er, that's a very cleverly worded question, Mr. Hirsch." Terry tried to force a smile. "It's like asking me if I still beat my wife." No one laughed.

"I'm not trying to be clever, sir," Hirsch said. "I think the American people deserve an answer to that question."

Terry looked off stage. He nodded to one of his assistants. The assistant left to call for some help.

Terry said, "I . . . ah . . . you're not asking a question. You're trying to be inflammatory."

"No, sir. I'm asking you how many people will be killed as a result of this policy you wish to continue."

"It's war, Mr. Hirsch. War is always tragic."

"Well, then, since you refuse to answer that question, I'll ask one more. Isn't it true that Pentagon documents prove that the McCormick administration fabricated the report that led to the Gulf of Tonkin Resolution? That you and your brother knew that the North Vietnamese had not fired on American ships and yet you led Congress to believe that they had?"

There was something of a collective gasp in the audience. People turning in their seats to look at Hirsch. Murmurs and shock filling up the room. It might have passed, that moment, but Terry McCormick could not keep quiet. He never did have his big brother's coolness in the face of fire.

"That's a lie!" Terry shouted. "Goddammit, that's a lie!"

Hirsch smiled. He had always known about the famous Terry McCormick temper. And now Terry had lost control of himself.

Terry gripped the podium with one hand. He pointed the other at Hirsch and said, "You're a goddamn liar, Hirsch! You're finished! How dare you! How *dare* you!"

An assistant pulled Terry away from the podium. Terry broke away and a student

415

took the microphone.

The student, looking shaken, said, "It's been a long evening and I think we've had enough questions for now. I want to thank Secretary McCormick for being our guest." There was no applause. The audience was shocked and confused, a sense of ugliness and doom had pervaded the proceedings. A sense that what had been new and bright might now become stained.

Two campus security officers approached Hirsch and held him. One of Terry's men told the campus cops that Hirsch was to be held until federal agents could arrive.

Hirsch was smiling. He would be arrested and taken to jail. But the worst of it was over for him now.

The conference broke up.

■ ■ ■ ■

PART 4

■ ■ ■ ■

CHAPTER THIRTY-EIGHT

1973 . . . in a country that might have been ours.

In a barber shop in Austin, Texas, a man known to his customers as Jack Reed cut a man's hair. The customer was an oil man who had previously told his barber he hadn't voted for either one of the McCormicks. He said the day he voted for a Democrat would be the day he'd have his throat cut.

On this warm day in May, the customer held the *New York Herald-Tribune* as his barber did his work. The story he was reading was written by a reporter named Simon Jacobs. The barber had met him once.

The customer said, "God Almighty. Who'd 'a' thought this Watergate thing would go so far? Terry McCormick's only been president for a few months and they're already talking about impeachment."

Kegan said, "Is that right?"

419

"Yeah. Says here one of his top assistants turned state's evidence against him. The guy's name is Mike Mayville. I guess Mc-Cormick tried to blame all this Watergate shit on him. So this assistant goes to the prosecutors and offers to help them so he won't have to go to jail himself." The customer turned the page. "Well, that's Washington for you."

Kegan grunted in agreement.

The customer said, "You know how this started?"

"How?"

"The police arrested some guy at the Watergate apartments. Someone shot him in the leg and he couldn't get away. Turns out he was there with this crew trying to kill some government analyst or something. He was supposed to keep quiet about who he was working for, but I guess they didn't pay him enough to keep his mouth shut. And he sang like Ethel Merman."

Kegan smiled. Hirsch had been right to prevent him from killing that little suck. Hirsch had been right about a lot of things.

Kegan had read the paper as soon as he opened up his shop that morning. There were two other articles the customer hadn't yet read, though Kegan had.

One of them said that Senator Andy

McCormick was now proposing legislation cutting off funding for all military operations in Indochina, including but not limited to bombing. Senator McCormick said, "It's time to put Vietnam behind us."

Andy McCormick would not respond to questions regarding the Gulf of Tonkin Resolution, except to say there was no point in dwelling on the past. Senator McCormick said he was confident of getting a two-thirds majority on the vote.

The other newspaper article said that Judge William Reif had dismissed the United States indictment against Albert Hirsch based on "the totality of government misconduct, including the suppression of evidence, the destruction of relevant documents, witness tampering, and disobedience of judicial orders." The judge's order concluded that a declaration of mistrial would not be sufficient to cure this misfeasance and the government's "utter disregard for the law." Therefore, the defendant's motion for dismissal would be granted in full and the case was hereby terminated.

A photo above the story showed Albert Hirsch kissing his wife in front of the courthouse.

ABOUT THE AUTHOR

James Patrick Hunt is the author of *Maitland, Maitland Under Siege, Maitland's Reply, Get Maitland, The Betrayers, Goodbye Sister Disco, The Assailant, The Silent Places, Bullet Beth, Reinhardt's Mark, Bridger, Police and Thieves, The Detective,* and *The Reckoning.* He lives in Tulsa, Oklahoma, where he writes and practices law.